Bolan triggered an HE round, watching it detonate on impact

The shout from Bolan's flank was fear and outrage, mingled in a wordless cry that drew his attention to the new threat. Buckshot rattled toward Bolan's position, but the Executioner had already dived through a forward shoulder roll.

He came up firing from the hip, his first rounds punching through the legs and pelvis of a gunner standing twenty feet away. The wounded Nazi fell across the warrior's line of fire as Bolan held down the trigger, the copper-jacketed rounds whipping his target through a spinning sprawl.

Sudden stillness descended on the killing field. The warrior was aware of traffic slowing at curbside, drivers scoping out the scene of mayhem. Sirens were already wailing in the distance, answering the crisis call.

Bolan had to go, but he couldn't leave until he checked among the dead for Justin Pratt. Deliberately retracing his steps, he visited the bodies in the parking lot, turning each one over to reveal a slack face, eyes glazed in death. But Justin Pratt wasn't one of them. Bolan's target had evaporated. Gone.

And that left the Executioner's work in Los Angeles unfinished.

MACK BOLAN®

The Executioner

DON PENDLETON'S
MACK BOLAN
THE EXECUTIONER

THE TERROR TRILOGY
Book I

FIRE BURST

A GOLD EAGLE BOOK FROM
WORLDWIDE®

TORONTO • NEW YORK • LONDON
AMSTERDAM • PARIS • SYDNEY • HAMBURG
STOCKHOLM • ATHENS • TOKYO • MILAN
MADRID • WARSAW • BUDAPEST • AUCKLAND

First edition June 1994.

ISBN 0-373-61186-2

Special thanks and acknowledgment to
Mike Newton for his contribution to this work.

FIRE BURST

Revenge is a much more punctual paymaster than gratitude.

—Charles Caleb Colton

The fires of hate, compressed within the heart,
Burn fiercer and will break at last in flame.

—Corneille

It takes a cleansing flame, from time to time, to settle some of our enduring debts. This time around, the paymaster is going to settle the accounts in full— with payment due in blood.

—Mack Bolan

PROLOGUE

Driving south from Mahattat al Qatranah, the open staff car felt like a broiler. One hundred and fifteen degrees in the shade, assuming there was any to be found, and there was no relief from the furnace blast of desert wind generated by their rapid progress on the two-lane highway. They'd seen nothing in the way of traffic since they'd passed an army convoy headed in the opposite direction twenty minutes earlier.

The blond American had all that he could do to keep from laughing—at his driver, at the country, at the whole damned Middle East. You had the Arabs, sitting on a lake of oil that everybody in the world was begging for, and barely one in ten of them would ever learn to drive a car. They had no auto plants to speak of, buying all their cars and trucks and farm equipment from the West.

It was a confirmation of the blond American's belief that progress only came to backward third world countries when the white man took a hand at setting things in motion. Where would any of the Arab nations be without the income and technology from firms like Shell, Exxon and British Petroleum? Still herding goats and pitching tents between two sand dunes when they couldn't find a water hole.

It barely made a difference, even so. This was his second visit to Jordan, and he still had trouble understanding how a group of people holding half the money in the world could still exist like savages. It was a land where people dined on monkey meat and sold their daughters to the highest bidder. Any crazy notion you could think of was cleared by Allah, just as long as you remembered to pray five times a day, facing the east and wailing like a sow in labor.

The slums in Amman made Bedford-Stuyvesant look like Rodeo Drive in comparison. Beggars squatted on the sidewalk in their own filth, most of them crippled or faking it pretty damned well. Children traveled in swarms, like grubby little insects, none of them acquainted with a bar of soap. And the smell...

It would have been intolerable, coming here, if some among the Arabs weren't allies in a common cause. He didn't have to like them; for the moment it was ample to consider their immense reserve of cash and military hardware. Deep, abiding hatred for the common enemy would do in place of mutual respect.

And come the revolution, he'd make a mental note to wipe the ragheads off the map.

The desert camp was situated thirty miles southeast of Mahattat al Qatranah, close enough to the Wadi al Hasa for trainees to draw their water by hand and haul it back to the compound in buckets. The pig state of Israel was dangerously close, a ten-minute flight for the deadly F-4E Phantom II fighters, but there were benefits to living dangerously. It kept the trainees on their toes, alert and constantly aware that they weren't involved in some elaborate game.

Their war against the Jews was deadly serious.

It was the one and only thing the blond American could readily admire about his raghead hosts: they hated Jews like no one else around. He thought there was a lesson in there somewhere, but his concentration was diverted as they left the highway for their final, dusty run into the camp.

He knew the timing of their journey was precise. The various guerrilla camps from Libya to Jordan, Syria and Lebanon were under daily satellite surveillance by the CIA, who used some kind of crazy cameras that had the power to pick out individuals or read a license plate from way to hell and gone in outer space. They couldn't eavesdrop, yet, but he wouldn't have been surprised to learn that they were reading lips.

Unfortunately for the powers that be in Washington, the orbits of their satellites were known throughout the world. And when you knew the satellites were coming in advance, it was a relatively simple matter to defeat their magic. Camp activities were scheduled to permit the satellites a view of standard basic training exercises, just enough to let them know the Palestinian resistance was alive and well, still doing business at the same old stand. More sensitive activities were timed to miss the overflights, sensitive personnel scheduled to arrive and leave the camp when there were no prying eyes in the heavens above. It was a minor irritation, ducking back inside the stifling tents when a whistle was blown, but the system worked, and personal inconvenience was a small price to pay for ultimate victory.

He could see the camp now, a smudge on the flat horizon at first, growing steadily larger as his driver accelerated, anxious to be back among his fellows. At three hundred yards he could make out the tents, mostly sandcolored, some of them cut from desert camouflage material. Chaotic rolls of concertina wire marked the perimeter, scraps of waste paper caught here and there on the razoredged barbs of the wire.

At two hundred yards he could pick out sentries walking their beats with Kalashnikov rifles in hand, tiny stick figures that took on unique, identifiable features as their staff car drew up to the gate.

There was no formal check of credentials, per se. The blond American and his driver were expected, their faces well-known to the men on the wire. They passed through the gate without slowing, braking only when they reached the camp command post. As his driver switched the staff car's engine off, the new arrival had a chance to look around the camp.

It seemed to him that nothing had changed since his last visit three months earlier. There were undoubtedly new recruits in the camp, watching their instructor dismantle a

DShK heavy machine gun, but ragheads all looked alike to the American. The layout of the compound was familiar, and he recognized the grizzled cook who stirred the contents of a blackened pot.

There was movement at the tent flap of the camp CP, drawing the American's attention from the barbed-wire perimeter. A squat, khaki-clad figure was emerging from the tent, putting on a crooked smile for the newcomer, hitching up the web belt that supported a holster and ammunition pouches below the bulge of his paunch.

Behind the Jordanian commander, a second figure stepped into the glaring sunlight. Taller, without the commander's bulk, the Iraqi wore a thick mustache that only partially concealed splayed, yellowed teeth. He also wore a pistol on his belt, butt-forward on his left hip to facilitate a cross-hand draw. Unlike the camp commander, the Iraqi didn't smile.

The German was third in line, the last to emerge from the tent. Long and lean, a classic blue-eyed Aryan, he wore blue jeans and a chambray shirt with the sleeves rolled up to his elbows, sweat stains spreading from beneath his arms. No weapons were showing, but the German's reputation had preceded him. He was a proved, stone-cold killer with at least seven scores to his credit. A warrior.

The American put on a smile as he stepped from the staff car, observing protocol as he approached the trio standing near the CP tent. He shook hands with the commander first, then the Iraqi, wishing he could wipe his hand before he shared a fervent grip with his German compatriot. He knew the man from Bonn would share his own contempt for their hosts, his sense of bowing to the inevitable, putting up with obnoxious company in pursuit of a higher goal.

"Welcome, friend." The commander's breath was foul, like something from the morning-mouth commercials on TV, back home. "You traveled well?"

"No problems," the American replied. He didn't ask about the satellite, knowing they wouldn't have been assembled in the open if the prying eyes were anywhere within range.

"We stand on the threshold of a great day," the commander said, looking full of himself. "After all this time, a decisive blow against the infidels."

The American didn't respond to that, making do with a noncommittal smile. He automatically tuned out the raghead's talk of Allah and the holy war, dismissing Islam just as he dismissed the Jew-dominated dogma of spineless Christianity. Racial purity was the young man's religion.

"We have much to discuss," the Jordanian said, "but first there is a tiresome matter to dispose of. Still, you might find it amusing. I have saved it specially for your arrival."

"Oh? What's that?"

"A filthy spy," said the Iraqi, spitting out the words as if they left a sour taste in his mouth. "A traitor who has sold his birthright to the pigs in Tel Aviv."

The American frowned, catching a steely glint in the German's eye as he listened. The muscles in his neck and back were tightening, and he took a deep breath, relaxing with an effort of sheer willpower.

"A spy." He tried to keep the sudden rush of panic from his voice.

"Have no fear," the commander said. "I am confident we caught the pig before he had a chance to betray us. He knows nothing of our larger plans."

"You're sure of that?" It was a risk just asking, skating up to the fine line of an insult that would demand satisfaction, questioning the commander's competence.

"No question," the Jordanian answered, graciously taking the question in stride. "He has been thoroughly interrogated. There is no mistake. He was alone."

"Reporting to the Jews, you said."

"Through a contact in 'Aqaba, a sandal maker. We will visit him soon. First, though, we shall punish the traitor in hand."

"I look forward to it," the blond American replied, meaning it.

"We knew you would. First, though, a cup of tea."

He didn't question the commander's sequence of events. The American had long since given up on trying to make sense of what the ragheads said and did. If the Jordanian wanted a cup of hot tea on this scorching afternoon before they got down to business, then tea would come first.

It was darker, but scarcely any cooler, inside the commander's tent. They sat in a circle, in folding camp chairs, waiting while a flunky brought the tea in metal cups and left the tent without a word. The four men sat and sipped their tea, discussing news from their respective homes, avoiding the central matter of their common goal, coming back time and again to the Jews and their parasitic role in human society. The Arabs got that right, at least, but hating Jews would never make them white.

They dawdled in the tent for close to forty minutes, making racist small talk until the commander decided that it was time to move. He made a show of checking his wristwatch, beaming a smile at his three companions.

"Almost ready."

The commander barked a command to the empty air, and his underling returned a moment later, his hands full of trailing checkered cloth. The American recognized the keffiyeh headgear worn by so many Palestinian guerrillas of the PLO and other militant factions. He frowned as one of the cloths was placed in his hands, the others distributed around the circle of his companions.

"In eight minutes the American satellite will be within range," the commander said. "I wish for this to be a public demonstration, but we do not want our faces seen, for obvious reasons."

The blond watched his associates, fitting the cloth over his head after the Jordanian's example, wrapping the tail of it around his face from right to left, so that only his eyes and the bridge of his nose were exposed. He was hotter than ever now, sweat beading on his forehead underneath the keffiyeh, smiling in spite of himself at the irony of an Aryan warrior dressing up like a wog.

All in a good cause.

"Shall we go?"

The Jordanian led them outside. Merciless sun beat down on the American's head, no protection to speak of from the useless rag he wore. Leave it to a mongrel race, living in one of the hottest lands on earth, to wrap their women up in black robes and hoods, while their men tramped around in the heaviest clothes they could find. Small wonder that everyone he met smelled as if they had gone for weeks without a shower.

The commander fired a burst of orders at his second in command, waiting with his arms crossed while the man ran to execute his orders. Minutes ticked away before the aide returned, leading two other guerrillas with a battered scarecrow slumped between them, dragging his toes in the sand.

The Jew-loving traitor had taken a beating, and then some. His eyes were swollen almost shut, and if his nose wasn't broken, it was the next best thing, dark blood crusted at the nostrils and across his lacerated upper lip. Two of the fingers on his left hand had been twisted back at impossible angles, snapping the joints, and no one had bothered to straighten them out again once the pig spilled his guts. His sweat-stained shirt was unbuttoned in front, revealing a patchwork of livid bruises on his scrawny chest and stomach.

The American wasn't repulsed by what he saw. There would be worse in store for the race traitors at home, when his party finally seized power. The Day of the Rope was coming, no doubt about it, and he would be pleased to join the execution squads when that day rolled around.

First things first.

He had a death to witness, and the camp commander wanted it on tape, via satellite, as a slap in the face for their enemies in Washington and Tel Aviv. It was a stylish touch, and he had to give the raghead credit.

The traitor's escort dropped him on all fours, retreating as the commander and his Iraqi sidekick drew their semiautomatic pistols, whipping back the slides to chamber live rounds. The American watched and waited, hands clasped behind his back, standing at ease.

He was surprised when the commander barked another order and the aide returned, carrying a pistol in each hand, thrusting one toward the German, the other toward his American companion. The blond examined his weapon, a Czech-manufactured M-52 pistol chambered for the 7.62 mm bottleneck cartridge, weighing the automatic in his hand. He drew the slide back and watched a shiny cartridge slotted home as it whipped forward.

Ready.

He let the Jordanian lead, babbling some raghead gobbledygook at the condemned while his one-man audience knelt in the dust, chin down on his chest, and offered no response. Almost as an afterthought, the commander checked his watch again, making certain the satellite was well within range, its high-powered lens locked on target, before he raised his pistol to full arm's length, sighting down the slide.

"On my signal," he snapped, three more guns lining up on the target in a rough semicircle.

The shot was crisp and loud, a sharp spike in his ear, and the American fired in reflex, the reports of three weapons rippling like an echo to the commander's first round. The M-52 kicked hard against his palm, and he saw the 7.62 mm round punch through his target's left eye socket. Blood and mangled tissue exploded from the wound as the Jew lover sprawled over backward, twitching in the dust.

All done.

The American felt good, the kill rating as a bonus payment for his pains in traveling so far from home to meet with savages and treat them as his equals. Now, if they could just get down to business, so that he could put the stinking camp behind him and begin his predestined task, carrying the battle to his enemies at home.

Even so, it had been a treat, dropping the race traitor like a sitting duck. He thought about the satellite, its camera whirring, sending pictures back to Washington or Langley. It would have been a trip to watch the tape, perhaps obtain a copy for himself, so he could show it to his friends and watch it on his VCR at home.

No matter.

There would be other targets and other opportunities to vent his rage against the mongrels who were ruining America and the world at large. Once they were rolling, he would have more films and tapes than you could shake a stick at. Bodies by the thousands, even millions. Enough to make Adolf's home movies look like a stand-up comedy routine.

Beneath the keffiyeh, he was smiling once again. For real, this time. The trip was worth it, if it brought him closer to his goal.

The Day of the Rope.

He could hardly wait.

1

David McCarter lay facedown in the sand, taking full advantage of the meager shade from boulders that flanked his hiding place on either side. The desert sun was merciless, its glare uncomfortable despite the sunglasses that covered his eyes. When he removed the shades, reluctantly, it was to use a pair of high-magnification binoculars. He scanned the ribbon of highway that wound past his stakeout and climbed briefly through rugged hills before it fell away to the wasteland beyond.

The trucks were coming, eight of them in convoy, making decent time. Without lowering the binoculars, McCarter brought a compact walkie-talkie to his mouth and mashed his thumb on the transmitter button, once, twice. They'd agreed on no spoken word in case their enemies had somehow locked in on the frequency.

Soon, now.

In theory Jordan's border with Iraq had been closed since the invasion of Kuwait, a part of the United Nations plan to cut off any commerce beyond the export of oil and delivery of humanitarian supplies. Of course, the world knew Jordan's King Hussein had been in league with his Baghdad namesake from the start, renting his country out as a conduit for military hardware before—and since—the conflict known as Operation Desert Storm. The king denied it, but the trucks were rolling daily, unopposed, and items ranging from Iraqi rugs and beaten gold to ancient, priceless works of art had turned up as far away as Sotheby's auction room in London. Jordanian banks were also involved in the clumsy scam, laundering billions of Iraqi dinars, reinvesting them from Tokyo to Wall Street under bogus corporate labels, funneling the profits back to Baghdad.

Everybody knew, from the UN Security Council on down, but no one had the intestinal fortitude to put his foot down and call a halt to the illicit traffic.

Until now.

McCarter reached out with his free hand and touched the steel tube of his RPG-7 portable rocket launcher. It was loaded, and two spare rockets rested on the sand beside it. On the other side, McCarter's left, a Russian-manufactured AKM assault rifle lay ready for action, fitted with twin 30-round magazines of 7.62 ammunition.

So far, so good.

There was no Soviet Union these days, but Russian hardware was still the basic armament of many Middle Eastern countries—and all of the irregular guerrilla bands who trained and loitered in the camps strung out between Algeria and Lebanon's Bekaa Valley. Using Russian weapons was a form of cheap insurance for McCarter and his comrades, hidden in the rocks on both sides of the highway. When the time came to discard their weapons, they would be leaving nothing of themselves behind.

The trucks were closer now, four hundred yards and closing. Still beyond the RPG's effective range, but getting there. He couldn't say what sort of cargo they were bearing, and he didn't care. An agent in Iraq had passed the word to his control, and it had gone from there to Langley, winding up by hook or crook at Stony Man Farm. From there the orders had come down to Phoenix Force: intercept and destroy.

All they had to do was ambush the convoy, inflict maximum damage and retreat to safety without engaging Jordanian security forces. It was all in a day's work.

McCarter could have stopped the first truck anywhere inside three hundred yards, with luck, but he would have to wait until his comrades had a shot from their positions in the rocks. Unless the trap was well and truly closed, the last few trucks in line would have a chance to cut and run, dodge back across the border to Iraq.

And that was unacceptable.

McCarter cherished no illusion that destroying eight trucks and their cargo in the middle of the desert would effectively disrupt black-market trading in Iraqi merchandise. The ambush was intended as a message, a beginning.

Two hundred yards and closing. McCarter laid his field glasses aside, pushed himself onto his knees and lifted the RPG-7 to his right shoulder. The rocket's bulky warhead was capable of penetrating armor to a depth of 12.6 inches, and had more than enough power to deal with the canvas-backed half-ton trucks in front of him. They were even slowing, as if to make it easier, drivers clashing gears as they shifted down for the short uphill run.

Perfect.

The lead truck had closed the gap to within sixty yards of McCarter's position, but his primary target was the last truck in line. To make the ambush work, he had to slam the back door tight, preventing any of the sitting ducks from taking wing.

The RPG-7 was simple to aim and easy to fire, constructed with semiliterate conscripts and third world guerrillas in mind. McCarter lined up his sights on the right front wheel well of the last truck in the convoy, knowing his rocket had the power to rip the vehicle's engine block free of its mountings and drop it in the driver's lap.

He took a breath and held it, counting down the final seconds, slowly tightening his index finger on the trigger, squeezing off. McCarter felt the blast of heat behind him, channeling through the cut between two boulders, scorching desert sand. The five-pound rocket sizzled toward its target, ripped off the truck's right front wheel at the axle, detonating with a smoky thunderclap beneath the hood.

McCarter wasted no time checking out the blasted truck as it began to burn. Reloading swiftly, he was sighted on the lead truck in the convoy by the time its driver realized his peril, nearly stalling out the engine as he hesitated over the decision whether he should brake or stand on the accelerator and attempt to flee.

Too late.

The second RPG projectile bored in through the passenger's door and detonated on impact. The truck nosed down in the sand, smoke and flame billowing from the shattered cab. The shock wave slapped McCarter's eardrums as he dropped the launcher and reached for the assault rifle on his left.

Time to go.

The Phoenix Force warrior braced the AKM against his hip and rose from cover, firing on the run.

THE BLOND AMERICAN WAS riding shotgun on the convoy as a trade-off, anything to keep the ragheads happy, and cash and hardware flowing to the troops back home. It amused him to play the diplomat, appeasing savages with phony smiles and words of welcome, knowing in his mind and heart that there would come a day when he could drop the mask and finally get around to kicking ass.

From his position in the third truck, riding with an AK-47 braced between his knees, he watched the open desert simmer at 100-plus degrees. His khaki shirt was plastered to his back with sweat.

His German comrade, Fritz, was three trucks farther back, and no doubt feeling much the same. Their mutual disgust at working with the Arabs had been aired in private conversations, well beyond the hearing of their sponsors at the camp. Both men were looking forward to the day when they could sever any ties with third world allies, but that day hadn't arrived.

Not yet.

The trucks were climbing now, his driver downshifting to handle the grade.

Another hundred miles remained before they reached their destination outside Az Zarqa, north of Amman. Call it two hours, minimum, at their present snail's pace. The tedium was grating on his nerves, but anything was better than sitting around the camp, killing time in a sweltering tent.

The first explosion came from somewhere at his back. He checked the side mirror first, picking out a drifting cloud of smoke behind the other trucks that blocked his view. He was craning out the window for a better look when all hell broke loose.

This time, he actually saw the rocket coming, almost panicked in the instant when he thought it might be meant for him. It took out the lead truck instead, a blast that squeezed a frightened whimper from his driver, bringing their progress to an abrupt halt.

Automatic weapons opened up from both sides of the convoy, raking the trucks with high-velocity projectiles. Scanning left and right, he tried to pick out the snipers, then gave it up as shiny divots marched across the half-ton's hood. One round cracked the windshield, smacked the vinyl seat beside him, but the American was already moving, bailing out in search of better cover.

He hit the ground running, with the sounds of combat ringing in his ears, the AK-47 heavy in his grip. How many snipers were arrayed against them? Who had sprung the trap?

No doubts on that score, any way you sliced it. It made no difference whose finger was on the trigger; scheming Zionist Jews had loaded the guns.

The battle had been joined, albeit prematurely, and despite his fear, the American couldn't suppress a smile.

CALVIN JAMES WAS READY when McCarter fired the first grenade. The Dragunov SVD sniper's rifle was braced against his shoulder, targets magnified by the PSO-1 telescopic sight. He waited for the second rocket blast, this one on his left, stopping the convoy cold.

The sixth truck in the line was James's target, idling directly opposite his rocky sniper's perch. The driver's profile filled his eyepiece. The Arab's lips were moving, but no words carried to the hillside where James lay in shadow, tightening his finger on the Dragunov's hair trigger.

The rifle bucked against his shoulder, the 7.62 mm round dead on target at a range of fifty yards. The driver's head rocked sharply to one side, away from James, as crimson spouted from a blowhole in his cheek. The dead man kept on going, slumping to his right, and James had his first glimpse of the passenger—fair hair above a Nordic face, the snarl dissolving into shock, bright flecks of crimson on the sunburned cheeks.

The Dragunov was semiautomatic, nine rounds waiting in the detachable box magazine, but James didn't have the chance to log a second kill that easily. The passenger reacted with surprising speed, bailing out and dropping out of sight.

James cursed and scanned along the truck's length with his telescopic sight. They had men on the other side— McCarter, Manning and Encizo—who could take the runner down. No reason James should sweat it out, but it still went against the grain, allowing any target to slip away.

He tracked to his left, the fifth truck in line, and caught the driver rolling out of his cab. Another Arab, frightened, reaching for a pistol worn beneath his baggy peasant shirt. His keffiyeh was askew, giving him the appearance of a hunchback at first glance.

James caught him on the run, sights lined up on the driver's chest as he stroked the trigger. Round two lifted the Arab off his feet and slammed his back against the side of the half-ton. He hung there for an instant, lost his contest to the pull of gravity and slumped into a seated posture, buttocks resting on the asphalt road.

Two down, and how many left to go?

The trucks were packing two men each inside their roomy cabs, no trick to multiplying two times eight, but James's math was thrown off as a gunner scrambled from the covered rear of number five. James had the Arab spotted as the guy hit the pavement, glancing left and right from his fighting crouch, the compact submachine gun looking almost toylike in his hands.

The Phoenix Force warrior shot the gunner through his armpit, from the target's right, and pitched him over sideways on the baking asphalt. Tremors shook the fallen shooter's legs before the spark of life was finally extinguished and he moved no more.

A darting movement at the corner of his eye brought James's head around, leaving the Dragunov's sight for a moment. Yakov Katzenelenbogen was shifting positions, scuttling down the rocky hillside to another vantage point, firing a burst from an AKM assault rifle as he ran.

Surviving gunners in the convoy were returning fire now, aimlessly at first, feeling their way toward elusive targets on the shadowed hillsides. James heard angry bullets pecking at the rocks somewhere above him, but he shrugged it off.

Scanning the convoy below him, he picked up the blood-flecked Nordic profile again, shadowed by a truck the stranger was using for cover. Not an Arab, clearly, but James had no means of guessing the blond's identity or mission. He saw the trooper's submachine gun—it looked like a MAT 49, of French manufacture—and that was all he had to know. There were no noncombatants on this lonely stretch of mountain highway.

James lined up the shot, adjusting his aim as the target shifted position, peering out around the truck in front of him to check the killing ground. The half turn put his back to James, but that was nothing. There were no Marquess of Queensberry rules in guerrilla warfare, not when you were facing terrorists who thrived on the pain and misery of innocent victims.

The cross hairs of his telescopic sight settled between the blond's shoulder blades, dead on at something close to fifty yards. He took a breath and held it, the pulse beat in his ears competing with sounds of gunfire from his right and below him, on the road.

No time to hesitate.

The Dragunov kicked again, its vented muzzle brake helping to hold the 21-inch barrel down and on target. The PSO-1 gave him a ringside view of the gunner's final moment, punched forward by the hammer stroke against his spine, covering the submachine gun with his body as he fell.

There was a moment when he seemed about to rise again, his body heaving, elbows tucked in tight against his sides, but it was merely reflex action. Nothing could repair the damage to his spine, the heart and lung. In seconds flat, a pool of rich, dark blood was visible beneath him, spreading outward from the hillock of his corpse.

The seventh truck in line exploded, spraying shrapnel in a killing radius of thirty-five or forty feet. Another rocket? Hand grenade? Perhaps a tracer entering the fuel tank?

James kept the Dragunov in motion, seeking targets through the drifting pall of smoke.

He still had lethal work to do, and they were running out of time.

MOPPING UP THE CONVOY was a relatively simple proposition. Every member of the transport team was armed, but they had no effective cover beyond their own trucks. They could huddle in the cabs, lie prostrate under canvas in the back, or wriggle underneath the trucks, but there was nowhere they could hide. Grenades and rifle bullets found them, singly or in pairs, and in a few more moments all had been accounted for.

An eerie stillness settled on the killing ground. It seemed to Gary Manning like the silence of the grave.

The Canadian spent another moment scanning the battlefield, watching for movement, finding none. When he was satisfied, he left his crevice in the rocks and moved down the slope, covering the nearest burned-out truck with his AKM assault rifle. Twice his boots lost traction on the slope's loose shale, but Manning kept his balance, moving crablike in a horizontal track across the hillside.

He reached level ground at last and could see the others closing on the convoy, where resistance had been smothered by suppressing fire. He passed the rear truck and spotted Rafael Encizo several yards ahead of him, crouching to check beneath the next vehicle in line. Nothing there, and the Cuban moved on, Manning following in his tracks.

Number three was coming up, and he could hear Katz speaking to Calvin James on the other side of the convoy. McCarter was nowhere in sight, but Manning knew the SAS veteran wouldn't be far away.

He was stepping up to peer inside the third truck in line, frowning at the Arab lettering that marked assorted wooden crates, when a call from Encizo distracted him. Manning moved to join his comrade, finding the Cuban staring at a silent figure crumpled in the dust.

"What's wrong with this picture?" Encizo asked.

No need to guess. The corpse obviously wasn't an Arab. He was blond and fair of skin, a stranger, armed and traveling with the Jordanians for reasons they might never understand.

"Hey, check this out!" The voice of Calvin James commanded their attention.

Manning stepped across the fair-haired corpse and went to join his colleagues, four trucks farther down the line. The body lying stretched out at their feet inspired a sudden flash of déjà vu.

Another paleface, this one dressed in sweat-stained desert camouflage fatigues, blood soaking through the shirt where armor-piercing rounds had drilled his chest. One arm was outflung in a kind of salute, while the other lay twisted underneath his body.

Without the blood, it would have been a peaceful scene, a weary tourist dozing in the shade.

Except, thought Manning, this one wouldn't be waking up.

"I'd better get some photos," Manning said. He lifted a compact camera from a pocket of his shirt and framed the lifeless face, snapped off two head-on shots, then turned the unresisting head to catch a profile.

Moving back along the line of trucks, he found the other paleface, dragged him from the failed hiding place and rolled the dead man over on his back. The camera clicked three times before he tucked it back inside his pocket and buttoned the flap.

He didn't recognize the two dead men—there was no reason why he should—but someone else might have a better chance. The files at Stony Man included terrorists and sundry criminals from every corner of the globe. If nothing came of that search, they could access files from Langley, Quantico and Interpol.

And if the search still drew a blank, what then?

It stood to reason that the two dead Nordic types were on some shady errand. They hadn't been drafted as shotgun riders on the Iraqi convoy by accident, that much was certain.

He knew the recent dead might never be identified. Their mission and motives might remain forever unknown. No data bank could ever hope to capture every piece of low-life scum on earth.

And if they failed to make a positive ID, so what? Their mission was accomplished, a clean sweep of the convoy as ordered. Anything else was gravy.

"We need to get moving," Katz told the assembled warriors. "Ninety minutes to our pickup, and we're still three klicks from the landing zone."

The helicopter would be punctual; its pilot had been ordered not to hang around if they were late. No time to waste.

It was a long walk back.

2

"Five minutes," Jack Grimaldi said. "I've got the beacon now."

Beside Grimaldi, in the copilot's seat of the Piper PA-34 Seneca, Mack Bolan made no reply. His eyes were fixed on the crest of the Blue Ridge Mountains below them, Skyline Drive following the ridge of high ground. They passed over a tiny pickup truck, leaving it behind at their cruising speed of 200 miles per hour.

Twenty minutes out of Dulles International, in Washington, they were closing on Stony Man Farm, two hundred acres of orchards and cultivated fields that screened the central base facility from prying eyes.

It was a long way from the streets of Pittsfield, where the Executioner had spent his childhood, but returning to the Blue Ridge station always felt like coming home.

He couldn't see the cyclone fence around the Farm from 7,000 feet, much less make out the signs warning would-be trespassers that they were approaching a restricted area, with use of deadly force authorized inside the wire. Most hikers took the warning seriously, and idle thrill seekers were further deterred by the fence's stunning electric charge. No one got beyond the fence by accident, and those who breached the perimeter deliberately were never seen again.

"Here goes."

Grimaldi spoke into the radio and waited briefly for his confirmation, banking into the approach. The Seneca's twin Continental TS10-360-E four-piston engines changed their pitch immediately, snarling as the pilot put the plane into a shallow dive. Treetops flashed past beneath them, giving way in moments to the lighter green of open fields.

On normal days, when no one was expected, a dilapidated mobile home sat squarely in the middle of the Farm's main airstrip, effectively blocking a touchdown. Even when the obstacle was drawn aside, like now, it didn't lose its bite. Inside, a sentry manned a bank of four GEC miniguns chambered in 7.62 mm, each with a cyclic firing rate of 6,000 rounds per minute. The flick of a switch would drop the mobile home's hinged walls and give the high-speed Gatling guns a full 360-degree field of fire. Any aircraft landing in the face of such a firestorm would be torn apart before its wheels touched down. And then there were the missiles...

The blind remained shuttered and silent as Grimaldi put the Piper down, pulling back on the throttle to cut their speed. An open jeep was waiting for them at the far end of the runway, a familiar face behind the windshield.

Leo.

Bolan felt the smile before he knew that it was coming. Old home week, for sure, but with a tang of apprehension nagging at him. The Executioner wasn't summoned to the Farm for social outings or to sit and pass the time. A call from Stony Man spelled trouble on a scale beyond the "usual." More often than not it meant someone was already dead—in mortal jeopardy, at the very least.

It was all in the stars or the turn of a card, life and death riding on the line each time he took his marching orders from the team of Stony Man.

The warrior waited for the Piper's engines to fall silent, finally leaving his seat and moving back toward the exit, and the folding steps between the open doorway and the ground. Grimaldi took another moment to secure the plane before he followed Bolan, and the two of them approached the jeep together.

Leo Turrin was on his feet beside the vehicle and coming forward to shake hands.

"You're looking good," Bolan remarked.

Turrin shrugged. "I'm going to the gym again, for what it's worth. I make some points with Angelina, anyway. This place is still the only sun I get, to speak of."

"Cloudy days in Wonderland?"

"It's the name of the game. Matter of fact, there's a storm front waiting for you right here."

"That bad?"

"You kidding me? I flew in with the weatherman."

"He's at the farmhouse?"

"Working on his second pot of coffee."

"Well, I guess we shouldn't keep him waiting."

On the ride to the farmhouse, Bolan didn't bother looking for the posted sentries. Some of them were dressed as farmhands and spent their days driving tractors and irrigating crops, while others lay up in the trees, all camouflaged, prepared to strike the moment an alarm was sounded. Even those who seemed innocuous at the first glance kept their weapons close at hand, and all of them had been through Special Forces training at Fort Benning, Georgia.

The farmhouse was a neat structure with attached garage, sixty feet across the front, complete with covered porch. Hal Brognola waited for them by the steps as Turrin pulled in and switched off the jeep's engine. The three men got out, and mounted the wooden steps, Bolan and Grimaldi shaking hands with the man from Justice.

"You made fair time," Brognola said.

"We're here."

"So, it's unanimous. Let's go inside."

The front door opened on an entryway, security headquarters to their immediate left, a den on the right. The stairs were just ahead, and Brognola led the way to the basement. Downstairs, they moved directly to the war room, passing through a coded access door and waiting as it whispered shut behind them.

Aaron Kurtzman had his wheelchair nosed into the horseshoe command console, turning his thick upper body to greet the new arrivals with a smile. Barbara Price was in her customary seat, near the head of the long conference table, glancing up from an open manila folder. Her smile encompassed all four men, but there was special warmth for Bolan, meant for him alone.

"We're it?" Grimaldi asked. His tone registered mild surprise at the small turn-out.

"Able Team has some unfinished business in New England," Brognola said, moving toward his chair. "The guys won't be joining you on this one. Katz is standing by in Tel Aviv to make the satellite connection."

They settled in chairs near Brognola, Bolan facing Barbara Price across the table, Grimaldi on his right, facing Leo. Memories of other urgent conferences came flooding back, and Bolan cut them short. No time for ghosts.

"Let's make the hookup," Brognola said.

"Roger."

Kurtzman's nimble fingers did a tap dance on the keyboard, and a giant wall screen came to life. Just snow for starters, then a blip, and Yakov Katzenelenbogen's face was frowning at them from the screen, three times life size. The wall behind him was a neutral shade, no posters, signs or artwork that would help identify the room. From the direction of the gruff Israeli's eyes, it was apparent that a viewing monitor was mounted just below the camera, level with his chest.

"Have we got audio reception?" Brognola asked.

"That's affirmative," Katz answered, speaking for himself before Kurtzman could field the question. "I read you five by five."

"Okay, let's get it done." Brognola had a slim file spread in front of him, and he glanced at the top sheet as he spoke. "You're all familiar with the UN's standing trade embargo on Iraq?"

"Oil out and Band-aids in," Grimaldi said.

"That's close enough. No weapons are supposed to cross the border going either way, no stocks or bonds, no cash— no nothing, basically, except for petroleum exports and humanitarian aid."

"Let me guess," Bolan said. "There's a leak."

"And then some," the big Fed replied. "Try thousands of leaks, with tons of hardware slipping through, billions of dollars in Iraqi cash and products flooding the international market."

"That's billions with a *B*?" Grimaldi asked.

"You heard me right the first time, Jack. Jordan's King Hussein might not be related to Saddam on paper, but they're brothers under the skin. Amman stayed neutral during Desert Storm, if you call it that, and now the Jordanians are moving anything that's not nailed down from Iraq to the world market...for a tidy commission, of course."

"Diplomatic inquiries?" Bolan queried.

"The usual. We accuse, they deny. We produce satellite photos, they shrug and play dumb. We show them trucks, they ask for proof of what's inside. When all else fails, the king goes on TV and does his see-no-evil act. Butter wouldn't melt in his royal mouth, but he's dirty as hell, and everybody knows it."

"So, why is the White House tiptoeing around?" Grimaldi asked.

"What did you have in mind?"

"Withdraw our diplomats, for openers. Extend the UN sanctions to include Jordan if we have to." There was anger and frustration in Grimaldi's tone. "While we're at it, maybe we should just go back and finish what we started in the first place."

"Sell it to the Congress and the voters, Jack. We're looking at a new peacetime economy, remember? Lots of red ink under the bridge since the USSR fell apart. Nobody wants their 'peace dividend' invested in another war."

"So, what's the answer?"

"Covert action," Bolan interjected, speaking for Brognola. "Tag a convoy on the border, maybe two or three, to drive the message home."

"We've been there," Brognola informed them.

"Phoenix Force?"

The big Fed nodded. "The day before yesterday. It hasn't made the headlines, and I don't expect it will. If anything, our friends in Amman are more likely to blame the Israelis, but I tend to think they're sweeping it under the rug entirely. Be that as it may, we're here because of what Katz and his people found."

"Which was?"

"Two ringers, riding shotgun. Let's take a look."

Kurtzman tapped the console, and a second screen, positioned at the far end of the conference table, lighted up with a close-range photo of a dead man's face. The corpse couldn't have been mistaken for a living man—blood flecked along the jawline, eyes half-open, filmed with gritty dust and not a tear in sight.

"We had to access Interpol to run him down," Brognola said. "Fritz Klenner, German national. Born August 7, 1967, in Heilbronn. Two juvenile convictions, for assault and burglary. For the past two years or so, before he bit the big one, he'd been running with the National Vanguard."

"That's the neo-Nazi outfit?" Grimaldi asked.

"Bingo. Organized in Stuttgart, just before the Wall came down, and growing fast since Germany reunified. They hate the Jews, of course, that's understood. Minorities, you name it. Anything to purify the so-called master race. They're also down on foreigners in general, to the point of mugging tourists on the street. GSG-9 had Klenner pegged as a participant in half a dozen raids—the Mannheim synagogue, that kind of thing—but they could never make it stick."

"Too late," Grimaldi said.

There was a new picture on the viewing screen, a candid telephoto shot showing three young men dressed in black. It was a common uniform of sorts, though it could pass for daily wear to satisfy prevailing German law.

"That's Gerhard Kasche in the middle," Brognola said, "the younger brother of the Vanguard's founder. He's been running things since Heinrich went away for arson three years ago. Somebody taught him how to hate like it's the only game in town."

"It is, for some," the Executioner replied.

"The joker on his left is Bruno Lauck, his number two. He was arrested last year on suspicion of killing a Mittenwald rabbi. The police had two witnesses, but one disappeared and the other clammed up. Case dismissed."

"They pull some kind of weight," Grimaldi said.

"Political connections help," Brognola told the room at large. "No one admits it publicly, but Kasche's Vanguard works hand in glove with the German National Party. You might have tracked their progress in the papers lately, doing what they can to slam the door on immigration and repeal the antifascist legislation dating back to 1948. They've picked up four seats in the national legislature, so far."

"Hitler started with less." Katzenelenbogen's voice was a growl from the hidden speakers.

"What's the link between Jordan and Germany?" Bolan inquired.

"We're working on that. Meanwhile..."

On cue, another dead man popped up on the viewing screen. This one looked slightly older than the first, but it could easily have been the grimace on his face, a sign that he hadn't died quietly or free from pain.

"Meet Mitchell Rudd," Brognola said, "a.k.a. Mark Roberts, Michael Reed, Mitch Reese—the list goes on. We picked his file up from the FBI in Washington. He is—was—a hard-core member of the Aryan Resistance Movement. California-based, an estimated fifteen hundred members nationwide."

"More Nazis." Jack Grimaldi's voice was heavy with contempt.

"Bureau files link the ARM with acts of terroristic violence going back three years or so," Brognola continued. "Gay-bashing, graveyard desecration, arson jobs, the usual. Three members went down behind an armored-car robbery last year, but we never got the money back. A million plus, that was. The word is, some of it was spent on arms, the rest on forging contacts with like-minded groups overseas.''

"Including the National Vanguard?" Bolan asked.

"Right the first time."

Brognola nodded to Kurtzman, and a new face came up on the screen. A police mug shot this time, numbers lined up underneath the pointed chin. Gray eyes stared back at the camera from beneath straight brows. The man's blond hair was too short to comb.

"Justin Arthur Pratt," Brognola announced. "This shot comes from his third arrest, on a charge of inciting to riot in San Diego. Bargained down to disorderly conduct. He served thirty days on a ninety-day sentence. Nothing much since, at least on the books. He's farming out the dirty work these days."

Another, younger face came on the viewing screen. Dark hair, this time. A thin-lipped mouth was drawn down on the left by a scar that ran to his chin.

"Pratt's number two, Chet Blackmun. He pulled eighteen months in the California Youth Authority for manslaughter at age sixteen. When he's not bashing Jews or blacks these days, word has it that he's dealing heavy flake. All in the interest of white power, of course. The DEA's been following his tracks for something like a year. They know he gets his product from Bolivia, but so far that's the limit. Two, three times they've taken down his runners, but they don't give anything away."

"So we've got Nazis dealing shit and chatting transatlantic," Leo Turrin said. "I still don't see the link to Jordan and Iraq."

"That's why we're here," Brognola said. "Black-market trade between Iraq and Jordan's one thing. If they're going international, with drugs and right-wing terrorism on the menu, someone needs to take a closer look. It might be nothing. Then again..."

Bolan's mind was already chasing the possibilities. He didn't have a handle on the motives yet, but he could see a dark potential in the merger of Arab oil money and professional bigots abroad. Israel was enemy number one for both camps, and neither cherished any love for the United States. The neo-Nazi movement in America had long since issued a declaration of war against "ZOG"—the "Zionist Occupational Government" in Washington, D.C.—and groups like the National Vanguard were testing Germany's hate laws on a daily basis, running up sizable casualty lists in the process.

The potential for catastrophe was there, all right, amplified by the involvement of drug money and large-scale dealers from Latin America. He was speculating now, but any way he turned the puzzle pieces over in his mind, there seemed to be no reassuring fit.

"So, what's the plan?" he asked Brognola.

"Phoenix is booked from Tel Aviv into Munich this evening. GSG-9 has an agent standing by to brief them on-site and point out the players. From there we'll see how it goes."

"It will go badly for the master race," Katz promised, still without a smile.

And Bolan didn't doubt that for a moment.

"What about the ARM?" he asked.

"Your baby, if you want it," Brognola replied. "The Bureau has a deep-cover agent close to Pratt, and DEA's been working the Bolivian angle for all it's worth. Both agencies have offered their cooperation—strictly unofficial, I should add."

"What else?" The Executioner couldn't suppress a small, sardonic grin.

"They don't know what it is we do," the big Fed reminded his team, "and they'd like to keep it that way. Congressional oversight committees have been crawling up their backsides as it is, double-checking every dime they spend on covert operations, talking civil liberties. No one official would touch this operation with a ten-foot pole."

"I never met a bureaucrat who had one," Grimaldi quipped, evoking muted laughter from Turrin and Kurtzman.

"Vital statistics aside," Brognola continued, "you'll essentially be on your own."

"Not quite," Grimaldi said. "I'd like to tag along, in case he needs some wings, whatever."

"Fair enough. My point is, that whatever help the regulars decide to give you will be limited, at best. I won't presume to dictate your approach or tactics."

SOP, Bolan thought. If he took the mission—make that *when* he took it on—he'd be dancing on the high wire by himself, without a safety net. The crew at Stony Man would offer full support, of course, but there was little they could do upon short notice, when the fat was in the fire. Southern California might not be a world away, but it could still get lonely for a soldier working on his own behind enemy lines.

"Let's do it," Bolan said.

The rest of it was independent briefings, Katzenelenbogen first, while they still had the satellite hookup in place. Bolan went out for coffee while the head of Phoenix Force was talking tactics with Brognola, scoping out the players on the German front.

Five men against how many, when they reached the target area? They would be violating every major statute on the books, opposed by the police as well as their intended adversaries in the National Vanguard. Still, there would be five, plus one or more from the German antiterrorist squad at GSG-9.

In California it would just be Bolan, with Grimaldi in reserve for any airborne operations that happened to materialize. The Executioner took it for granted that the FBI's deep-cover agent would be more concerned with protecting himself and his contacts than helping out some wild-ass warrior who dropped in out of nowhere, looking to upset the apple cart. Orders were one thing, but communiqués from Washington on this one would remain ambiguous, at best. Nothing in the files suggested that FBI headquarters had countenanced an illegal search-and-destroy mission on American soil.

Bolan's briefing lived up to its name, fifteen minutes in and out, finessing the available details from Brognola's dossier on the Aryan Resistance Movement. The big Fed had little to add, beyond some character assessments of the opposition and their status as a fighting force. Most of the rank-and-file members were skinheads and thugs, high-school dropouts with a king-size grudge against life in general, anxious to lay the blame for their own miserable failures on convenient scapegoats. At the heart of the movement, though, there was a hard core of dedicated haters, politicized misfits with a deadly ax to grind. They viewed themselves as frontline soldiers in a war of national liberation from the tentacles of ZOG, and they had demonstrated willingness to die in that pursuit.

Okay.

The Executioner could help them out, if it was martyrdom they craved.

In fact it was his specialty.

When he was finished with the briefing, Bolan retired to his quarters and took a steaming shower. He was stepping from the bathroom with a towel around his waist, when someone knocked on the door.

Barbara Price stood on the threshold, a bottle of red wine in one hand, two glasses in the other.

''Room service,'' she told him. ''You called, sir?''

Bolan smiled his welcome.

''You're just in time.''

3

Horst Bochner checked his wristwatch for the third time in as many minutes, his eyes flitting back to the Volkswagen's windshield, checking the flow of traffic on Friedrichstrasse. His pigeon was running late, but it made no difference in the long run. He was ready, and his men were ready. All had been prepared. Nothing was left to chance.

In the driver's seat, Rudi Plisl hummed softly to himself, one hand covering the short-barreled Walther P-38 in his lap. Behind him, Hermann Braun was armed with a Heckler & Koch 9 mm MP-5 submachine gun, identical to the one braced across Bochner's knees.

All ready.

The Israeli would be coming soon. Five minutes late, but that was nothing in Berlin these days. Since demolition of the Wall, the city was revitalized, but urban growth couldn't occur without a fair degree of chaos on the side. New construction delayed and diverted traffic, police were swamped with everything from auto accidents to robberies and homicides, but all of this was progress, in its way.

Reunification of the Fatherland was a first long step in the right direction, moving inexorably toward the day when Germans would rediscover their national pride, reach out to grasp their destiny from tumbling foreign hands. It wasn't the last step, by any means, but every triumphant victory march had to start somewhere.

Bochner's march to glory had already started, but this night's engagement would advance the cause quite handsomely.

Besides, it was a matter of revenge.

He didn't know exactly what had happened in the desert wastes of Jordan. Horst Bochner wasn't privy to top-level strategy of the National Vanguard. It was enough for him to think of Fritz, a friend and fighting comrade, cut down in a savage land, surrounded by strangers, inferiors. Fritz Klenner was a human sacrifice for the cause of racial purity, and his loss wasn't taken lightly at home.

It never crossed Horst Bochner's mind to exonerate the Israelis from complicity in Klenner's death. The Zionists were everywhere, throughout the Middle East and around the globe, pulling strings with their Jew-loving allies abroad. Tel Aviv snapped its greasy, money-grubbing fingers, and the other countries fell in line, parroting Zionist slogans and vying with one another for the chance to kiss Israeli ass. The German government was no better, but at least the fatherland still had a nucleus of hard-core patriots on hand to stem the running tide of treason.

Starting now.

Their source had guaranteed that the Israeli would be coming; he had even specified the route, aware that any mix-ups or mistakes would have dire repercussions for himself. Horst Bochner knew the source, a closet Nazi who was sickened by the way his job required him to associate with Zionists and other trash. Still, everybody had to make a living, and his access to the enemy was sometimes helpful to the cause.

He knew, for instance, that the minister from Tel Aviv was scheduled to attend a reception at the Berlin Museum. Some kind of cocktail party for an "artist" who specialized in decadent obscenities, the kind of thing that Jews enjoyed supporting, anything at all to undermine society and spread their taint to members of the master race.

The minister from Tel Aviv wouldn't have recognized Fritz Klenner's name. It was ridiculous to think that every bureaucrat and flunky in the Zionist establishment was privy to the inner strategies of government. No matter. An example was needed, and any Yid would do, as long as he was in the public eye. A cultural attaché fit the bill, and the communiqué prepared to follow his elimination would remove all doubt.

The hand-held radio beside Horst Bochner squawked and sputtered three delicious syllables.

"Approaching."

Plisl reached for the ignition key and brought the Volkswagen to life, but kept the headlights off. When the Mercedes came into sight, they would be ready, waiting.

Bochner cocked the MP-5, but left the safety off, his index finger resting on the trigger guard. The submachine gun's metal stock was folded. He wouldn't be firing from the shoulder this time, not a requirement for an expert marksman when it came to laying down a screen of automatic fire at point-blank range.

He saw the sleek Mercedes rolling south on Friedrichstrasse, late but coming, rapidly closing the gap. Behind him, Hermann would be lifting the American M-79 grenade launcher from its place at his feet, slipping a 40 mm high-explosive round into the stubby weapon's firing chamber. Just the thing for opening an armored vehicle, the sort that even low-level Israeli diplomats used in this day and age of high security.

"On my command," Bochner said.

He counted off the seconds in his head. One thousand one. One thousand two. One thousand—

"Go!"

ASHER BLUM WASN'T concerned about a tardy entrée to a cocktail party that would doubtless leave him bored to tears before he found an opportunity to slip away. His wife was six months pregnant, and she took advantage of the fact, quite sensibly, to dodge engagements with a "yawn potential" well above the average. It almost made Blum wish he was a woman, anyway, until he thought about the crap most women had to take from day to day.

On balance, Blum would take his chances with the cocktail party and attempt to slip out early, when the hosts were suitably distracted. As it was, at least the food and drinks were free.

His service in Berlin, the past two years, hadn't been uneventful, but he had been spared the dangers encountered by some of his colleagues in other countries. Germany's effective antiterrorist squad had suppressed Palestinian violence and much of the Red Army Faction since the early 1980s, but security remained tight for the Israeli embassy and its personnel. Of late, especially since reunification, there had been other stirrings, from the right-wing underground, echoes from Dachau with younger voices belting out the old, familiar marching songs this time.

It worried Blum, though he couldn't lay claim to any relatives annihilated by the Nazis during World War II. He understood the pain, regardless. It was part of every Jew on earth, their nationalities irrelevant to understanding of the man-made tragedy that made them one. He understood why it was necessary to retaliate in force against the Palestinians each time they crossed the border with their AK-47s and grenades.

His country's fighting motto said it all: Never Again.

On the surface there was little that a cultural attaché could contribute to security for Israel. He was paid to nod and smile, make small talk with a wide variety of artists, businessmen and diplomats throughout each working day. Blum told himself that he was making Israel stronger by procuring friends in every walk of life, and sometimes he believed it.

Sometimes.

Other times, Blum thought he might feel better in another line of work. Two years of mandatory service in the military generated no desire to spend his life in uniform, but there were countless other things he could have done with his degree in political science and languages. Diplomacy had sounded romantic at first, and by the time reality set in, well, Blum was hooked and working on his pension, with a young wife to support.

And he was safe. As safe as any Jew could hope to be, these days. He would be far down on the target list for anyone nursing a grudge against the embassy, assuming that he made the list at all.

Security and the trappings of stability were important to Blum, more so to his wife. She made no secret of her hope that he would someday rise to the rank of a full-fledged ambassador, commanding the prestige and respect that accompanied that title. As for Blum himself, he thought that it might be enough to simply do his time, retire on schedule to a farm in the Negev and finish out his life in peace.

He was ten minutes late, but that was nothing in the beehive of Berlin society. If he was only late by twenty minutes, Blum would bet that some two-thirds of the invited guests would still be missing, dawdling with their mistresses and gigolos, intent on staging just the right dramatic entrance at a social function where photographers would catch their good sides in a flash. Recorded for posterity.

All for show.

Blum relaxed, pushing the requirements of diplomacy from his mind with an effort. Tonight could be amusing, in a simpleminded way, if he could only let himself unwind to some degree. Picking up a woman was out of the question, of course, with so many strange eyes upon him, but an innocent flirtation always helped to pass the time if Blum found something interesting around the bar.

Ruth had grown increasingly distant through the weeks of her pregnancy, seeming to notice her husband only when she had complaints to make. Blum loved her dearly, as he would surely love their child when it was born, but in the meantime.

A smile played across Blum's face as he watched the flow of traffic on Friedrichstrasse. Just ahead of the Mercedes was an opening before they reached the next traffic signal. Blum saw his driver check the rearview mirror, felt the pressure of acceleration as the car surged forward, closing the distance.

The late-model Volkswagen came out of nowhere, veering across their path and cutting the Mercedes off. Blum's driver hit the brakes, cursing, his passenger rocked forward by the sudden stop. They had been driving in the inside lane, and now the right front tire of the Mercedes jammed against the curb. Blum muttered an oath as he was nearly vaulted from his seat.

In front of him, the Volkswagen formed an effective roadblock, its doors flapping open, young men with grim faces piling out of the car, weapons in their hands.

Blum felt his stomach twist into a painful knot.

"Dear God!"

HORST BOCHNER'S PULSE was pounding as he hit the pavement, leveling his submachine gun at the sleek Mercedes. He knew there was no point firing yet. Israeli diplomats went nowhere these days without their armored cars and bodyguards. The Mercedes would be a tank, and as such it required special antitank munitions.

Rudi Plisl stepped forward with the M-79 grenade launcher, aimed directly at the tinted windshield and squeezing off a 40 mm round. The shock wave rocked Bochner on his heels, but he stood fast, raising his weapon and firing a short burst toward the driver's seat through a pall of swirling smoke.

Small need of that, he thought. The bastard would be shredded after that explosion, probably his passenger as well, but they would take no chances. Thoroughness was crucial in guerrilla warfare. Enemies allowed to walk away from one engagement might surprise you next time, coming out on top.

But not this pig from Tel Aviv.

Plisl's second grenade ripped the left rear door from its hinges, opening the smoky interior of the armored car. Bochner stepped forward, Plisl close behind him as his comrade laid the M-79 aside and hoisted his machine pistol into firing position.

Asher Blum was visible inside the car, a rag-doll figure slumped across the back seat, looking limp and lifeless. Bochner took nothing for granted, stepping closer, and cutting loose with the MP-5 at a range of ten or twelve feet. Blum's body twitched and trembled with the impact of 9 mm parabellum slugs, crimson bursting from his many wounds.

Another heartbeat and the magazine was empty. Bochner stepped forward, leaning inside the Mercedes, making sure. He could feel the heat that radiated from the door frame, where the grenade had punched through, holding his breath against the smoke and stench of fecal matter from the dead man's bowels.

Bochner tucked the MP-5 under his arm, reaching inside his windbreaker for the classic Luger automatic. His grandfather had carried such a weapon in the last great war against the Jews—not this one, granted, but an identical model—and Bochner wore the Luger with pride. He cocked it now, drawing back the toggle action, leaning across the back of the driver's seat.

Blum's driver was missing his head from the jawline upward, obviously dead, but Bochner shot him anyway. Three bullets in the chest to emphasize the point.

No sanctuary for the Zionist oppressors of the master race.

He backed out of the shattered Mercedes, feeling the smile on his face, and retraced his steps to the Volkswagen. Traffic was stalled for blocks behind their ambush, drivers gaping at him from behind a dozen windshields. Bochner blessed the traffic jam that would delay police response, and made no effort to conceal his face.

The drifting smoke and the shock of witnessing a double murder would serve him as well as a ski mask. And if the pig detectives managed to compile a workable description of the raiders, what was that to him? Horst Bochner felt no shame for his participation in the struggle. He was proud of his achievement, would have sung it from the rooftops given half a chance.

His time was coming, Bochner told himself, but not just yet. Today they were compelled to flee and hide, leave others to release the proud communiqué.

Another slap at Israel and her slavish lackeys all around the world.

Fritz Klenner was avenged.

For now, this moment, Bochner thought it was enough.

MOSSAD HEADQUARTERS in downtown Tel Aviv, Israel, is a nondescript low rise designed with utility and security in mind. The windows are double-thick bulletproof glass, specially tinted to prevent a passerby from seeing in at any time of day or night. An eight-foot fence and concrete dragon's teeth surround the office block to minimize the risk of suicide attacks. Armed guards are posted at the exits, and a rooftop sniper team stands watch around the clock, nestled among sandbags, surrounded by a small forest of aerials and satellite-dish antennas.

For all the aboveground security, most of Mossad's sensitive business is conducted below street level, in a cocoon of reinforced concrete designed to withstand direct hits from any nonnuclear warhead or bomb.

Uri Dan was familiar with the building's layout and its various layers of security. Over the past twelve years, on average, he had reported to Mossad headquarters three days a week, displaying his laminated ID card for the sentries at three separate checkpoints before he reached his tiny office on the second floor. When he was working in the field, he was in daily contact with headquarters by radio or telephone.

In most respects the ugly low rise was his home.

He had no family to speak of—parents both deceased, no children, never married. Uri Dan's one sibling was a sabra, midway through her sixth year in the military, but they seldom spoke. He missed her sometimes, mostly during holidays, but it was abstract pain, minute and soon dismissed from conscious thought.

Dan lived for his profession, focusing on counterintelligence and the suppression of anti-Israeli terrorism to the virtual exclusion of all else. What woman would be willing to accept a man on those terms, when she knew that he would always put his country first, its enemies second and his private life last?

The summons to report for work at night—11:45 p.m., to be precise—wasn't unusual. It told him there had been some kind of flap, a crisis of the sort that came along for Dan every two or three months. He didn't try to guess the problem, knowing speculation was fruitless. He would be told exactly what he had to know when he was briefed by his superiors.

Dan showed his ID to the outer sentry, retrieved it and passed through the gate. He walked fifty feet to the headquarters entrance, where an armed guard buzzed him through and gave the plastic-coated card a second look. He used a hand-held scanner to read the bar code printed on the flip side, confirming Dan's top-secret clearance. Dan surrendered his Beretta side arm, his car keys and pocket change, stepping through the fixed metal detector without producing a squawk.

"Proceed."

There was no sentry on the elevators, but a closed-circuit television camera followed Dan that far, another picking up his progress when he stepped inside the car. If he displayed any sort of suspicious behavior in the elevator—producing an undisclosed weapon, for instance—the car would be stopped between floors, its passenger isolated and sealed off while armed defenders rallied to the silent alarm.

He pressed the button for the basement and waited impassively while the car took him down. He passed through a third checkpoint as he disembarked, the sentry making no attempt to hide his Uzi submachine gun or the semiautomatic pistol on his hip. The laminated ID card received its third and most intensive check before Dan was passed along an antiseptic hallway to the briefing room.

His chief was waiting for him, gray and taciturn. Meyer Levin had served the Mossad for over thirty years, and office wags were fond of joking that he hadn't left his basement hideaway in twenty-five. He smoked incessantly and seemed to shun the daylight like a vampire. If Meyer ever stepped outside, a colleague once remarked while dining in the cafeteria, he would disintegrate.

"We have a problem, Uri." Levin lighted a fresh cigarette from the butt of his last one, drawing the smoke deep into his lungs.

Dan took a seat across the desk from Levin, leaned back and crossed his legs. "What is it?"

"Asher Blum, the cultural attaché, was murdered in Berlin tonight with his driver. That was three hours ago, and now the German police have a communiqué from the killers."

Levin passed a flimsy sheet of fax paper across the desk. The message was brief and direct: Blood demands blood. Death to Jew-Zionist leeches—NV

"NV?" Dan thought he knew the answer, but it never hurt to ask.

"The National Vanguard. You're familiar with the movement, I assume?"

It was a rhetorical question. Dan nodded, running through the mental dossier on Germany's latter-day fascist underground. "Neo-Nazis," he replied. "Political connections to the German National Party. Involved in anti-Semitic terrorism and violence against foreign visitors for the past four years, approximately."

"Near enough." Levin's face was a mask carved from colorless stone.

"You accept the communiqué as genuine?"

"We have no reason to doubt it," Levin replied. "The Vanguard has killed before today. This time, they might think they have a reason."

"'Blood demands blood'?"

"Three days ago, in Jordan, a black-market Iraqi convoy was ambushed by persons unknown."

Dan raised a skeptical eyebrow. "Sir?"

"The action wasn't ours, I am assured by those I trust. The weapons used were Russian, this we know. Beyond that, all is speculation."

"And the Vanguard?"

"One of their men was riding with the convoy. Jordanian authorities picked him up with the rest of the bodies, nineteen in all. His name was Fritz Klenner. Nothing in our files, but GSG-9 made the Vanguard connection. Another rider with the convoy was American, a member of their Aryan Resistance Movement."

"And the rest?"

"Iraqis and Jordanians, roughly half-and-half," Levin told him. "Nothing noteworthy."

"The cargo?"

"Art objects, for the most part, bound for shipment through Amman to European markets."

"So."

"We cannot tolerate a challenge of this sort," the handler said. "It must be dealt with."

Dan knew what was coming. Once upon a time, Israel had maintained a special unit for revenge and counterterrorism, dubbed the Wrath of God. That group had been disbanded in the late 1970s, but Tel Aviv retained a strict policy of retaliation for each and every terrorist attack, regardless of the time or place. At any cost an injury must be repaid, enemies stalked and eradicated from the face of the earth.

He smiled and asked, "When do I leave?"

4

It had begun.

Midnight was approaching when Shiraz Najaf received the bulletin at his flat in Iraq. It called for no response, and so he sent the messenger away with nothing but a nod for the performance of his duty. Coddling subordinates was an insidious habit, eschewed by Najaf as destructive to order and discipline.

In fact the messenger had brought good news. The plan was paying off, small dividends to start with, but he hadn't counted on a massive chain reaction in the early stages. Anything worth doing well took time. As it was with the construction of a house or the production of a classic sculpture, so it was in striving for revenge.

So many targets, but the ax would fall on each and every one of them in turn.

It was fitting that Israel should feel his wrath first. As far as Najaf was concerned, every major conflict in the Middle East was traceable to the arbitrary creation of the Zionist state long ago, in the year before his birth. The uprooting of Palestinian Arabs to create a Jewish "homeland" was the first shot in a war that wouldn't end until the scourge of Zionism had been purged with fire and blood. The rest of it, from British actions in Suez to the American display of might in Operation Desert Storm, all stemmed from the painful, traumatic birth of Israel.

Too late for an abortion, and the bastard child had grown into a bully, stealing land and self-respect from Arab neighbors. Oil-poor Israel called the tune for American policy in much of the Middle East, evoking the specter of Jewish voting blocs at home whenever aid to Israel was debated in Congress, plucking at liberal heartstrings with references to the so-called Holocaust.

Under different circumstances, it might have been amusing for Najaf to watch a postage-stamp country with no resources to speak of dictating foreign policy to the United States. Truly, as the Americans would say, it was a case of the tail wagging the dog. In fact, however, he could find no cause for mirth as he surveyed the forty-six years of history since Israel's creation. Iraq and her Arab neighbors had been repeatedly humiliated, forced to grovel in the style of poor relatives begging for a plate of table scraps. When they turned against each other, as in the Iraqi war against Iran, agents of the United States and Israel funneled hardware to both sides, thus promoting fratricide.

But times were changing. Israel and her lackeys didn't know it yet, but they were riding for a fall. The enemies of Zionist imperialism were working night and day to free the millstone from around their necks, and this time they would triumph.

The dead Jew's name was Asher Blum, a cultural attaché in Berlin. He was a flyspeck in the larger scheme of things, less than insignificant to the master plan, but his death would put Tel Aviv on notice. The Zionists and their allies had nowhere to hide. Not in Berlin. Not in Washington. Not in Tel Aviv itself. The arm of righteous vengeance was long and powerful, inescapable.

At first it had gone against the grain for Shiraz Najaf to work with Germans and Americans, but he had overcome his prejudice in the interest of expediency. Great risks were involved in sending Arab gunmen into western Europe, all the more so in America, but each and every one of the selected target nations had its own hard core of dissidents who hated Jews on their own account, militant warriors who had pledged their lives to combating the Zionist scourge.

The best thing about Jews, Najaf thought, was the way in which they managed to alienate total strangers, almost overnight. Potential enemies of the Zionist regime were everywhere, more of them appearing with each new day. If they could somehow be coordinated, organized into a worldwide fighting force...

The convoy's loss had been a minor setback, irritating when it happened, but Najaf had a new perspective now. The massacre of nineteen men could prove to be a blessing in disguise, the trigger incident for widespread reprisals against Israel and her cronies.

Indeed, the payback had already begun.

He had to give the Germans credit. They had moved swiftly, effectively, without hesitation. Something in their national experience, perhaps, predisposed them to ruthless action against the Jews.

Najaf had never met a Nazi before this year, and he wasn't impressed by their peculiar, egocentric interpretations of world history. The goose-steppers held his own people—all nonwhites—in utter contempt, but they were willing to bargain for cash and arms, whatever the source. Betrayal would come later, if they got the chance.

But that would never happen.

Shiraz Najaf was no ignorant desert nomad to be duped by false friends. He had his own agenda, and he meant to see it through.

But first, regardless of the hour, he had a call to make.

TARIM SUDAIR CRADLED the telephone receiver, his fingertips lingering briefly on the plastic instrument before he drew back his hand. Jordanian intelligence had confirmed the message from Baghdad, tapping an embassy source in Berlin, but Sudair was still uncertain how he felt about the news.

Of course, he was pleased any time a blow was struck against the Zionists, regardless of the source, and this move had come from one of his own. The Germans were first on the scoreboard, avenging the loss of their man on the convoy.

Payback.

Granted, Sudair still had no clear idea of who had ambushed the Iraqi convoy. There was every chance that he would never know, but that didn't prevent his speculating on the subject. Sudair's prime suspects were the Zionists in Tel Aviv. Their spies were everywhere, including Arab traitors who would readily sell off their birthright for a handful of coins. It would have been a simple thing for the Mossad to learn the convoy's scheduled route, the time of its departure, and to lie in wait along the trail.

A simple thing... but were the Jews, in fact, responsible?

If one absolved the Zionists, albeit theoretically, then the field was wide open. Anyone from the Iranians to Britain's MI-6 or the American CIA would jump at the chance to punish Iraq and embarrass Baghdad's Jordanian front men.

Which meant that they were taking aim directly at Tamir Sudair.

Truth be told, the agent in Amman wasn't enamored of Saddam Hussein's regime. The man was an insufferable bully, with his neighbors and his native population, but that label hardly set him apart from other Middle Eastern rulers. Sudair despised the Beast of Baghdad for his crass opportunism, spouting support for a Palestinian homeland when it served his purpose, ignoring his homeless, hopeless brothers most of the time. Given a choice, Sudair would have preferred to work with almost anyone besides the spokesmen for Saddam Hussein.

But there had been no choice.

His king dictated full cooperation, and Sudair obeyed. It would be foolish, even suicidal, to do otherwise.

And he agreed with some of what the bold Iraqis said. Their animosity toward Israel matched his own, and he wouldn't mind striking out at the United States for once, reversing the usual trend in international events...provided, always, that it didn't place his own neck on the chopping block.

The Iranian mullahs might be overstating matters when they damned America as ''The Great Satan,'' but there was still a hard core of truth in their words. Without support from the United States and Britain, Israel would surely wither and die on the vine like some overripe fruit.

In one role or another, Tarim Sudair had been dealing with Baghdad since the end of Operation Desert Storm, in 1991, facilitating black-market shipments of cash and salable objects from Iraq, through Jordan, to banks and open markets in the West. Evading the United Nations sanctions was a relatively simple matter, given the time-honored privacy stipulations of banks in Switzerland, Liechtenstein and the Caribbean. Iraqi cash was welcomed in the button-down world of numbered accounts and overt investments, all the more in South America, where money spent on cocaine shipments to America could be increased a hundredfold in hours or days.

It wasn't such a small world, after all. In fact, Sudair believed the world had grown too large and too complex for any single country—even the United States—to effectively strangle an enemy's financial prospects. Greed was the true international language, spoken fluently from Baghdad and Zurich to Bogotá and Los Angeles. Even the zealots, rabid Jew haters who stockpiled their weapons and worshiped the spirit of Hitler, found time to fatten their own bankrolls with illicit trafficking in drugs, arms, anything at all.

Sudair understood such men. He had been dealing with their kind all of his adult life, and what he lacked in personal admiration was made up in grudging respect for their power and influence. King Hussein was such a man, himself, keeping Jordan afloat in a sea of red ink by accommodating his rapacious neighbors.

Even so, the present game was different. Instead of simply acting as the middleman, Sudair found himself thrust into a leadership role, of sorts, helping to direct a global terrorist campaign. Now the Germans had set the ball rolling, and there could be no turning back.

It was a brand-new feeling for the civil servant in Amman.

He only hoped it wouldn't get him killed.

"A TOAST!"

Gerhard Kasche raised his foaming beer mug, waiting while the others did likewise. He was surrounded by grinning faces, but the momentary center of attention was Horst Bochner, their conquering hero.

"To Horst and his commandos, for their service to the fatherland," Kasche said. "They have struck a heroic blow against the Zionist parasites among us. One more step in our long march to victory. Heil Hitler!"

The small room bristled with stiff-arm salutes, a chorus of voices barking their praise of the führer. The dozen men present were focused, spiritually united in their determination to establish a Fourth Reich in reunified Germany. Hitler had failed, through no fault of his own, to establish the Thousand-Year Reich, but Gerhard Kasche had faith in his personal destiny.

The day was coming, that much closer for their new co-operation with like-minded elements in the Middle East. They weren't the allies Kasche would have chosen on his own, but war—like politics—made for strange allies. Once the hated Jews had been disposed of, anything was possible. Before the Arabs knew it, a revitalized fatherland would control their precious oil fields, crushing their ragtag armies and heathen mosques beneath a polished jackboot.

There was still a long way to go, but Gerhard Kasche was a patient man at heart. He longed for the day of victory as much as any of his comrades—more so—but he understood that no lasting triumph was won overnight. The great fortresses were built one brick at a time, with a craftsman's loving attention to quality and detail.

One brick at a time.

And they had dropped a large one on the Jew pig's head tonight, no doubt about it. Nothing could bring Fritz Klenner back, but in his private thoughts, Kasche knew that Klenner had merely been a cog in the war machine, an expendable soldier who laid down his life for the fatherland. Klenner was worth more to the movement dead than he ever had been alive. He was a martyr now, a symbol for the other

Vanguard members to hold in abstract high esteem. His name would become a battle cry for those who followed after.

And there would be other martyrs, soon enough. Kasche had no doubt of that. You couldn't fight a war without suffering casualties, and he stressed that point in his speeches to the faithful, doing his best to prepare the frontline brownshirts for arrest or worse. He relied on his own charisma and their adulation for Hitler to put steel in their spines at the crucial moment.

"It was a pleasure to eliminate the Jew," Horst Bochner said. "I only wish it could have been more challenging. Like spearing trout in a bucket, it was. We took them absolutely by surprise, and they had nowhere to run."

"Next time, we'll let you try the embassy," Bruno Lauck said. More laughter from the troops, as Bochner drew back his shoulders and thrust out his chin.

"Just tell me when."

"Every victory is precious," Kasche interrupted. "If we have a chance to hit the Jews without sacrificing one of our own, so much the better. We need soldiers who will live to fight another day, not like the Arabs who are hungry for the chance to kill themselves."

"I'm not afraid," Bochner said, a flicker of disquiet in his eyes.

"No one is questioning your heroism," Kasche replied. "You have done well tonight, and we are grateful for your contribution to the cause."

The comment generated a round of boozy cheers from the assembled warriors. Kasche waited for the moment of hilarity to die away before he spoke again.

"We still have far to go," he told his troops. "Tonight is but a single step, and we must not let down our guard. Our enemies will do their best to crush us, but I guarantee that they will fail if we remain united in commitment to our duty for the fatherland. Each blow we strike will bring us that much closer to the final triumph. When the bastard state of Israel lies in ashes and the traitors to our race are swept away, we will recall this moment as a starting point and honor those who made it possible."

"Except the ragheads," Lauck interjected, drawing laughter from his audience.

"Their day is coming," Kasche promised, taking back the floor from his subordinate. He valued Bruno's muscle but wouldn't have given two cents for his tact. "In time, we will dispose of all our enemies, without exception."

"This should give the Yankees something to consider," Lauck said, refusing to be silent. "They are used to playing games with homosexuals and blacks. The time has come for them to recognize and deal with their true enemies from strength."

"Death to the Jews!" Horst Bochner shouted, hoisting his half-empty beer mug toward the ceiling, a sloppy grin on his face.

The rest took up his chant, some turning toward the portrait of the führer as they drained their pewter mugs. Kasche could feel the electricity crackling among them, bringing them together as one, his living weapon, aimed at the heart of his enemies at home and abroad.

There would be static from his contacts in the German National Party, their customary aversion to dramatic action in the streets, but Kasche felt certain he could put their minds at ease. They all had common goals, and any action that advanced one group would ultimately help them both.

He didn't fear the phone call, knowing that the party still depended on his brownshirts for its strength. If one group or the other failed from lack of trying hard enough, it wouldn't be the Vanguard.

They were on a roll, as the Americans would say, and the day was coming when they would roll right over their enemies, leaving crumpled bodies in the dust.

THE LATE NEWS out of Germany had faded from the television screen, and Justin Pratt switched the set off, staring at the blank wall opposite his chair for long, silent moments. Kasche's National Vanguard had put the Jews on notice, counterpunching for the loss of his man in Jordan, and what had Pratt accomplished in his own backyard?

Mitch Rudd was dead and rotting in a desert grave. There was no opportunity for them to bring him home and treat him to the hero's funeral he deserved, because it would have brought the FBI down on their necks at once. The Aryan Resistance Movement had enough problems with agents of ZOG as it was, everything from tax audits to paid infiltrators, the Judas goats who talked a good battle and sold their brothers out to Jew-loving federal agents at the first opportunity.

The year before, it had been Pratt's pleasure to preside at the interrogation of a federal spy. The session had been videotaped for posterity, the cassette tucked away in his safe-deposit box downtown. Pratt conjured up the pig informer's screams from time to time, amusing himself and drawing solace from the memory.

There would be more such golden moments in the days ahead, but Pratt had other matters to concern him now.

Revenge, for one, and how to let his people know that he wasn't indifferent to their loss. Payback was the name of the game, and he couldn't afford to stall forever.

A second issue was Pratt's commitment, on behalf of the ARM, to their Arab allies of the moment. Despite his single-minded commitment to racial purity, Pratt wasn't above working with nonwhites when it served his purpose. The previous year, he had sat down for meetings with spokesmen from the Nation of Islam, Black Muslims who shared Pratt's contempt for the Jew parasites, preferring his overt racism to the mealymouthed hypocrisy of so-called liberals.

So it was with the Arabs. There was no pretense of mutual admiration or affection. The ragheads had money and hardware that Pratt's troops would need for their final push to victory at home, and in return for those strategic contributions to the cause, they simply asked him to do what he planned on doing anyway, with or without their support. If Middle Eastern aid advanced his timetable, so much the better. It was fitting irony, Pratt told himself, that third world mongrels should contribute to America for once in their miserable lives.

Revenge for Mitch Rudd's death was high on his list of priorities, but Pratt wasn't naive enough to place a dead man before the living soldiers of his movement. They were growing stronger, granted, drawing new recruits from the Klan and competing paramilitary factions, but he didn't have bodies to waste on empty, hopeless gestures.

Any move he made would have to be well planned, with an above-average potential for success.

And he would have to make it soon.

The Germans had scored a definite coup, with their strike at the Israelis' diplomat. Pratt had no men in Washington, D.C., and anyway, the Yids would be doubly on guard after the loss of their stooge in Berlin. He would need another target, one to drive his point home with a vengeance, while allowing his commandos a good prospect for escape.

Pratt ran the mental checklist, ticking off assorted synagogues and schools, the Simon Wiesenthal Center in Los Angeles, businessmen and politicians known for their public support of the Zionist state.

He needed something special, even dramatic, something that would drive his point home without bringing down too much federal heat on the faithful.

His troops were getting restless. Pratt could see it in their faces, hear it in their angry questions since the news had come of Rudd's death. No matter that the triggerman was unidentified, perhaps an Arab bandit totally divorced from any link to Tel Aviv. Pratt's men wanted the Jews to be responsible; it fit their preconceptions of the world at large and fueled their righteous anger toward the common enemy. They didn't have a hope in hell of tracking Rudd's actual assassin, but there were plenty of targets at home, just begging for attention.

It was time for Justin Pratt to make a choice, select his hit team and unleash them on the enemy. The longer he waited, the weaker he seemed in the eyes of his soldiers.

And weakness was fatal.

In an organization like the ARM, there was always a new warlord waiting in the wings, anxious to seize the top spot for himself. But Pratt wasn't about to step down or let himself be pushed aside.

Time to choose, and let the chips fall where they may.

He reached out for the telephone beside his chair and punched up a number from memory, marshaling the troops.

5

Bolan followed the San Diego Freeway north from L.A. International Airport, pushing his Ford at the legal speed limit. He watched his rearview mirror for highway patrol cars, conscious of the hardware bundled in the trunk. A speeding ticket would offer no excuse for a search of the car, but Bolan refused to take chances with so much at stake.

From this point on, his life was riding on the line.

And he wasn't alone.

He picked up Interstate 5 near San Fernando, following it north to the cutoff for Highway 14. The state road took him west as far as Vincent, north from there through Lancaster, Rosamond, Mojave, across the high desert, climbing into the foothills of the Sierra Nevada. It was a long drive to follow a cross-country flight, but Bolan was glad to be moving, homing on a concrete target in the first phase of his new campaign.

As yet, he hadn't met his deep-cover contact from the FBI. That would come later, after he had taken time to get his feet wet, shake up the Aryan Resistance Movement a little on his own, a sucker punch from out of nowhere, just to keep the Nazis guessing.

Driving through Lancaster, he was reminded that this was where the virulent Aryan Nations got its start, the brainchild of an aging Ku Klux Klansman and convert to the bizarre "Christian Identity" cult. Stripped of its pseudo-scriptural trappings, "Identity" religion taught that Nordic races—the classic "Aryans"—were actually the "lost

tribes of Israel.'' Jews, in turn, were the subhuman offspring of Eve and Satan, conceived in the Garden of Eden,
direct ancestors of the nonwhite ''mud people'' who populated so much of the globe. Racial purity demanded revolution against the sinister ''Zionist Occupational
Government,'' a holy crusade to be pursued by any and all
means available.

It was incredible, in Bolan's view, that any thinking person in the last decade of the twentieth century could enter-
tain serious commitment to the ''master race'' philosophy
of Adolf Hitler and his minions. After World War II, the
ghastly revelations of the death camps, logic dictated that
all sane men would turn their backs on organized hatred en
masse...but such was not the case.

Today, on the eve of a new era, self-styled scholars and
candidates for national office denounced the Holocaust as
a myth, deliberate fiction concocted by Jewish propagan-
dists, supported by perjured affidavits, doctored photo-
graphs and bogus newsreels filmed in Hollywood.
Thousands, perhaps millions, of would-be Aryans swallowed the fallacious argument, accepting discredited out-
lines of the ''Jewish world conspiracy'' at face value, never
questioning the source or the statistics. Some of those believers—admittedly a small minority—lapsed into fanati-
cism, donning sheets or uniforms and taking up the gun to
help defend their concept of a ''white man's country.''

Madness.

Bolan's target for the morning was a mountain training
camp constructed and maintained by the Aryan Resistance
Movement. Information from the Bureau files in Washington had put him on the scent, and he saw it as the perfect
opportunity to make his presence felt in California without
taking the critical step of revealing his identity to the enemy.

The last town he passed through was Little Lake, a wide
spot in the road where a full-service gas station competed for
attention with a mom-and-pop burger joint. Bolan passed
them both and found his turnoff a mile north of town. The

side road was narrow, maybe a lane and half in a pinch, but he met no traffic coming down the mountain.

Fine.

The last thing he needed at the moment was company.

Two miles off the highway the pavement ran out, giving way to hard-packed dirt and traces of gravel. Bolan watched the odometer, navigating on the directions he had been given. A quarter mile beyond the asphalt's cutoff point, he started looking for a place to hide the car. It took him fifty yards, but he found a slash between the conifers with ancient tire tracks pressed into the weeds, some makeout artist's high-security retreat. He nosed in the Ford, double-checking to satisfy himself that it was hidden from the road before he killed the engine.

Time to change.

His camouflage fatigues were in the trunk, along with items from the lethal shopping list he had submitted to Brognola back at Stony Man. He shed his street clothes and dropped them in beside the spare, enjoying the feel of a cool mountain breeze on his body before he slipped into battle dress.

Bolan wore the sleek Beretta 93-R underneath his left arm in a shoulder sling. The .44 Magnum Desert Eagle automatic rode his right hip in military leather, and surplus magazines for both side arms were slotted into pouches circling his waist. The Executioner's lead weapon for the probe was an M-16 A-1 assault rifle, sporting an M-203 40 mm grenade launcher mounted underneath the barrel. Ammunition for the double-threat weapon crossed his chest in drooping bandoliers.

His compass, hanging on a lanyard strung around his neck, pointed him north-northwest.

The California mountain forest bore no resemblance to Vietnam, but it took Bolan back, all the same. Birds flitted through the branches overhead, while scuttling rodents cleared his path. The warrior concentrated on the overall environment, alert for the sounds that would betray a larger animal, man-size, and possibly alert him to an ambush while he still had time to save himself.

If Bolan's information was correct, he had a mile or so to cover before he reached his target. There would be no point in planting bobby traps so far away, but the Executioner watched his steps regardless. He wasn't dealing with professional soldiers, and the built-in paranoia of political rebels might dictate unorthodox tactics. Likewise with sentries—they could be anywhere—but Bolan met no opposition as he made his cautious way through the woods, closing inexorably on his mark.

He had no way of predicting how many targets—if any—he would find when he reached his destination. The camp might be deserted, manned with a skeleton maintenance force, or teeming with new trainees. Bolan would have to take the odds as they came, and if he was left with an empty net, well, that was the luck of the draw.

If nothing else, the Executioner would leave his mark behind for all his would-be enemies to see.

As for the ones who got away, they would be meeting Bolan soon enough.

SCOTT MAYHALL LIGHTED a thin cheroot and tugged the shoulder sling of his Ruger Mini-14 into a more comfortable position. Wind rustled in the trees behind him, whispering in voices he, a city boy at heart, could never hope to understand.

He scanned the open compound from behind his mirrored aviator's glasses, tracking from left to right and back again. On his left, or north, was Silhouette City, the camp's target range that simulated urban combat conditions; then the row of six portable toilets, painted olive drab in keeping with the camp's paramilitary motif; a prefab metal shed containing the generator, cables snaking out from there around the compound; the mess tent and field kitchen; clapboard barracks for three dozen troopers in a crunch, plus the smaller cabin reserved for officers.

In fact, there were only a dozen men on-site at the moment, half of them visible as they went about their daily appointed tasks. Camp Victory rarely operated at full capacity, leaders of the Aryan Resistance Movement preferring to limit exposure of their troops at one place and time. A stranger might have called it paranoia, but Mayhall knew firsthand about the long arm of ZOG, tapping telephones and spying on private meetings, opening mail and interrogating loved ones in relentless pursuit of damaging information.

He wouldn't have put it past the FBI or CIA to raze Camp Victory, maybe write the incident off as a freak forest fire or electrical storm. Standing watch wasn't an empty exercise for Mayhall, even though he had a tendency to let his guard down sometimes, like this afternoon, when all was calm and quiet in the woods.

There were 250 members of ARM in the Los Angeles-Orange County area, give or take, each required to spend one weekend out of every six at Camp Victory. The regimen included grueling exercise, target practice, political lectures and seminars on the fine points of sabotage, demolition and assassination.

Preparation for the Day of the Rope.

There was no fence around the camp's perimeter, no high-tech security devices. The mountain forest was their shield, and in the three years of Camp Victory's existence, only one hiker had stumbled on the compound by chance. He was buried a hundred yards due south of the camp, a rotten log marking the grave. If anyone had ever taken time to look for him, they never reached Camp Victory.

The hiker had been Mayhall's first kill, and he had considered it a privilege to execute a total stranger for the good of the movement. Loose lips were deadly, and no amount of threats or negotiation could guarantee silence with the same iron-clad assurance as a rifle bullet in the brain.

Case closed.

His second kill, the last to date, had been a random drive-by in Watts. With two companions, wearing ski masks, he had cruised past a crack house staffed by the Crips, hosing down the jungle bunnies with a full clip from his Ingram machine pistol, seeing two of them go down in a heap. Newspapers told him that one of his victims had died, predicting Crip reprisals against their arch enemies, the Bloods.

And that had been the whole point of the exercise to start with.

There were different ways to launch a racial revolution. One of them was stirring up the enemy, provoking him to violent actions that would put his animalistic behavior on public display. Let the police mop it up, instead of wasting their time on harassment of patriotic Americans. The more blacks and Mexicans sniped at each other in the street, preferably catching innocent bystanders in the cross fire, the better it was for groups like the ARM.

Propaganda hit home more effectively when you had living examples of the enemy on TV every night, beamed into the sumptuous living rooms of Bel Air and Beverly Hills.

Film at eleven, damn right.

Mayhall followed his beat around the perimeter, coming up on the latrines. Portable toilets eliminated much of the stench he recalled from the early days of slit trenches and swarming flies. He took a last drag on his cheroot, dropped it and ground it out with the heel of his boot. He shifted the folding-stock Ruger to his left shoulder, scanning the tree line in search of enemies.

They were out there, he knew, but the odds against meeting one here were a million to one. Not like L.A., where he was forced to rub shoulders with mongrels and mud people each time he set foot outside his apartment. Cleaning up the streets would be a Herculean task, but they would get there, given time.

And from that day onward, nothing would ever be the same again.

The streets would run with blood before they finished cleaning house, and that was fine. Fresh blood was the best disinfectant that Mayhall could think of. The more you spilled, the fewer enemies were left to undermine the progress of white civilization.

The next camp Mayhall helped erect, with any luck, would be the kind that Hitler had constructed to eliminate his enemies in Europe. He could picture the facility now, New Auschwitz, rising from the desert east of Yorba Linda, trucks and trains running around the clock to deliver fresh meat for the fires.

Of course, there would be resistance; that was to be expected. Mayhall was looking forward to it, the sweeps to round up human garbage, wasting those who decided to fight. The more the merrier. Every mongrel cut down on the streets was one less to clog the machinery of execution when they hit their stride with the Final Solution.

Caught up as he was in the dream of a whiter tomorrow, Mayhall missed the flicker of movement directly opposite his position, on the southeast perimeter of the camp. His first warning of imminent disaster was a muffled popping sound from the undergrowth, some sixty yards away, immediately followed by a rush of birds in flight.

The sound was hauntingly familiar, something he should recognize, but Mayhall had no time to mull it over. A heartbeat later, he was stretched out on his face, thrown prostrate by the shock wave of a powerful explosion leveling the generator shack.

Grenade launcher!

Mayhall lurched to his feet, grappling with his rifle as he cleared the shoulder sling and thumbed the safety off. His mind was racing, conscious thoughts piling up on one another like cars on a foggy stretch of highway.

The enemy had found him somehow. This was not a drill.

"Roll out!" he bellowed to the camp at large. "Red alert, for Christ's sake! Red alert!"

BOLAN DROPPED the shouting sentry with a 3-round burst from his M16, tracking in search of new targets before the body touched down. He caught two Aryans flat-footed in the mess tent, scrubbing pots and pans, their jaws slack in surprise at the unexpected sound of gunfire. One quick burst, and both of them were down.

Scratch three.

A couple of the troopers he could see were firing now, without clear targets or direction, drawing confidence from the staccato sound of their own automatic weapons. One of them was crouching near the outdoor toilets, while his comrade huddled in the shadow of a barracks hut, across the way.

Bolan thumbed another 40 mm round into the launcher, sighting quickly on the nearest adversary of the two, squeezing off as soon as he made target acquisition. The high-explosive round impacted on the second toilet in line, toppling the rest like dominoes and flattening the gunner crouched behind them. Bolan watched him for an instant, waiting for a sign of life, but then the bullets started to reach for him, edging closer, and he turned to face a more immediate threat.

The shooter near the barracks had him spotted now, firing short bursts from a submachine gun as he tried to get the range. The warrior edged to his right several paces, letting stout trees absorb the incoming fire, looking for a better angle of his own. He found it as the gunner hesitated to reload his weapon, changing magazines, and Bolan framed the human target in his rifle sights.

A gentle squeeze was all it took, the 5.56 mm tumblers ripping into flesh and fabric at a range of something over forty yards. He saw the shooter topple backward, his subgun airborne as it slipped from lifeless fingers, cartwheeling through the air.

No shortage of targets now, as would-be soldiers of the new *reich* scrambled from their quarters, clutching weapons, torn between the urge to fight and a survival instinct verging on near panic in the face of a surprise attack.

Bolan lobbed an HE round into the nearest barracks for the sake of added confusion, watching part of the tin roof lift off as the grenade detonated on impact. Wooden slats and shrapnel flew across the compound, stinging several of the runners, dropping one in midstride. Most of the others were firing now, on general principles, hosing the tree line with disorganized suppressing fire.

The Executioner shifted locations again, threading his way between trees as wild rounds whispered through the undergrowth around him. He went to ground behind a fallen log and risked a glance across the compound to his left, spotting targets on the run.

He loosed another 40 mm round, directed toward the center of the camp. The smoky thunderclap swallowed two runners and spat them out again, vaulting then through the air to land in crumpled heaps, their arms and legs twisted at impossible angles. Close by, another punk in camouflage fatigues was grappling with his automatic rifle, trying to clear a jammed round, when Bolan stitched him with a burst across the chest and knocked him sprawling in the dust.

The warrior rose from cover, moving in for the mop-up. He caught one of the ARM commandos just emerging from the shadow of a cabin on his left, the Nazi taken by surprise and gaping as his enemy was suddenly revealed. The shooter tried to raise his pistol, but he never got there. Bolan's burst of 5.56 mm shockers drilled into his face, blowing him away.

And that left two.

He had the targets spotted, ducking back inside a cabin on the far side of the compound. From his early recon, Bolan knew the structures had been built without back doors; there was no other exit once the troopers were inside. He slipped a fresh magazine into the M-16's receiver, thumbing another HE round into the grenade launcher as he closed the gap. Two windows were in the front wall of the cabin, and one of his adversaries had a weapon thrust out the closer window, angling for a killing shot.

Bolan got there first, firing his M-203 from the hip. He missed the window, but it made no difference. The grenade shattered woodwork, dropping part of the wall and roof into the cabin's single room. Smoke billowed from the open door and windows, thinning as HE blew across the compound.

The Executioner triggered a short burst through the nearer window, keeping the gunner's head down while he reloaded the M-203. His next grenade sailed through the door and detonated inside, drilling holes through the thin walls with shrapnel, producing a strangled cry of pain from within.

A tattered figure burst from the doorway, trailing smoke as he ran. Bolan hit him with a rising burst that punched the runner through an awkward pirouette and dumped him facedown in the dirt.

Bolan circled toward the cabin, taking his time on the approach, closing from the blind side. A quick glance through the window showed him all he had to see. The second gunner was stretched out on his back, blood seeping through his camo shirt where jagged grenade fragments had pierced his chest.

All done.

Ringing silence descended on the camp. Bolan stood in the midst of carnage and breathed the odor of gun smoke. Surrounded by death, he felt no peace of mind. His work had only just begun, and there was no end in sight. The opening shots had been fired in a new campaign, but no one could predict how it would end.

Twelve bodies scattered in the compound meant he had reduced the Aryan Resistance Movement's strength around Los Angeles by roughly five percent. It was a start, but nothing more.

Bolan understood that hatred could never be eradicated by bullets and grenades, but he wasn't concerned with winning hearts and minds. He dealt exclusively with terrorists and other human predators whose virulent behavior set them apart from civilized society. In Bolan's view, it was too late to counsel the savages or set their feet on the straight and narrow path. They had gone too far, cost humanity too much, and nothing short of extermination would render them harmless.

That was where the Executioner came in.

The leaders of the Aryan Resistance Movement didn't know it yet, but they had stubbed their jackboots on a hornet's nest, and they were just about to feel the sting of retribution.

Bolan found a can of olive spray paint in the smallest of the cabins, laid out like a CP hut, and took it back outside. He left his message on the wall in foot-high letters. Two words said it all: SCORCHED EARTH.

He left the can—no worry on the fingerprints, since no one from the ARM would dare to get in touch with the police—and started to retrace his own steps through the woods.

It was a long walk to the car, and he had far to go.

6

Yakov Katzenelenbogen had booked five tickets on Cyprus Airways out of Tel Aviv, breaking the obvious link to Israel with a stopover in Nicosia before Phoenix Force reached Berlin. Their flight was thirteen minutes late at Tegel Airport, but the rental cars were waiting, and their reservations were confirmed at the Sylter Hof, on Kurfurstensdam.

So far, so good.

Their weapons had been left behind in Israel, and they hit the ground unarmed in Germany, preventing the risk of setting off alarms in one of the world's most security-conscious airports. Traveling naked was safer, in terms of slipping through police and customs, but it left them at a disadvantage from the moment of arrival at their destination, and the Phoenix warriors felt it, going in.

Item number one in a new battle zone: acquisition of hardware.

The dealer's shop was located on Grunewaldstrasse, near the intersection with Pacelli Allee. His name was Dieter Engstrom, and the tax returns he filed each year listed his occupation as ''antique merchant.'' It was true that Engstrom made a living—a fairly handsome one, at that—by selling ancient furniture and family heirlooms, but his best-selling items were new, in perfect working order... and nowhere on display.

Dieter Engstrom liked to tell his customers that a second cousin by marriage was the personal secretary of a second vice president in one of the country's top-ranking firearms companies. No one bothered checking out the story, which was wholly false. The groups and individuals who dealt with Engstrom on the sly had secrets of their own, and plenty of them. They were more concerned with quality and quantity of merchandise than where the weapons came from. Engstrom, for his part, refrained from asking where the items he sold were going, and how they would be used.

No questions meant fewer tracks to cover, no comebacks or paybacks if something went sour beyond the point of sale. Engstrom posed no threat to his customers, and they left him in peace if their own negligence led to arrests. As for the German government, officially it had no knowledge of Engstrom's sideline. In fact, his private arms bazaar was tolerated, with occasional covert surveillance, in return for services rendered during twenty years of Cold War tension, when Engstrom performed certain unspecified favors for the CIA and the West German government in Bonn.

One hand washes the other, Katz thought, but does either hand ever come clean?

The Phoenix Force warriors went to Dieter Engstrom with a Langley endorsement and cold cash in hand, a combination that guaranteed prompt service with a guarantee of satisfaction. The shopping list was relatively simple: three Heckler & Koch MP-5 SD-3 submachine guns with built-in silencers and two of the shorter MP-5 K models; five of the new Browning Double Mode—BDM—semiautomatic pistols, an improvement on the classic P-35 Hi-Power with their double-action capability and 15-round magazines; for distance work, if necessary, two Heckler & Koch G-3 A-3 assault rifles, the standard-issue weapon of the German army. And last but not least, a crate of the excellent Dutch V-40 "mini-grenades."

Katz paid the full amount up front, at Engstrom's office, and they took delivery from the loading dock of a warehouse in the Charlottenburg quarter. The rifles, spare magazines, grenades and MP-5 SD-3s were divided between their rental cars, while the Browning autoloaders and the stubby MP-5 Ks went upstairs to their rooms at the Sylter Hof.

Compromise.

The Sylter Hof's garage was as secure as they could hope for, in the circumstances, and Katz judged the risk of a theft from the cars to be less than the hazard entailed in dragging military hardware through the lobby of an upper-class Berlin hotel. In the worst-case scenario, if their cover was totally blown and they were forced to shoot their way out of the hotel, he reckoned they had enough firepower between them to get a fair start on the job.

Phase one accomplished, and they had barely entered the starting gate.

The task had seemed relatively simple, at first. Penetrate Jordan and intercept a black-market Iraqi convoy, perhaps two or three, to drive the point home in Iraq. It had been an object lesson, as much as anything, but that perspective was radically altered with the discovery of German and American neo-Nazi involvement.

Katz knew Nazis inside out and despised everything about their ideology of hatred and exclusion. As a Jew of European descent, he'd lost relatives in the death camps and therefore had a personal investment in preventing the brown-shirted savages from making another run at global genocide. Racist, anti-Semitic groups had proliferated in the past ten years, and Katz never missed an opportunity to grind the haters underfoot when they crossed his path.

Like now.

Phase two of the ongoing Phoenix mission in Berlin was contact with their local guide, a representative from the elite counterterrorist squad known as GSG-9. Organized in the wake of the Munich Olympic massacre of 1972, drawing its initial recruits from the ranks of German police, the army and frontier guards, Grenzschutzgruppe 9 scored its first publicized success four years later, liberating the passengers of a hijacked airliner from Baader-Meinhof terrorists at Mogadishu. The crack guerrilla unit had earned its no-nonsense reputation for giving short shrift to terrorists of left or right, cutting them down without distinction when innocent lives were at stake. For every radical who damned the counterterrorists as Fascist agents, there were disgruntled Nazis who damned them as left-leaning tools of the Jews.

On occasion, as now, GSG-9 cooperated with outside agencies toward a common goal. In this case, Katz knew the official cooperation would be strictly limited, but their liaison with an agent of the German government would grant Phoenix Force a measure of insurance against police or military intervention.

So much for theory, at least.

Their meeting with the German contact was set for 9:00 p.m. in Potsdamer Platz, where once the British, American and Soviet sectors had met. Nearby, at the intersection of Friedrichstrasse and Zimmerstrasse, foreign visitors had, from 1945 until 1991, passed in and out of East Berlin through Checkpoint Charlie, scrutinized by uniformed troops and surveillance cameras of two hostile regimes. Arriving at the contact site, Katz could have walked ten yards to stand astride the track of the former Berlin Wall.

Times change, for some...but here Katz stood with Gary Manning at his side, McCarter watching from a distance, waiting to launch his campaign against a philosophy of evil dating from the 1920s.

Katz saw his contact coming from a block away. The men had never met, but he was on alert for someone in a leather jacket, with a copy of *Der Spiegel* folded underneath his arm. Katz half turned toward the nearest streetlight, letting the new arrival catch a glint of stainless steel from the claw that was his right hand.

Recognition accomplished.

The man in leather sidled up to Katz, checked Manning with a glance that took in everything at once and filed the information away for future reference.

"How is the weather in Washington?" he asked, the German accent barely audible.

"It snows year-round," Katz replied.

The German smiled at that. "Here also it is sometimes getting deep, as you would say. My name is Rudolf Wetzel."

Maybe, maybe not, Katz thought. He gave the cover name that fit his current passport, introducing Gary Manning with another pseudonym. They shook hands all around, Wetzel offering his left to Katz, and started walking east on Skalitzerstrasse, Wetzel in the middle of the sandwich. Katz knew without checking that David McCarter was tracking their progress, following at a discreet distance in one of the rental cars.

"You've come about the Vanguard, yes?"

"That's right," Katz said.

"I wish you luck."

"We're hoping for a little something more substantial."

"Understand that those you seek are well connected with the German Workers Party, which in turn has many friends in private industry. The party is small, yet, but growing. Now that communism is dissolved in Europe, they say things many people wish to hear."

"It sounds familiar," Manning said with thinly veiled contempt.

"I wonder, sometimes," Wetzel answered. "This is not my father's generation, but it seems that many feelings in my country do not change. A strong tide of nationalism, for instance... and other things. We have laws on the books proscribing certain conduct, symbols, everything but thoughts. Old habits die hard."

"Maybe they need a helping hand," Katz said.

"Perhaps. And you, I think, will need a place to start."

"That's why we're here."

"You know the Vanguard's leaders?"

"More or less."

"I have some photos here." Wetzel passed his folded magazine to Katz. "Likewise, names and addresses. A few homes, some common meeting places for the Vanguard and the German National Party."

"We're not interested in rigging elections," Katz said.

"All the same. You might find some of the connections... interesting."

"Any current operations running with the Vanguard?"

"There is always something," Wetzel answered. "Let me think."

They spent another forty minutes strolling while he thought and talked, listing recent Vanguard crimes from memory, projecting likely targets for the immediate future. It was nearly ten o'clock when they separated, exchanging emergency telephone numbers and agreeing to keep in touch.

The Phoenix Force warriors had much to think about, no shortage of potential targets for their initial move against the Vanguard. No end of possible choices.

All Katz had to do was flip a coin and decide where to start.

BOLAN'S DESTINATION after nightfall was a smallish tavern on La Brea Avenue in Hollywood. He made a drive-by, checking out pedestrians and cars against the curb for any indication of surveillance or an ambush in the making. Nothing caught his eye, and on the second pass he pulled into the tavern's parking lot, spent another moment sitting still before he left the car and locked it, then moved casually in the direction of the entrance.

He was clean, so far.

The message had been waiting for him at his hotel in downtown Los Angeles, when he returned from his side trip into the Sierras. No name or number for a callback, just the message RICK'S IN HOLLYWOOD—8:30—DANCER.

"Dancer" was the code name for his Bureau contact in L.A., and Bolan had to take for granted that his cover wasn't blown. Not yet, at any rate. The Yellow Pages told him where to go, and he had spent the early evening in a form of relaxation, showering, dining on room service, biding his time until the next move.

It would have been relatively simple for Bolan to launch an assault on the Aryan Resistance Movement by himself. The ARM maintained a bookstore open to the public in Torrance, and the home addresses of its leaders were public knowledge. He could have run them ragged for a while, perhaps driven the Nazis underground, but Bolan wanted more from his California campaign. To make a lasting difference, he would have to hit the fascists where they lived, and that required assistance, guidance, from the man inside.

He wore a navy blazer, covering the Beretta 93-R in its shoulder rig. The crimson handkerchief in his breast pocket was the recognition signal, coupled with a verbal exchange to eliminate the possibility of false starts.

A doorman in his early twenties relieved Bolan of five dollars and ushered him into a smoky room where dancers and tables competed for minimal floor space, hard-rock music issuing from ceiling-mounted speakers. The warrior found a bar stool that would leave him visible from the door and from the dance floor. Waiting.

He ordered a beer and made it last, sipping directly from the bottle while he made a slow visual scan of the crowded nightclub. Most of the patrons were younger than Bolan by several years, sharp dressers who lounged in their chairs with the same style they displayed on the dance floor.

One woman in particular caught Bolan's eye, a hard-bodied blonde of twenty-six or twenty-seven, wearing a thigh-high red minidress that fit her curvaceous body like a layer of paint. She knew the moves, and then some, drawing sufficient attention from male spectators at ringside that some of their dates were moved to glare and pummel ribs with angry elbows.

Style.

One number bled into another, the lyrics wasted on the Executioner. He scanned past the blonde and back again, knowing there was no way he could spot his contact in the milling crowd. As long as he was forced to sit and wait, he might as well enjoy the view.

Five minutes passed, and then another five. Twice, he established fleeting eye contact with the blonde, there and gone as she twirled away from him, her body undulating with the sinuous grace of a reptile. He shot a glance toward the door, resisting an urge to check his watch. In fact, he could have stated the time with a fifteen-second margin of error, and he thought he could afford another fifteen minutes in the club before he had to split.

A hundred different problems could prevent his contact from keeping their appointment, anything from trivia to tragedy. Bolan wasn't about to second-guess the unknown, projecting new, speculative dangers on top of the obvious.

He felt the blonde beside him, caught a heady whiff of her perfume before she settled onto the adjacent stool. Up close, her skin was flawless, light on the cosmetics. She had startling violet eyes.

"I haven't seen you here before," she said. It could have been a standard come-on line; what mattered now was his response.

"I just got in this afternoon," he said. Step one completed.

"Are you staying long? Business or pleasure?"

"As long as it takes. A little of both."

She relaxed visibly, waving the bartender off when he drifted by to get her order. "I'm Janice Flynn. And you are . . ."

"Mike Belasko," the warrior replied, using the cover name he chose for this mission.

"We can't talk here," she said. "Let's take a ride."

"Suits me."

He left five dollars on the bar and followed her outside. The night was warm, and after several hours in the L.A. basin, he could hardly smell the smog at all.

"Which one?"

"Over here."

He let Flynn into the passenger's seat, circled around and slid behind the wheel.

"Anyplace special?"

"Just drive."

He pulled out of the lot and turned left on La Brea, then right onto Beverly Boulevard, cruising without direction.

"You're alone?" she asked, when they had put the first two blocks behind them.

"It's the way I work."

"I don't suppose you would have been in the Sierras earlier this afternoon?"

"Could be."

"We caught a squeal. One of the troopers rolled in late for weekend exercises and he found the whole place trashed. Camp Victory they call it. Used to, anyway." She hesitated, staring at his face in profile. "Twelve men dead. Is *that* the way you work?"

He had a feel for what was coming, and he didn't try to skirt the issue. "Going in I like to have their full attention."

"Well, you have that, anyway." She paused again. "Are you clear on who I am?"

"You're FBI. Deep cover, as I understand it."

"Then you know I'm in the business of preventing crimes, not setting up assassinations."

"Any questions you might have can be relayed to Washington," the Executioner replied. "If you'd prefer to drop out of the loop right now, that's fine."

He felt her bristling. "I've got seven months invested in this case," she told him. "You don't want to know the things I've done to get this far. I'm not about to have some one-night drop-in blow me off."

"That's not the plan," Bolan said. "There are limits, off the top, to what I can tell you. It's need-to-know, all right? The ARM is working on some international connections that you might or might not be aware of. That's where I come in."

"We're talking Middle East, I gather."

"That's affirmative."

The lady's frown was as attractive, in its own way, as her smile.

"I won't pretend to know the details, but I've heard some talk," she said. "It sounded like hot air at first. A lot of gas about some kind of coalition with the 'rags'—Jordanians, I think, but Justin keeps it vague with skirts around. That's Justin Pratt. I've tried to work on Chet—"

"Chet Blackmun?" Bolan interrupted.

"Right. He doesn't give that much away. I know Mitch Rudd, one of the goons from Santa Ana, made a few trips east. The last time out he didn't make it back."

"Reaction?"

"Justin damn near blew a fuse. He doesn't know who pulled the trigger, but he blames the Jews for everything, so that's an easy out. In fact—" she paused "—he's got some payback lined up for tonight."

"You've passed that on?"

"My supervisor's sitting on it. You're supposed to take it off our hands, I guess."

"I'm listening."

She looked embarrassed for a moment, finally shrugged it off, surrendering to the inevitable.

"Justin has a hit list on diskette," she said. "I haven't seen it, but I understand it runs to several hundred names for Southern California—wealthy Jews, black spokesmen, politicians, take your pick. He's looking forward to what he calls the Day of the Rope. That's payback time on a national scale, when the movement takes over and settles accounts with ZOG."

"Tonight," Bolan pressed.

"They slipped on that one. Chet was bragging, couldn't keep it to himself. The mark's a lawyer, Aaron Bluestein, very active in civil rights work and the Anti-Defamation League of B'nai B'rith. Last year he threw in with the Southern Poverty Law Center on a civil suit against some local skinheads in a gay-bashing case. The sluggers got off with ninety days in the county lockup, but Bluestein socked them for a million-five in court. They had to sell their clubhouse, liquidate the gang's marginal assets. They'll be in hock till they die."

"Connections to the ARM?" Bolan asked.

"Before the lawsuit, only philosophical. Justin kicked a few bucks in for the defense, but he stopped short of getting sucked in to the limit. It's more his style to lie back in the weeds and hit you when your guard's down."

"Where and when?"

"Bluestein's got a place in Coldwater Canyon," Flynn replied. "The goons are rolling in at midnight. If I couldn't get in touch with you by then, I was supposed to call my supervisor back and let the sheriff's office take the squeal."

The dashboard clock told Bolan he had just under three hours left.

"I'll have to drop you off," he said.

"My car's at Rick's."

He turned back toward the bar, accelerating through a gap in traffic, catching the light as it turned from green to amber.

"How do I keep in touch?" he asked.

She rattled off a number and Bolan repeated it once, committing it to memory at the same time.

"Is the hotel okay for messages?"

"Should be," he said. "If there's a change, I'll leave the number."

"Right." They rode in silence for a moment, drawing closer to the bar. They had a block to go when Flynn spoke again. "You know, I still don't like this."

"That just proves you're sane," the Executioner replied. "Pratt likes it. He's the problem."

"I understand the problem. It's the solution I'm not sure about."

He turned into the lot at Rick's and parked beside the Chevrolet she indicated. "If you want out," Bolan told her, "now's the time to make the call."

"I'm sticking, damn it! Just be careful, will you?"

"It's my middle name."

"I'm sure."

She left the car without a backward glance, striding purposefully toward her car. Bolan had the Ford in motion before she got her keys out, trusting the lady Fed to take care of herself.

He had other concerns at the moment, a murder—perhaps multiple murder—to prevent. His contact was sticking, reservations aside, and she would have to work out her own misgivings.

Her voice came back to Bolan as he drove: You don't want to know the things I've done to get this far.

He had a hunch, but that was none of his concern.

The game was going into sudden death, and Bolan had an appointment to keep, turning the ARM's hit list around.

It was, he thought, as good a starting point as any in the hellgrounds.

7

From Rick's, Janice Flynn drove back to her apartment complex in Culver City, three short blocks from the Fox Hills Mall. She drove on instinct, barely noticing familiar landmarks on the way. Her conscious thoughts were dominated by thoughts of the newcomer, Mike Belasko, and the new twist his presence had put on her already-complicated job.

Working deep cover had been a fantasy for Janice, coming out of the FBI academy at Quantico. It was the kind of glamour job you saw in all the movies, high adventure and nonstop excitement, flirting with danger from time to time, the good guys always coming out on top.

Except that real life didn't work that way.

Her fantasies hadn't included listening to diatribes of racial hatred day in and day out, swallowing bitter retorts as Justin Pratt and his cronies railed against blacks, Jews, Hispanics, homosexuals and anyone else they could think of. Their enemy amounted to some eighty percent of mankind when you ran down the list.

More to the point, her notion of flirting with danger had never included the relationship in which she found herself with Chet Blackmun, Pratt's second in command at ARM headquarters. Never in her wildest nightmares...

And now, Belasko, coming out of nowhere with a covert hunting license, validated out of Washington or who-knew-where. A dozen brownshirts were dead already, and more fireworks were due before the night was over, if Justin's hit team kept its date with Aaron Bluestein in Coldwater Canyon.

Nothing in Flynn's training or experience had prepared her for the way this job was shaking out. First Blackmun, and the compromise that stood a chance of scuttling any case she tried to make in court, then orders from her supervisor to cooperate with the directions of a total stranger who, she found out now, was bent on launching all-out war against the Aryan Resistance Movement in L.A. The Hoover era's dirty tricks paled by comparison, when she thought about it. With a simple phrase—"I'm sticking, damn it"—she had placed herself outside the law.

And if it blew up in her face, the Bureau would be quick to cut her loose. She knew that in her heart, a certainty that left her virtually on her own.

Except for Mike Belasko.

He didn't feel like CIA. The Company was barred from operating on American soil, at least by statute, though Clandestine Ops had seen fit to ignore the law at times, when it suited Langley's purposes.

Still, there was something about Belasko that ruled out CIA involvement. His air of independence, perhaps, not so much the arrogance she normally associated with Company operatives as a deep-seated confidence in his own ability to get the job done.

He had done a job on Camp Victory, and no mistake. Even as the violence repulsed her, Flynn felt an urge to stand up and shout. Not for the loss of life, per se, but at the thought of someone—anyone—standing up and striking back at the goons on their own terms. There was an undeniable sense of exhilaration, despite her natural revulsion at the thought of so much violence committed under cover of official sanction.

She turned into the parking lot of her apartment complex, keeping to the right and circling around back to reach her assigned space. A sports car was parked in her slot, nothing she recognized, and she let it go with a curse muttered under her breath. She found an open curb space, locked the Chevrolet and moved along the lighted concrete pathway toward her ground-floor flat.

The lights were on, which generated a quick hitch in her breathing. Instead of barging in, she played a hunch and walked back to the parking lot, paying closer attention now as she scanned the ranks of vehicles. On her left, six spaces down, sat Chet Blackmun's BMW, nosed in to the curb.

He had bullied her into letting him have a key. Flynn had no convenient way to refuse, short of blowing her cover. Her Bureau credentials were now secure in a safe-deposit box, downtown, but she left the standard-issue Smith & Wesson 10 mm automatic pistol in the top drawer of her nightstand, knowing the gun would fit her cover as a would-be member of the master race.

Blackmun was lounging on the sofa as she entered, a sweaty bottle of Michelob beer leaving rings on her coffee table. From the crooked grin on his face, Flynn knew it wasn't his first of the evening.

"You're late," he said.

"Is that so? I didn't know we had a date."

"So, now you do."

"I guess that's right."

"Where were you?"

"Rick's." There was no point in lying.

"New dress?"

"You like it?"

"It's all right. I'll like it better when you take it off."

She locked the door behind her, set her purse down on the breakfast counter as she passed the tiny kitchen and headed for the bedroom.

"So—" she turned and faced him from the open doorway "—are you coming?"

"Hell, we both are, babe. You wait and see."

COLDWATER CANYON IS ONE of those spots in L.A. where coyotes and raccoons still turn up after dark to sniff at the trash cans outside million-dollar homes, a touch of wilderness in the heart of America's second-largest city. These are the hills that give Beverly Hills its name, and residents pay dearly for the privilege of settling here.

Bolan's first glimpse of the Bluestein residence told him that the ARM had selected a high-profile victim, while keeping ready access in mind. The house, a long split-level in a vaguely Spanish style, was set back twenty yards or better from the street, screened by hedges, weeping willows and the natural contour of the hillside. There was no protective wall around the property, no gate across the entrance to an asphalt drive. The closest neighbors were situated one hundred yards south of the Bluestein estate, another house some 150 yards to the north.

A hit team could be in and out in moments, if it knew its business and performed efficiently. The neighbors might or might not be at home, might recognize the sound of gunshots and respond with calls to 911 or simply let it slide.

He estimated that police response time in the high-rent district would be fairly prompt, but there was no way he could estimate that lag time with anything approaching accuracy. In the absence of dry runs, he would have to stay alert for sirens and react accordingly before the cavalry arrived.

Parking was a problem in Coldwater Canyon, and deliberately so. The last thing wealthy residents desired was traffic piled up on the shoulder of the road, rubberneckers or potential thieves and vandals lining up to scrutinize the homes. Bolan was sweating it out when he stumbled on a narrow, unpaved access road fifty yards north of the Bluestein estate, on the opposite side of the road. He double-checked the highway—clear in both directions—and backed his car into the narrow track, rolling in reverse until his Ford was hidden from the view of passing motorists.

For the second time that day, Bolan stood beside the open trunk of his car, stripping down to the skin, dressing swiftly in combat garb. His chosen gear this time was the formfitting blacksuit, military webbing at his waist and the sleek Beretta snug beneath his arm. Battlefield cosmetics blacked his face and hands before he reached inside the trunk to find an Uzi submachine gun. He threaded the squat suppressor onto the subgun's muzzle.

Ready.

He had time to kill, so the warrior used it on a cautious recon of the Bluestein property, confirming to himself that any raiders interested in speed would have to come in from the road. An overland approach meant parking miles away and hiking through the woods both ways, a fearsome risk on the return trip if police were on the prowl with helicopters and attack dogs.

If they intended to escape, the hit team needed wheels, and that meant they would come in from the street. The Bluesteins had no guard dogs on the premises, no visible security devices to sound an alarm or slow down intruders. Common sense told Bolan that there had to be some kind of alarm for the house, but his cause would be lost if the gunners got close enough to breach a door or window.

Bolan meant to stop them in the trees or in the yard, no later. Gunfire or explosives in the house could mean civilian casualties, and his touch-tone research told him the Bluesteins had three children living at home, ages seven to thirteen.

He could have simply blown the whistle, bringing uniforms on the scene or at least alerting the Bluesteins to their peril, but he had opted for silence. The raiders would abort their mission at the first glimpse of a squad car, and for all he knew they could have backup targets ready in the event of a snafu. If Bolan hit the panic button prematurely, he stood a chance of condemning some unknown third party to death.

Instead he meant to stop the raiders cold and give their leaders something else to think about before the sun rose the next day. By the time the smoke cleared, Aaron Bluestein and his family would have police protection, time to think about their options and evacuate for the duration if it came to that.

He settled down to wait, at home in darkness, stretched out under cover of a juniper hedge. The landscape blocked his view of approaching cars, but he would see their head-lights coming, hear them in the stillness if they came in running dark.

Or so he hoped.

If he was wrong...

The warrior stopped that train of thought before it had a chance to run its course. Defeatism had no place in Bolan's philosophy. He would deal with any problems as they came, and damn the risk.

Five innocent lives depended on Bolan's skill and deter-mination.

He didn't plan to let them down.

CHRIS STURBAUM WISHED that they could stop somewhere for him to take a leak, but that was stupid, like some little kid who couldn't hold his water at a scary movie. He had to concentrate on business now, and keep his wits about him. This would be his one big chance to shine for Justin and the others. If he blew it... well, he'd damn well better not, and that was all.

As late as half-past seven, he had been afraid that Justin would decide to scrub the mission, put it off until they had a chance to sort out what had happened at Camp Victory. Some kind of crazy fuck-up that was, twelve men and half the buildings trashed, with rumors of a message painted on the wall that Justin still refused to share with any of his men.

Twelve dead, and no one had a clue who pulled the trig-ger. Not that it made any difference, in the long run. When you thought about it, if you read *Mein Kampf* and listened to the führer's message, you would know there was only one real enemy. The Demon Jew was at the root of all their problems, whether he used spics or niggers or the god-damned FBI to do his dirty work at any given time.

Going ahead with their mission was the right decision, Sturbaum knew. It was right for Mitch Rudd and the twelve boys who lost it that morning. More to the point, it was right for the movement, a shot in the arm when they needed it most. No more backslapping rallies and long hours wasted running off leaflets on the photocopier in Justin's basement.

It was time for action, and Sturbaum had been aching for it when the word came down. They had a big Jew in their sights, the kind of hit that made the liberal media moan for days on end. He could already hear the wailing and gnashing of teeth as the Yid lovers said farewell to one of their guiding lights.

Good riddance.

But now, rolling through the darkness with three men crammed in the back seat behind him, clutching a rolled-up ski mask and an Ingram submachine gun in his lap, Chris Sturbaum was having second thoughts. Not fear, he wouldn't call it that, but reservations. That was better.

Suppose the pigs were waiting for them? What if Bluestein had a party going, or the family was away from home? Suppose—

Enough, goddamn it!

Sturbaum focused on the moves they had rehearsed together, working from an Arco street map, estimating times and distances. They would be running on the razor's edge, and that was fine, because it meant he would have no more time to think or worry. Only time to move, to act, and carry out his mission as he had been ordered by the leader of their sacred movement.

One step closer to the Day of the Rope.

Turning onto Coldwater Canyon Drive, they slowed a little. He started reading numbers, painted on the curb or fixed on streetside mailboxes in luminous digits. Sturbaum's bladder started tingling again when they had closed the range to something like a hundred yards.

"Kill the lights."

It went dark all around them suddenly, his driver navigating by feel and the faint light offered by a quarter moon. Before they even glimpsed the Jew's driveway, Sturbaum was rehearsing the play in his mind. He saw the four of them hit the ground running, his wheelman remaining with the car, a headlong dash across the lawn and bust the house before anyone inside knew what was happening. Screw the alarms, relying on speed and accuracy, wasting anything that moved.

One of the troopers in the back seat had a can of spray paint, issued with instructions for signing their crude work of art.

"Coming up," he warned the driver, stating the obvious. "Make sure you keep it running when we bail."

"I hear you."

Nerves were making him repeat himself, and Sturbaum shut his mouth to keep from sounding like an idiot. Better to finish the trip in silence than to have the men—his men—questioning Sturbaum's resolve.

They swung into the driveway of Bluestein's estate, the driver hitting the brakes right away. Sturbaum lurched forward in his seat as he reached for the inside door handle. Then he was out and running, cursing the flare of the dome light, wondering why no one had thought to pull the frigging bulb.

An oversight, but nothing critical.

They raced across the blacktop, running as the crow flies, manicured grass spongy beneath his boots. Sturbaum had traveled no more than a dozen strides when a clap of thunder exploded behind him. The shock wave pitched him forward, off balance, and he went down on his hands and knees.

He spun to face the street and found their vehicle in flames, a twitching scarecrow pinned behind the steering wheel. It took another heartbeat for the image to register, and then a secondary blast ripped through the flaming car. The gas tank going, sure as shit.

Chris Sturbaum waited for his life to flash before his eyes, but all he saw was smoke and fire, his night vision shot to hell by the glare of the flames. One of his troopers started firing, a staccato sound of automatic fire, and he wondered what the stupid bastard found to shoot at.

In another thirty seconds, give or take, Sturbaum found out for himself.

THE RAIDERS CAME IN DARK, as Bolan had expected, fifty yards and closing when his ears picked up the sound of tires on asphalt. He was primed and ready when they swung into the Bluesteins' driveway.

Choices. He could hose them with the Uzi where they sat or let their pointmen leave the car, making better targets on the open lawn. He opted for the latter course of action with a twist, releasing a fragmentation grenade from his web belt, jerking the safety pin free with his thumb.

A quick flash from the dome light revealed four men out and running as the doors swung shut behind them.

The driver had his window down, and it was all that Bolan needed. An overhand pitch from twenty feet, and he had time to register the wheelman's shocked reaction before he broke cover, peeling off to intercept the others.

A high-pitched squeal issued from the car, swallowed by the crash of a contained explosion as the grenade went off. Bolan ran with the shock wave at his back, letting it power him forward, as his human targets froze in midstride, pivoting to face the ruin of their vehicle.

Bolan hit the nearest gunner with a short burst to the chest, lifting him completely off his feet and dropping him flat on his back. The shooter's Ingram submachine gun spat a short burst toward the sky, jerked free of lifeless fingers and fell silent on the lawn.

One down, then the muffled stutter of Bolan's Uzi was covered by the secondary detonation of the hit car's gas tank. Something—possibly the muzzle-flash from the warrior's weapon—alerted one of the survivors, brought him around to face Bolan with gun in hand.

There was no silencer on the Aryan warrior's machine pistol. A loud ripping sound tore though the night as Bolan's adversary opened fire without waiting for a fix on his target. Angry hornets swarmed away to the Executioner's right, chopping divots in the lawn before his Uzi spat an answer. Parabellum manglers dead on target from a range of thirty feet stitched tidy holes between the gunner's belt and clavicle.

The two survivors broke in opposite directions, one sprinting toward the Bluestein home, his comrade dodging toward the hedge that separated lawn from street. Both men were firing on the run, their weapons hammering the canyon's former stillness.

Bolan swiveled toward the shooter on his left, a greater threat to innocent civilians as he neared the house. A light was visible around in back, perhaps a bedroom window, but the raider had his eyes fixed on the door. A short burst for the locks, if he could get that far, and he would be inside.

The Executioner cut the runner's legs out from under him with a short burst of 9 mm slugs, holding the Uzi's trigger down as the sprawling target fell across his line of fire. The raider twitched and shuddered, twisted over on his back, arms outflung in death. He was still three steps from the Bluesteins' porch, as close as he would ever come to victory.

One left, and Bolan ditched the Uzi's empty magazine and reloaded. His quarry had already breached the roadside hedge, running for his life, and the warrior had a choice—to let him go, or to try for a clean sweep.

No contest.

He crossed the lawn in loping strides, pushed through the broken hedge and out onto the shoulder of the drive. His target had given up on tactics, running flat-out down the center of the two-lane blacktop, elbows pumping in the quest for greater speed.

Bolan made his choice in a heartbeat, palming the Desert Eagle .44 Magnum as he stepped into the middle of the road. His target was a bobbing silhouette, framed in his sights. He thumbed the automatic's hammer back, his index finger tightening around the Desert Eagle's trigger.

The warrior fired one round at a range of forty yards, which drilled a crimson spout between the runner's shoulder blades. The explosive impact pitched his target forward, sliding on his stomach like a base runner coming in under the throw.

Too late.

Bolan was already moving as he holstered the pistol, retracing his steps to the access road fifty yards north of the Bluestein estate, where his Ford was concealed. He wasted no time changing, left the war paint on his face and hands as he slid in behind the steering wheel. The engine turned over on his first try, and he powered out of his hiding place, turning south on Coldwater Canyon Drive, accelerating away from the killing ground.

He swerved around the dead man lying in the middle of the road, navigating by moonlight for the first hundred yards or so, in case one of the neighbors made it streetside and looked for a license number. He was well away before he switched on the high beams to light his way.

Someone had managed to reach a telephone, that much was clear. Bolan met the first police cars on Santa Monica Boulevard, sirens screaming and colored lights flashing as they raced toward the scene of the action. He held his speed to the legal limit, pulling over as required by law when two more squad cars passed him, heading north.

Too late for anything but mopping up.

And that made seventeen of Bolan's adversaries down and out.

He found an all-night service station on La Cienega, pulled around in back and made it to the men's room unobserved. It took some scrubbing with the gritty powdered soap to clean his face and hands, but Bolan got it done. A hasty change of clothes, and he was ready to pass inspection, all his hardware except the Beretta safely stowed in the vehicle's trunk.

The time was 12:40 a.m. It was a brand-new day in Los Angeles.

His Nazi adversaries didn't know it yet, but they were starting their last day on earth.

8

The ringing telephone was a relief to Janice Flynn. She had lain awake since Blackmun finished with her, wishing for a hot shower, unable to sleep with the memory of his hands and mouth on her flesh. It was always the same, a mixture of repulsion and self-loathing, whenever he wound up spending the night. With any luck, an early breakfast might get rid of him.

She fumbled the receiver from its cradle on the second ring, her voice coarse from hours of silence.

"Hello?"

"Give me Chet."

Justin Pratt, no amenities, straight to the point. From his tone, she could tell he was angry—or was that the sound of fear?

Belasko.

What had he been up to overnight?

She clutched the sheet to her chest as she rolled toward Blackmun, shaking him roughly, thrusting the handset into his face as his eyelids came open.

"What—"

"Justin's on the phone. He wants you. Now."

Blackmun grumbled something unintelligible, rubbing sleep from his eyes with the back of one hand before he accepted the telephone.

"Yeah?"

She rolled away from him, taking the sheet with her to cover her breasts, avoiding any obvious attempt to eavesdrop. Her first impression of Pratt's mood was borne out as

Blackmun stiffened and pushed himself up on one elbow wide-awake now.

"You're shitting me! When?"

Another moment of silence as he listened, scowling over what he heard.

"Okay, right. I'm on my way. I heard you, damn it Yeah, okay."

He dropped the receiver in Flynn's lap as he rolled out o bed, reaching for his shorts and jeans on the floor. He wa muttering a string of curses as he dressed himself, nearly ripping his T-shirt when he got it backward on the first try

"What's wrong, Chet?"

"Fucking numbskulls blew it," he responded, tugging on a boot.

"Blew what?"

"The Bluestein gig," he snapped. "They got their asse kicked."

She felt a tremor of excitement, laced with guilt. "Po lice, you mean?"

"Somebody else. I don't have time to chew the fat righ now, okay?"

"Well, sure. I only thought—"

"Don't think, babe. Stick with what you know."

She swallowed a retort and saw him out the door. No need to follow him; he knew the way out. Relief washed over her sweet and warm, as she heard the front door swing shut be hind him.

Gone, but not forgotten.

Flynn flipped a mental coin and cradled the receiver long enough to clear the line, tapping out a number with her fin gertips. It rang twice at the other end before a gruff, famil iar voice came on the line.

"Hello?"

"It's me. What happened last night?"

Her control wasn't an early riser by disposition, bu something told her he had managed no more sleep last nigh than she had.

"Crazy bastards made a run at Bluestein, like you said they would."

"What happened?" she repeated.

"What happened is, they bought the farm. Five up, five down."

"They're dead?"

"As dead can be. You got the squeal from Blackmun?"

Flynn felt herself flushing furiously. She tugged the sheet up to her chin, as if the older man could somehow see her through the telephone.

"I gather Justin's calling out the troops."

"I wouldn't be surprised. You'll keep me posted, right?"

"If I hear anything."

"Your boy kicks ass." A hint of admiration was in the other's tone.

"He's not my boy."

"I didn't mean it that way. Anyway, ours not to reason why. The word comes down, that's it."

"I'll keep in touch," she told him, dropping the receiver before he could say any more.

Flynn ran the shower as hot as she could stand it, soaping herself three times over to be rid of Blackmun's filth, remaining underneath the stinging spray until her flesh was lobster red. Cold water next, to shock her mind awake and clear the final vestiges of cobwebs.

Toweling off, she tried to organize her thoughts and program for the day to come. Belasko might need help, though there was nothing in his performance so far to indicate weakness or indecision.

"Your boy kicks ass."

"He's not my boy."

But fate or pure dumb luck had cast the two of them together. Whatever happened next, there could be no turning back. She had a job to do, and for the moment that included helping Mike Belasko.

Helping him kick ass.

Staring at the rumpled, sweaty sheets, she was surprised to find the prospect somehow less repugnant than it had seemed the night before.

THE ARYAN RESISTANCE movement's White Power Bookstore was located on Crenshaw Boulevard, in Torrance. It was the shop's third location in two years, the first having been firebombed by persons unknown, the second padlocked after repeated threats put the landlord on edge. Eviction from the present quarters had been threatened six months earlier, before the American Civil Liberties Union had pitched in with a lawsuit charging violations of the First Amendment.

As for Bolan, he didn't give a damn what the Nazis published, or who read their mindless drivel. He was blitzing, and none of the ARM's property was exempt from destruction on constitutional grounds.

The shop wasn't scheduled to open for another hour, and that was fine with Bolan. He parked two doors down, outside a triple-X-rated video store, and lifted a nylon gym bag from the floorboard as he left the car. An easy stroll around in back, along the alleyway, took him to the shop's back door. Bolan used his pry bar on the lock and let himself inside, to the accompaniment of a jangling burglar alarm.

He found the master circuit inside, ripped it out of the wall and restored blessed silence. There was no way to know if the alarm would keep ringing at the nearest police station, but he didn't plan to linger at the scene. One minute, in and out, should be enough.

He checked the tiny back-room office quickly, not expecting any confidential paperwork and finding none. He took one of the compact incendiary sticks from his gym bag, primed it and dropped it on the desk. Another for the filing cabinet, just in case, before he pushed into the claustrophobic sales room at the front.

He spent ten seconds checking out the shelf stock. Most of the material on hand was published by the ARM, but there were several items from the Klan, the California

Rangers, sundry other groups of the lunatic fringe. Screaming shoutlines proclaimed the end of white civilization, precipitated by a worldwide cabal of leftists, homosexuals, "mud people" and the Learned Elders of Zion. Salvation for the master race would only be achieved when white patriots got off their backsides and picked up the torch.

Right, Bolan thought, tossing four incendiaries toward the corners of the room, a touch of cleaning fire to wipe the filth away.

He was back in the alley, retracing his steps toward the Ford, when the first incendiaries started to pop, spewing white phosphorous coals in a radius of thirty feet.

White heat against white power.

Scorched earth.

It was a minor victory, all things considered, but Bolan was playing no favorites.

Driving back toward L.A. proper, he considered all he had accomplished since his touchdown in the city, some sixteen hours earlier. The enemy hardforce had been reduced by seventeen, a major blow delivered to the monumental Nazi ego. Spokesmen for the self-styled master race didn't take insults lightly. Soon, perhaps immediately, Bolan's adversaries would be moved to take some action of their own.

At that, they would be handicapped by ignorance of who their adversary was. Without a special target, Justin Pratt's stormtroopers might be unleashed against any number of targets from the ARM hit list. Random strikes against minorities at large couldn't be ruled out absolutely, but the Executioner was beginning to get a feel for his opposition.

When Pratt lost a man in the Middle East, he struck back at a prominent Jewish leader in Los Angeles. No plausible connection, to be sure, but it was close enough to satisfy a die-hard anti-Semite. Pratt had not unleashed his troops in Watts or East L.A., preferring a high-visibility target whose elimination would beef up the ARM's killer rep. Frustrated in that attempt, he would feel compelled to try again . . . but where? And when?

Janice Flynn might help narrow the range of targets, and he started watching for a public telephone away from traffic, set back from the street, where he would have a modicum of privacy. Meanwhile, it occurred to Bolan that there was only one way to keep his enemies off balance, to prevent them from getting organized enough to score against some target he could never hope to reach in time.

He had to keep the pressure on, turn up the heat and keep them reeling with rapid-fire blows until they began to fall apart. Obsessive hatred was one thing, but he knew from experience that groups like the ARM did their primary recruiting from the dregs of humanity—thugs, deviants and mental cases with a private ax to grind. Khaki uniforms and polished jackboots didn't make a soldier, not in any of the ways that mattered.

Under pressure, thugs and psychos fell apart, began to turn on one another and desert their leaders in pursuit of self-preservation. Half-assed training aside, Pratt's "Aryan warriors" were still motley rabble, unprepared for the Executioner's brand of warfare.

Bolan spied a likely phone booth, and thought it wouldn't hurt to speak with Hal Brognola briefly before he got in touch with Janice Flynn.

BROGNOLA WAS STIRRING sugar into his first cup of coffee of the day when the telephone began to ring. It was his private line, the number shared among perhaps three dozen people in the country. He waited for the third ring, sipping at the steaming mug before he hoisted the receiver to his ear.

"Hello?"

"It's Striker. I'm on a public line."

"How's La-La Land?" Brognola asked.

"It's warming up."

"That's what I hear. They're squealing in the Führerbunker."

"All the way to Wonderland?"

"And then some. Any problems with your contact at the Bureau?"

"None so far. The gender took me by surprise."

"It's not a man's world anymore."

"I guess that's right."

"Good job last night," Brognola said.

"They won't be giving up."

"I shouldn't think so."

"Is there something I can help you with?"

"Connections," Bolan answered him. "Our playmates might be looking for a source of income overseas, but they've been getting by all right until now. Somebody must know where the money comes from."

"I could ask around."

"It wouldn't hurt."

"What else?"

"That's it, for now," Bolan said.

"Still at the hotel?"

"Till further notice."

"Right, I'll be in touch. Stay frosty, eh?"

"I'll see what I can do."

The line went dead. Brognola hung up on the dial tone, rocked back in his swivel chair and raised his coffee mug. The brew had cooled a little, but it still had bite.

He knew what Bolan wanted. Since the 1930s, when the native Nazi movement first took root in the United States, there had been closet sympathizers in the background, propping up the frontline bigots with their checks and sage advice. Henry Ford had done his bit for the cause in another generation, and there were a host of lesser lights who chipped in through the years—captains of industry, fundamentalist preachers, retired military officers, the occasional used-car dealer. They had bankrolled Lincoln Rockwell in the 1950s, chipped in for the Klan's legal defense fund a decade later, lined up at the back door with their tax-deductible donations to this or that far-right political campaign.

More to the point, their names were on record—if not at Stony Man, then with the FBI. Their identities would have been culled from tax returns and wiretaps, surveillance of rallies and clandestine meetings, the notes of undercover agents and civilian informants. It was all a matter of pushing the right buttons, asking the right questions.

Brognola's stock-in-trade.

He knew what lay in store for those whose names he passed to Striker, but the man from Justice felt no sympathy. They had chosen their own course, cast their lot with racist lunatics, and it was payoff time.

At least for some.

Brognola tried to picture Bolan in Los Angeles, thought back to days when they had worked the streets together, albeit on opposite sides of the law. They had been allies, even then, but it had taken time to make the link official. Even then, the man from Pittsfield had retained his independence, choosing targets as they suited him, shying away from the federal ties that bind.

It was a new day, but the more things changed, the more they stayed the same. The enemy put on a different face and answered to a different name each time around, but they were all the same at heart. The predators who lingered on the fringes of society, waiting to thin the herd.

Some of them tried to justify their deeds with politics, while others fell back on religion, national security or simple greed. It all came out the same, when everything was said and done. Some men were born to prey on others, and the only way to stop them was with force.

It was the only language that a savage understood.

And what did that make Bolan, or Brognola? When they stepped outside the law, was there a difference between themselves and the enemy?

Damn right, there was.

A soldier did his job, whatever that entailed, and if he lost a measure of his own humanity in the process, that was the price he paid for answering duty's call.

A poet once said that each man's death diminishes us all, but he was wrong. Some men were so far gone inside themselves, their own pure evil, that wiping them off the face of the earth could only benefit mankind. A lifetime in law enforcement had taught Brognola the fallacy of "cures" and "rehabilitation" for the predators he dealt with every day. Such men were lost, beyond the reach of reason or simple humanity, utterly without value to the civilized community. Worse, each day that they survived ran up a tab in pain and suffering that no amount of retroactive justice could repay.

Better to let the brushfire run its course in California and be done with it. With any luck at all, something better would rise from the ashes, untainted by the hate and bitterness that went before.

Brognola drained his coffee mug and set it aside, reaching for the telephone.

JANICE FLYNN WAS STRAINED but civil on the telephone, her cryptic comments a concession to the open line. Bolan noted a trace of sarcasm when she congratulated him on his night's work, but there was something else, as well. Not admiration—that would be too strong a word—but something in the neighborhood of grudging acceptance.

And that was progress, of a sort.

He wouldn't ask her openly for other targets, too much chance of being overheard by one side or the other, but he mentioned visiting some friends in town, and Flynn rattled off some more addresses. It was a mixed bag, some familiar from the files he had reviewed at Stony Man, some others new to Bolan, options for him to consider as he laid his plans.

It was still early in the day for solid scores, unless he started hunting for the brownshirts in their homes, and that could wait. He chose a meeting hall on Crenshaw Boulevard, in Inglewood, within spitting distance of the horse track at Hollywood Park. The ARM held public rallies there the second Tuesday night of every month, year-round, and

Pratt addressed his troopers from the dais once a week, or Wednesday evenings.

Until now.

The Nazis didn't know it yet, but they would need another place to strut their stuff next Wednesday... if enough of them remained to rate the designation of a gathering.

He drove through morning traffic, south on Crenshaw, going with the flow. No rush on this one, time to sit back and reflect on what he had accomplished so far, what was coming. It was early in the game to make a stab at keeping score, but Bolan liked to know exactly where he stood at each step in a life-and-death campaign. It wasn't always practical—or even possible—but at the moment, he was still ahead of the game, running in the open, with no one close enough to bring him down.

Not yet.

All that could change with lightning speed if Bolan let his guard down, but he meant to seize on the advantage while it lasted, make it count.

The meeting hall stood by itself, a vacant lot on one side, separated from its closest neighbor on the other by a narrow alley lined with trash cans. Good enough for Bolan's purposes. He parked in the near-empty lot, took his gym bag with him and made a beeline for the side door.

It was open. Bolan's first hunch had paid off. He followed sounds of sweeping to the main room, where he found a middle-aged janitor busily pushing his broom along the center aisle. The man caught sight of Bolan moments later, and hesitated, his eyebrows raising.

"There something I can do for you this morning?"

"You can leave," the Executioner replied.

"Say what?"

He drew the sleek Beretta from its armpit holster. "Leave, as in get out, haul ass, take five."

"I hear you."

"If you've got two quarters," Bolan told him, "call the fire department first. There won't be much for the police to do."

"Yes, sir. I'm out of here."

It felt good, dropping the incendiaries at strategic points around the meeting hall, pitching some far out across the rows of theater seats, saving a few for backstage. The place would be insured, so the owner would be okay, but its loss would send another message to the Aryan Resistance Movement. Pausing on his walk back to the car, the warrior reached inside his gym bag for the can of crimson spray paint he had purchased from a convenience store three blocks away. The message Bolan left behind, written large across the outer wall, would be familiar to his enemies: SCORCHED EARTH.

He left the side door standing open, oxygen to feed the flames, and smoke was dribbling from the portal by the time he put his Ford in gear, nosing out of the lot onto Crenshaw. Much of the old brick structure would survive to face a wrecking ball, and that was fine. Bolan was holding his high explosives in reserve, for more significant targets.

A fiery gesture was enough, for now, but it wouldn't be good enough for long.

Compared to his initial strikes, the last two stops had been a letdown, minor digs at the opposition, with no lasting damage inflicted. Bolan was on the scoreboard, still well ahead of his opposition, but it was not his style to sit back and coast on an early lead. Any break in the action could only work to the enemy's advantage, and the Executioner wasn't in the business of giving points away.

Time to roll, but he would feel better when he heard back from Brognola, filing some unexpected names with the diehard neo-Nazis as potential targets. When he started reaching out beyond the brownshirts, tagging their "legitimate" supporters in the rear echelons, it would be a whole new ball game.

But the stakes were still the same as always: life and death.

Some things, it seemed, would never change.

Hell had come to the City of Angels, but so far, it had only been a taste of things to come for Bolan's enemies.

Their most paranoid fantasies hadn't prepared them for the hours ahead.

But they would learn, oh yes.

A few of them might even live to profit from the lesson, if the stars were on their side.

The hellfire warrior wished them luck.

All bad.

9

"What kind of shit is this? Can anybody tell me that, for Christ's sake?"

Justin Pratt was livid, raging, thick veins pulsing at his temples as he paced the room before his three-man audience. Chet Blackmun was seated in the middle, Ronnie Mills from Santa Ana on his right, Ed Cratty from Alhambra on the left—Pratt's chief lieutenants in the Southern California ARM, for what it might be worth.

Not much, this morning, in the leader's estimation.

Not that much at all.

"I'm waiting!"

"Someone's got us scoped," Cratty said. "Fuckers doing everything they can to take us down."

"What was your first clue, Einstein?" Pratt's tone was bitter acid, scorching Cratty's ego, but the burly skinhead kept a sharp retort dammed up behind his teeth.

"I'd say it all goes back to Mitch and what we're doing with the rags," Blackmun stated. "Someone sprung a leak—my money's on the Arabs—and it got back to the Yids. They've got a hundred different ways of reaching out, if they want to tag somebody."

"Fair enough." Pratt hesitated in the midst of pacing, his cold eyes pinning each of them in turn. "So, who leaked last night's action, can you tell me that? You think they ever heard of Aaron Bluestein out in Tel Aviv? It's not like we went gunning for the only kike in town."

"A traitor." That from Ronnie Mills, three syllables that came out sounding like a curse.

"Agreed, but who? We didn't take out ad space in the *Times,* okay? You may have noticed that the hit team didn't make it back, but I don't figure they committed suicide. That trims it down. Fact is, I only talked it over with the three of you."

Pratt waited, feeling the silence, studying the faces of his three lieutenants. They were tense, on edge, and with good reason. There was only one penalty for treason to the movement, meted out on two occasions in the past, with each of these three in attendance to witness the ritual. He knew that each would be replaying those moments right now, casting himself in the role of the condemned.

"You think *we* leaked it?" Cratty was the first to ask, his expression incredulous.

"What the hell am I supposed to think, Ed?"

"Jesus, Justin—"

"Eight guys knew that we were hitting the Jew. Five of them got wasted on the hit, and I can tell you that I didn't talk to anyone outside this room."

"I briefed the troops," Blackmun said. "That's it. You can't rule out the possibility that one of them was bragging to his squeeze, or someone in the cadre. No damn reason in the world it has to be one of us."

"If you want to sell that line, you'd better prove it, Chet." Pratt left no room for argument. "I want whoever sold us out, you read me? I don't give a shit if it was someone's girlfriend or a limp dick in the ranks. We're down seventeen men in less than twelve hours, with nothing to show for it. I don't like the odds."

"We'll ask around," Cratty said.

"Do that. Ask around and keep on asking till you have the answer, understand me? I refuse to take this lying down. We've come too far and risked too much to blow it now. I *will not* stand around here with a thumb up my ass while some loose-lipped son of a bitch sells us out!"

"No problem," Cratty muttered.

"Oh? I'm glad to hear that, Ed. Seems to me like we've had nothing but problems, so far."

"I didn't mean—"

"Fuck what you didn't mean, all right? Just nail it down, and if we have another leak, I'll be looking for someone in this room to take responsibility."

The muttered assent from his three lieutenants was meek enough to placate the ARM leader, bleeding some of the heat from his mood.

But only a little.

"What about these other hits?" he asked. "The bookstore and the meeting hall on Crenshaw?"

"Could be unrelated," Ronnie Mills put in. "The public knew about both places, Justin. You remember last time someone burned the bookstore out."

Pratt bit his lower lip, counting to ten before he responded.

"You think it's a coincidence? Is that it?" Frank derision laced his tone. "Six or seven hours after someone scrubs the Bluestein mission, we've got fires, a witness at the last one who gave the cops a clear description of the bastard, and you're telling me you think it was coincidence?"

"I said it could be."

"Could be, shit! The day coincidence comes four times in a row, you'll see me buying kosher."

"Well—"

"Somebody knows what's going down," Pratt told his officers. "You'd better tell me who, or I'll find someone else who can."

He let that soak in for a moment, watching them nodding, three heads bobbing up and down as one.

"I don't like being in the dark," he said. "Even if I have to set the three of you on fire to shed some light."

WEAPONS, ALONG WITH CASH, were the lifeblood of the Aryan Resistance Movement. Without the hardware, Pratt's brown-shirted commandos were reduced to little more than barroom brawlers, full of outmoded malice and hot-air bravado. But with guns in hand...

Justin Pratt wasn't foolish enough to put all his eggs in one basket, by any means, but he did believe in a concept of strategic centralization, stashing firearms, ammunition and explosives in several carefully guarded locations, available to his stormtroops at need, secure for the most part against federal seizure.

One such arsenal, according to the FBI in Washington and Janice Flynn, was a waterfront warehouse in Hermosa Beach. The location had been known to Bureau leaders for the best part of a year, but they refrained from notifying ATF or raiding the arms depot on their own, out of concern for Janice Flynn's deep-cover status in the ARM.

Mack Bolan, by contrast, had nothing to lose and everything to gain from a pointed strike at the movement's single largest arms cache in the state.

And unlike the White Power bookstore, unlike the Torrance meeting hall, this target wouldn't be left unguarded. In no sense would it be a risk-free piece of cake.

Bolan turned his car off Highland Avenue and cruised past the warehouse at a casual twenty-five miles per hour, scoping the scenery, checking for guards. His target was set back from the street, behind a six-foot chain-link fence, but the gate didn't appear to be secured by locks or chains. No sentries were visible, no dogs in sight, but he would have to get in close before he had a firm fix on the odds.

The warrior parked downrange in a vacant lot with tough grass sprouting through the broken asphalt. He had already changed clothes for the strike, stopping off at a gas station two miles back, donning a workman's coverall with spacious pockets and a zip down the front. His hard hat and toolbox completed the picture, one for show, the other purely functional, containing his Uzi submachine gun and a mixed bag of grenades, some fragmentation, some incendiary.

He was right about the gate: no chain, no padlock. Bolan risked a low-pitched whistle, waiting for the dogs, relaxing not at all when they failed to materialize. Canine patrols were the least of his worries on this stroke, one well-placed bullet more deadly than any four-legged assailant.

He breezed through the gate, leaving it ajar behind him. Keep it casual all the way, lips puckered in a silent whistle as he made his way across the broad expanse of asphalt toward the loading dock.

Where were they?

Janice Flynn advised him that the stash was never left unguarded, but so far he was unopposed.

Would there be a warning before they opened fire? Could the ARM afford the risk of gunning down a hapless workman in broad daylight, without first asking his business?

The shout of warning came from Bolan's right, snapping his head around toward the point where a man in blue denim stood watching, a pump shotgun gripped in his right hand, muzzle down, the piece held flush against his leg.

Bolan veered in that direction, putting on a crooked smile, pretending not to see the shotgun.

"Who the hell are you?"

"Cal Power," the warrior answered, closing the gap with measured strides. "We got a call about some kind of problem with your meter."

"Bullshit. Any problem here, I would've known about it."

"I don't want to argue with you, friend. I've got the work order here, if you'll give me a second."

It was all down to split-second timing now, as he slipped a hand inside the open front of his coverall, seeing the shotgun's muzzle start to rise, coming out with the Beretta 93-R in a single fluid motion. Trusting the custom silencer to cover any noise he made, he fired a double punch from twenty feet, his target reeling backward, going down.

The warrior turned the corner in a rush, prepared to face the gunner's backup, finding no one. He took the time to holster his Beretta, then fished the Uzi out of his toolbox before he continued on his way. Around the back he mounted a flight of steps and crossed the loading dock, an access door unlocked and waiting for him. Music led him inside, along a narrow corridor, into the warehouse proper.

Two more guards were seated opposite each other at a smallish card table, one of them calculating his bet on a hand of seven-card stud. "I'll see that five," he said, "and raise you one."

"I'd fold, if I were you."

The two heads snapped around as one, faces lapsing into shock at the sight of Bolan's automatic weapon. He gave them a fighting chance, both men reaching for pistols in the split second before Bolan stitched them with a dozen rounds, tracking the Uzi's muzzle from left to right and back again, blowing both of them away.

He wasted no time checking them for vital signs, intent on finishing his business swiftly. The firearms, ammo and grenades were ranged against one wall in wooden crates, mislabeled as machine parts and appliances. He cracked several cases at random, making sure of his find, before he stepped back, removed four thermite grenades from his toolbox and set about wedging them between strategic cases. That done, he loosened the safety pins of each in turn, securing them to ten-foot lengths of twine, double-checking the set to assure himself that the simple trick would work.

When everything was ready, he backed off to the limit of the twine's length, ditched his hard hat, gripping the lightened toolbox in his left hand, bundle of twine in his right. With a sharp tug the safety pins came free as one, spoons flying, seven seconds on the fuses counting down as he sprinted for the corridor and daylight.

He was clear before the thermite cans exploded, spewing white-hot coals that would reduce the guns to melted scrap, detonate the ammo and grenades on contact. He could hear them blowing like a string of giant fireworks, shrapnel punching through the warehouse walls and roof, as he retreated to his waiting car.

Scorched earth.

Damn right.

JANICE FLYNN GOT an early start on working the streets. It wasn't the same as her days working out of the Bureau field office in neatly pressed suits, rolling into a suspect's home or place of business and flashing the credentials to put a torque in his shorts. Working undercover was a whole different ball game, and Flynn was still getting used to the rules.

For openers, she had a part-time job to help explain the small apartment she had rented using Bureau operating funds. Three nights a week, she was a barmaid at a redneck club on Wilshire Boulevard, where Blackmun and a number of his fascist cronies met to pass the time. It was the place where she first made connections with her contact in the ARM, coming on to him as subtly as possible while she dodged groping hands and tried to keep two dozen orders straight in her mind.

And it had worked.

She took no pride in that, per se, believing Blackmun would have gone for any willing woman, just as long as she was white enough to pass the Nazi pigment test. He never asked about the flat, how she could afford it with a part-time job, but she was ready with an answer if he did. She had inherited some money when her parents died three years ago, a lucky break.

It made her skin crawl, working on that cover story, with her parents both alive and well in Wheeling, West Virginia. They understood her work, to a point, realizing that she couldn't always phone them twice a week like "normal" daughters would, but speaking of them in the past tense never failed to produce a twinge of guilt, as if she were somehow wishing them dead.

Her system for collecting information, when she wasn't working at the Wilshire club or killing time with Chet Blackmun, consisted primarily of hanging out in the politically correct places.

Politically correct for fascists, that is.

Los Angeles might not qualify as a melting pot, but it is certainly a smorgasbord. It is difficult to imagine a religion or political fringe group that has not taken root in the L.A. basin since World War II. Moonies and Krishnas, satanists and born-again ''Jesus freaks,'' anarchists and grim totalitarians, black revolutionaries and paranoid white supremacists—L.A. had them all, and then some. Each clique had its personal refuge or watering hole—attics and basements, reading rooms and storefront churches, bars.

So much of it came down to bars, as if the fellowship of alcohol was all that held some groups together, fueling their bizarre delusions. When you wanted information on a certain group and couldn't ask directly, you were best off hanging in the bars, keeping it subtle, nice and easy. No pushy questions to set tongues wagging the moment your back was turned. The best approach was simply clinging to the sidelines, soaking up the gossip, culling it at leisure for any useful bits of trivia. Take your time, put it together one piece at a time, determining what was critical and weeding out the garbage before you submitted a report to headquarters.

There are at least eight racist bars and nightclubs in L.A., jukeboxes stocked with the recordings of skinhead bands, walls decorated with Confederate battle flags, vintage German military posters and the occasional black rubber head, mounted to resemble hunting trophies. No one was excluded from the bars, per se—a practice that would certainly have landed the proprietors in federal court and put them out of business. Blacks were generally wise enough to shun the clubs on general principle, and if the young bloods came in looking for a rumble now and then, well, that was fine.

The redneck clubs opened around 10:00 a.m., and Flynn started making her rounds at 10:30, nursing a drink here and there, taking it easy and chewing the fat.

Flynn was surprised to note that talking to Belasko early in the morning seemed to perk her spirits up. She didn't know exactly what to make of that, and she wasn't convinced it rated any serious consideration. They were working on a job together, and she didn't like his methods, even though they seemed to get results.

And yet . . .

She let it go, went back to following the drift of conversation, dropping innocuous questions into the pot when she saw an opening, willing them to give her something, anything, a handle.

Please.

Anything at all to get this nightmare over with.

ELEVEN-THIRTY, Elwood Gainer noted, glancing at the stylish clock on his office wall. With no appointments scheduled until one o'clock, he could permit himself an early lunch, perhaps a drink or two, to soothe his nerves.

He had it coming, certainly. The past twelve hours, give or take, had brought enough new problems to persuade a Southern Baptist minister that he would find salvation in a whiskey glass.

Not business problems, though; that would have been too simple. He had problems in the one part of his life that Gainer did his best to keep a secret from the world at large.

If that part of his life should be exposed . . .

He shrugged the thought away and concentrated on the task of covering his tracks. He had been cautious, all the way, routing his donations through a paper company in different names. He stayed away from meetings, never talked to anyone suspicious on his home or office telephones, ordered literature through a dummy postbox that he rented in a name he picked at random from the telephone directory.

Still . . .

Elwood Gainer hated Jews, blacks, Asians—every nonwhite ethnic group that he could think of, when it came to that. The feelings were a legacy from his father, a first-class hater if there ever was one, drilling the message into his only son from the time Elwood got up in the morning until he retired at night. Jews were greedy, scheming Christ killers, the architects of godless communism. Mud people weren't human at all, and there were medical studies to prove it, cleverly sidelined and suppressed by the Jewish media in New York and grafting politicians in Washington. It was a wise man who kept to his own and knew where his roots were, constantly tending the delicate flower of white supremacy.

In fact, Gainer did business with Jews and other minorities every day, pocketing their money with a broad smile on his face. If anyone had grilled him on the point, he might have told them it was sweet revenge, taking back a measure of the wealth that various minorities had stolen from the white man over time.

Poetic justice.

Gainer's friends called him Woody, and none of those he mingled with on business or social occasions had ever heard him pass an anti-Semitic remark. None would have guessed that Elwood Gainer ranked among the top-four domestic financial supporters of a crackpot private army called the Aryan Resistance Movement. They would have laughed the notion off.

And they would have been wrong.

Time to go. Gainer smiled at his secretary on the way out, told her that he would be back from lunch in ample time for his one o'clock with the developers from Agoura Hills. No problem. As he was running down a mental list of restaurants while he waited for the elevator, Sherry buzzed down to have his driver waiting at the curb. Coordination and efficiency were Gainer's hallmarks. They had put him where he was today.

He rode the elevator down with a couple of "career women" from the seventh floor—snotty dykes—and breezed out through the office tower's lobby, emerging onto Tenth Street, one block from Olympic Boulevard. The car was waiting, a charcoal-colored Mercedes with smoked glass to match. His driver-bodyguard circled around the vehicle to get his door.

Gainer hesitated, letting a couple of Asians cross his path, shying away from the risk of physical contact. Nothing obvious—he could shake hands with mud people in a business setting, if he had to—but why take chances with the exotic bacteria they carried around?

The sidewalk was clear now, and as he strode toward the open back door of his car, something incredible happened. Gainer couldn't place it at first, the loud banging noise that left a shiny divot in the hood of his Mercedes, as if a mailed fist had slammed into the charcoal-gray steel. The engine was running, and something sparked under the hood, catching light. The hood blew free with an earsplitting crack, and smoke rolled out of the engine compartment as Woody Gainer tried to make sense of the scene.

His driver had a gun out now, half crouching in the shadow of the car, staring up at rooftops on the far side of the street. Gainer had missed the first rifle shot, lost in the sounds of impact and destruction, but he saw the second one strike home. His wheelman vaulted backward, as stiff as a bludgeoned trout, wearing a fine halo of crimson mist around his shattered skull.

God Almighty! Someone was shooting at him here, downtown, in broad daylight!

Gainer turned to run for the office block's lobby, had already taken the first wobbly stride, when that same mailed fist slammed into his left knee from behind. No pain at first, but he was spinning, falling, feeling a bruising impact as he touched down on his back, staring at the vertical slab of architecture above him.

Gainer braced himself for the killing stroke, tried without success to recall a prayer from childhood.

Nothing happened.

After something close to forty seconds, Gainer sat up, scanning the street in all directions, noting the vultures who formed ranks at a distance of fifty, sixty feet, waiting to see what would happen next.

With a sudden shock, Gainer realized that he had wet his pants.

And he began to cry.

10

The National Vanguard's public headquarters was situated on Kantstrasse, west of the main post office. It was a smallish building, early-1960s-vintage architecture, roughly contemporaneous with the now nonexistent Berlin Wall. It was dwarfed by adjacent buildings, showing its age, but it was reasonably well maintained. The sign beside the door was polished brass, illegible from where David McCarter stood on the opposite side of the street, but it showed him that the Vanguard felt it had nothing to hide.

Times change.

Since World War II, public expressions of Nazi sympathies had been outlawed in Germany, but enforcement of the law depended on local prosecutors, varying from one era to the next. Many Germans—especially in their new, reunified homeland—were anxious to forget about Adolf Hitler and get on with their lives. The Holocaust was ancient history in their estimation, a closed book, best left to gather dust on the library shelf. Any surviving war criminals were old men by now, staring death in the face, and they would garner their reward or punishment on the other side.

For others, like the National Vanguard, Hitler was alive and well in modern Germany, his master-race philosophy the one true answer to a host of problems plaguing Germany in particular, and Europe at large. If only certain unjust, antiquated laws could be repealed, the German people would be able to select a righteous leader for themselves, break the cycle of red terrorism and left-leaning corruption. Perhaps, when the German National Party rose to power...

McCarter knew the arguments by heart, from long exposure to the aberrant, destructive thinking common to fanatics. He dismissed the pseudologic, concentrating on the task at hand, the first step in a new campaign.

The Briton wore an earpiece and a small lapel-clip microphone to keep in touch with his Phoenix Force comrades. His jacket, deliberately full-cut, concealed the Browning BDM automatic in a shoulder rig, the silent MP-5 SD-3 submachine gun in a swivel mount on his right. He was ready to go.

"All clear in front," he said into the microphone. "No traffic in or out."

"All clear in back," the voice of Yakov Katzenelenbogen came back in his ear. "We're set."

"I'm ready on the west," Gary Manning almost whispered.

Katz and Calvin James had the rear exit covered, Manning positioned on a fire escape at the building's west side, ready to enter by force. The odd man out was Rafael Encizo, waiting in the car two blocks east, the engine ticking over, ready for a hasty getaway.

Rudolf Wetzel had directed them to the target, but he wasn't taking part in the raid. The man from GSG-9 refused to involve himself in Phoenix Force's campaign at the street level, recognizing the risk to his own career, let alone his life. The neo-Nazis were Wetzel's concern, but only to a point, and he wasn't prepared to sacrifice himself for strangers, much less foreigners with an agenda of their own.

"Let's do it," Katzenelenbogen announced to the team at large.

McCarter crossed the street with easy strides, slipping a hand inside his jacket to grip the barrel of his subgun. He wasn't about to waste time with the doorbell, waiting while a sentry scrutinized him through the peephole and tried to send him on his way. Without a backward glance toward the street, McCarter swung the SMG out from under his coat, shattering the lock with a 3-round burst at point-blank range.

He followed with a kick and stepped across the threshold, nudging the bullet-scarred door shut behind him. Twenty feet away, a thin young man was just emerging from a doorway on McCarter's left, gaping in shock at the new arrival, lips working silently, hands frozen in the split second before he went for the autoloader at his waist.

McCarter got there first, a short burst from his submachine gun slamming the young Nazi backward, bouncing him off the doorjamb and bringing him down on his face. As if in answer to the muffled shots, he heard Katz and James kicking in the back door, coming to join him.

They had no clear fix on the number of occupants present, no idea if there were women present or, if so, whether they would stand and fight with the men. Wetzel had given them some background, with the address and a basic floor plan, but the head count on Vanguard personnel was flexible.

They would have to play it by ear.

McCarter started for the staircase in front of him, leaving the ground floor to James and Katz. He had business elsewhere, and his time was running out. The former SAS commando didn't have a moment to spare for indecision.

It was now or never.

URI DAN HAD CHOSEN his hotel room carefully, insisting on a sixth-floor room with western exposure. He had counted off the floors and verified the presence of the fire escape in advance, before he ever approached the registration desk with his false but technically flawless passport and credit card. An extra tip got him the room he required.

All things considered, he decided it would be a relatively easy jump. There was a narrow alleyway between the hotel and the National Vanguard headquarters, perhaps twelve feet across, but the advantage lay in altitude. His onetime training as a paratrooper would be good for something, after all. And this time he wouldn't require a parachute.

His contact at the Israeli embassy had provided the hardware: a mini-Uzi with customized suppressor, a Walther PP semiautomatic pistol, and four extra magazines for each weapon.

With any luck at all, it would be enough.

His orders had included no specific details. Tel Aviv was calling for a gesture to put the National Vanguard on notice, punish the neo-Nazis for their murders of Israeli diplomatic personnel. It wasn't a matter for the German police, who would probably find themselves unable to prosecute the gunmen in any case.

An eye for an eye, in biblical terms. Or, more precisely, a head for an eye.

There were no specific limits on his errand of vengeance, but Tel Aviv would trust him to do enough without going too far. A fine point, perhaps, but Dan was experienced in such matters. He had gone on such errands before, and there had been no complaints from his superiors concerning tactics or body counts.

Locating the National Vanguard headquarters had been simplicity itself, child's play in comparison to tracking down an Arab terrorist in Lebanon or Syria. The racist bastards had such faith in their innate superiority that they made no real effort to hide.

It was a mistake that some of them, at least, wouldn't live to regret.

Dan considered waiting for nightfall and decided against it, worried that the building might be vacant after dark. The strike would be a onetime thing, and he didn't intend to waste his effort on empty rooms or a senile night watchman.

His window opened directly on the fire escape. When he had scanned the alley below and found it clear of foot traffic, Dan stepped out on the metal staircase, happy for the sunshine on his face and shoulders. The Uzi came with a shoulder sling, and he wore the piece under his jacket on the right. The Walther fit comfortably inside his belt, snug against the small of his back.

Dan worked his way down to the next landing, passing another window on the way, blinds drawn against the daylight. If any tenants noted his passing shadow, they gave no sign. He picked his spot, swung first one leg over the railing, then the other. For a moment he was balanced on the precipice, a spine-cracking drop to the alley below, and then he leaped, arms spread, his jacket flaring behind him like a cape.

He remembered to tuck and roll on impact, coming up in a crouch with the Uzi in hand. No immediate reaction from the floors below, as he approached the access door nearby. The door was locked, and he went to work on the latch with a clasp knife, cracking it in fifteen seconds flat. The open stairwell yawned in front of him, as inviting as a grave.

He reached the top floor unopposed and glanced left and right along the corridors, seeing four doors in each direction, staggered to the left and right. He waited, watching, listening. Nothing moved in the hallway, no scuffling, furtive sounds behind the doors. He contemplated checking out each room in turn and shrugged it off.

No time to waste.

He started for the fifth-floor landing, moving on the balls of his feet, striving for a minimum of noise. Halfway down he froze, bracing himself as the sound of clomping boot heels assaulted his ears.

The gunman seemed to come from nowhere, charging up the stairs, lips drawn back from his teeth in a snarl of exertion. The automatic pistol in his hand was pointed at his shoes.

"Was ist los?"

Dan answered with a 3-round burst that took his moving target in the chest and punched him backward down the stairs. The Nazi landed in a crumpled heap, unmoving, and there was no more time for caution now. If they were on alert below, he would have to hurry.

He leaped across the huddled corpse and swiveled to his left, pulling up short at the sight of a second body stretched out on the floor. Blood soaked the front of his dress shirt, abstract crimson patterns on a field of white. The second corpse clutched a Skorpion machine pistol in his out-stretched hand.

Two dead?

He was about to turn and scan the opposite direction when a soft voice froze him in his tracks.

"That's far enough."

The voice was male, and it spoke in English.

"Drop the gun," it said, "and turn around. No tricks, or you'll be dead before you know it."

CALVIN JAMES WAS READY when they went in through the back door, Katz in front of him, a hulking bear. A startled member of the Vanguard met them, stumbling from a closet-sized men's room, grappling with his trousers.

Katz hit him with a short burst from his subgun that slammed the dead Nazi backward and into the toilet.

They swept along a musty corridor, moving toward the front of the building and a reunion with McCarter. En route, they passed an office with the door standing open, one man gaping at them from behind a cluttered desk, his companion standing, turning to see what had drawn the sitter's attention.

The targets broke in opposite directions, almost saving it.

The standing figure swiveled on his heel and made a dive toward the nearby file cabinets, where an assault rifle lay across the metal boxes, sporting a 30-round banana clip. Katz helped him get there with a burst between the shoulder blades, punching the runner forward with extra momentum, smashing his face against the topmost metal drawer.

The man behind the desk, meanwhile, had launched himself to his right, ripping a compact semiauto pistol from its shoulder rig as he went low and outside. James tracked him with the stubby MP-5 K submachine gun, triggering a burst that caught the gunman's shoulder.

The gunner went down on his uninjured side, impact spoiling his aim as he pumped a wild shot into the bottom drawer of his own desk. James wasn't waiting for the Nazi to recover, squeezing off another burst that snuffed out the hardman before he had a chance to scream.

They met McCarter in the entry hall, just stepping over the prostrate corpse of a Vanguard sentry. "Up or down?" the former SAS commando asked.

"I'm going up," Katz said. "We're on the clock. Let's make it count."

"I'll take the basement," James announced, heading out.

He found the access door beneath the staircase, with steps leading down into a cellar that was roughly half the size of the ground floor. Lights were burning down there, but that could mean anything. It could be a washout, no opposition at all. On the other hand...

He picked up on cautious footsteps, drawing closer to the staircase, but the scowling moon face at the bottom still managed to surprise him. The Nazi was glaring, pulling back his head and blurting out a warning.

"Schwartze!"

Black. James got that much as he triggered a burst from the subgun, scoring plaster and thin air for his pains. At least two voices spoke excitedly now beyond his line of sight, and James knew that he would have to root them out before he could pronounce his job finished.

He palmed one of the Dutch V-40 minigrenades, yanking the safety pin and giving it a sidelong toss, caroming off the wall and wobbling away out of sight. The voices took on a different timbre, rising to a frantic pitch.

James retreated swiftly to the head of the staircase, crouching to make himself small as the minigrenade exploded, peppering the basement walls and ceiling with razor-edged shrapnel. A scream erupted from below, winding down into agonized moans, but it could be a trick.

No way around it. He would have to check the casualties up close and personal. Speed was the ticket, and he had no time to waste.

The banister was smooth, painted wood, and James rode it like a child, dropping into a crouch at the bottom, letting momentum take him down in a shoulder roll, coming up ten feet from the place he touched down. He held the subgun steady in a firm two-handed grip.

He scanned the smoky basement, noted that one man was down and clutching at the bloody ruin of his stomach. No fake there. Another man knelt in the corner, looking slightly dazed but coming back, already groping for the pistol he had dropped when the grenade went off.

Just two.

James took the kneeling figure with a rising burst that zippered him from crotch to collarbone and punched him back in the corner, a leaking rag doll, limp and lifeless.

The wounded Nazi saw James coming through a haze of smoke and pain. His lips were drawn back in a snarl, defiant in the face of death, muttering fiercely at his nemesis. James didn't understand a word of it, but there was no mistaking the tone. Bitter hatred, compounded by mortal pain.

James silenced that voice with a 3-round burst from his machine pistol, snapping the head back in midsyllable, pulling the plug.

A last visual sweep, double-checking to confirm that he had left no one alive down there, and James hit the stairs. He was a bit slower on the ascent, but still pushing it, listening for sounds of combat from the upper floors.

He emerged from the basement stairwell just as his comrades were descending from the second floor, apparently finished with their sweep. He heard their voices first, plus one he didn't recognize.

He did a head count and discovered four, when there should have been three.

"Who's this?" he asked Katz, nodding toward the dark, athletic figure sandwiched between McCarter and Manning.

"That," Katz replied, "is what I intend to find out."

THE NARROW LANE in Grunewald Park was overshadowed by trees, deeply shaded and cool. The Phoenix Force warriors had it to themselves. They spilled out of their crowded sedan, taking the stranger with them while Rafael Encizo remained with the car.

"All right, let's hear it," Katz demanded, when they had put twenty yards behind them, trees and hedges screening their view of the drive.

"I have nothing to say."

"Suit yourself," McCarter said. The Browning BDM automatic was in his hand before he finished speaking, cocked and leveled at the stranger's face.

"Hold on," Katz ordered. He faced the stranger, stepping close enough to read the younger man's eyes. "We will not hesitate to kill you if you threaten us, but I suspect that we have more in common than you know. You came to fight the Nazis. So did we. I think you came from Tel Aviv."

"Think what you like."

"Could it be you are here because of Asher Blum?"

The stranger hesitated, frowning, staring back at Katz. "You're not American."

Katz shook his head. "Israeli. Ex-Mossad."

The stranger looked around. "And these?"

"With me. We have a common goal."

"Which is?"

Katz knew that he would have to give a bit more of himself away before he could discover who this stranger was and what had brought him to the National Vanguard headquarters with an Uzi submachine gun in his hands.

"It is our mission to destroy the Vanguard. I cannot divulge the reasons, but you have my word that nothing we intend will jeopardize Israeli interests."

"Your word."

Katz nodded, waiting.

"So," the stranger said at last, making up his mind. "My name is Uri Dan. I work for the Mossad. My mission, as you say, is to avenge the death of Asher Blum and his associate."

"You're finished, then," Katz said. "You can go home."

The Mossad agent's smile was more ironic than humorous. "Perhaps not yet."

"Why not?"

"I am encouraged to apply initiative. It seems a shame to let you do my work and then go home before the job is done."

"What did you have in mind?" McCarter asked. His Browning automatic had been tucked away out of sight.

"Perhaps cooperation of a sort. I have resources at my disposal that might be mutually beneficial. Why should we not work together, rather than at odds." The smile took on a quirky twist. "I wouldn't mind five extra pairs of hands."

"Some bloody cheek," McCarter groused.

"We just might have a problem with security," Calvin James pointed out.

Katz nodded. "I'll have to speak with my superiors."

"And I," Dan replied. "The red tape is a bane of our existence, yes?"

"It feels that way sometimes."

"If you could grant me access to a telephone . . ."

"In time. We must discuss the matter first."

"Of course."

He stood aside, withdrawing a cautious few paces while the men of Phoenix Force formed a huddle around Katz, one or two of them keeping the Israeli constantly in view. They had disarmed him back at Vanguard headquarters, but none of them relished the prospect of a wild chase through the Grunewald Park.

"You think the Farm will go for this?" James asked.

"Why not? It helps us get the job done, and we won't be giving anything away."

"Who needs him?" McCarter asked. "All we've got is an Israeli playing catch-up for the men we lost. That's a distraction, not a contribution."

"I've been thinking that our mission might not be confined to Germany," Katz said. "It didn't start here, and I have no reason to believe our enemies are confined to Berlin."

"So what?"

"A friend in Tel Aviv might come in handy if we have to take it back to Jordan," Katz reminded them. "I take it from his hardware that they also have munitions laid by in the city. Something in reserve, perhaps, without falling back on the Farm."

"It couldn't hurt," Manning said.

"Do it," James put in.

McCarter nodded, but he didn't lose the frown. "All right."

The vote was part of it, a spirit of cooperation, even though Katz could have made the choice himself and used his rank to ram it down their throats. It was a part of teamwork, going through the motions when you had the time.

"Okay," he said, "I'll make the call and find out what Brognola thinks."

He led them back to Uri Dan, found the Israeli waiting for them with a calm, relaxed expression on his face. He seemed to be expecting nothing, ready for anything.

"Your decision?" he asked, sounding almost disinterested.

Katz smiled. "Let's find that telephone."

11

By half-past eleven o'clock, Janice Flynn was burned out on cruising redneck bars, disappointed by her lack of progress so far. She had touched base with Mike Belasko briefly on the telephone, and they were set to meet in two hours' time at a fast-food restaurant on Olive Avenue in Burbank.

Great.

Except that so far, Flynn had nothing new to share with her short-term ally, and she hated the thought of turning out for the meet empty-handed. It was bad enough being forced to work with a rogue, finding herself drawn to his no-holds-barred tactics against her own better judgment, without appearing incompetent on her own behalf.

Belasko clearly had his own sources of information that Flynn knew nothing about. Working a crazy deal like this with the Bureau took pull, for starters, and he hadn't come into L.A. flying blind. The strike at Camp Victory was all on his own, before they ever got in touch, and something told her the tall man would get along just fine if she decided to drop out of the race.

But she was sticking, and not because her field control had stressed the need for close cooperation with this stranger in his private war.

The thing that grabbed Janice Flynn, made her reconsider her own role in the Bureau, was a feeling of progress, a sense that she was gaining significant ground against her chosen targets for the first time—not because of her link to the Bureau, but in spite of same.

Filing reports with the local field office was one thing; getting down in the dirt and slugging it out on your adversary's own terms was something else entirely. It surprised and galled Janice Flynn to discover that her new feeling of accomplishment came from breaking the rules, instead of playing by the book, carefully dotting her i's and crossing her t's.

And speaking of rules, she was about to break another one, albeit minor in comparison to Mike Belasko's bloody tactics. If she couldn't pick up the information she required through normal channels, hanging out around the clubs, then she would try the horse's mouth . . . or, perhaps, some other portion of that animal's anatomy.

She placed a quick call to the field office, leaving a vague message for her control officer and hanging up before he could come on the line. She didn't want advice or backup at the moment, but a measure of insurance never hurt.

She called ahead from a phone booth on La Brea Avenue, satisfied that Chet wasn't at home. A two-mile drive took her to his apartment, and she checked the lot for a glimpse of Chet's car before she parked.

All clear, but she would have to hurry, even so.

Flynn didn't have a key to Blackmun's flat, but she picked the lock in seconds and let herself inside. It was her second time in the apartment, and she knew where he kept his personal computer. From the terminal in his smallish bedroom, Blackmun could plug into the Aryan Nations' "Liberty Net" and a variety of other computerized bulletin boards reserved for like-minded "patriots." He could also access files of data from the ARM's central computer, controlled by Justin Pratt, calling up membership lists, overseas contacts and God knew what else.

She switched the computer on, connecting the modem, and waited for the initial menu to show up on-screen. It was slow going without the mandatory passwords, but she could follow directions as well as anyone, better than most. Within fifteen minutes, she had progressed from the basics to stage one of the Aryan Resistance Movement's "Patriotic Record."

Flynn scanned the possible choices, recognizing some from common usage, puzzling over others. They included:

(1) Jewish Ritual Murders, by Justin Pratt
(2) The New American Revolution
(3) . . . no title line . . .
(5) A History of the Mud Races
(6) Crisis Survival Skills
(7) More Topics . . .

Flynn saw two immediate options, the blank line following Number 3, or the new topics offered by Number 7. She tried the first option to start, punched the requisite keys and saw a new legend materialize on the screen: Type Password Now.

"Well, shit."

She puzzled over the request for another full minute, trying to come up with something of significance to the ARM, something even a slug like Chet Blackmun could remember.

She took a shot and typed four words: Day of the Rope.

A tap on the Enter key, and the one-line message dissolved into a list of names. Not members of the ARM, she knew that much from skimming down the list. For one thing, she recognized none of the names. For another, some of them were obviously Jewish, others plainly Hispanic.

A hit list, sure.

"Well, now."

Blackmun had no printer connected to the computer. She would have to take notes or memorize as many of the names as she could.

No good.

She had her chair pushed back, already rising to look for a pencil and paper, when a shadow fell across the open bedroom doorway. She glanced up and froze at the sight of

Chet Blackmun watching her, his thin lips twisted somewhere between a manic grin and a snarl.

"See anything you like there, bitch?" he asked.

THE TRANSATLANTIC CALL to Stony Man Farm was routed to Brognola's desk through cutouts, an investment of fifteen extra seconds to render the call untraceable. Brognola spoke to Aaron Kurtzman first, a word of introduction, ready for anything as Katz came on the line.

"Hello?"

"I'm glad I caught you," the Israeli said.

"What's happening?"

"We've run into a friend out here."

"Oh, yes?"

"It came as a surprise, but I think we can work together."

"That's a bit unorthodox," Brognola said.

"But not unprecedented."

"No. Who is this friend?"

"You wouldn't recognize his name," Katz said. "We went to synagogue together, way back when."

Brognola grimaced. The Mossad. It was all he needed at the moment, one more chef to spike the broth.

"That's some coincidence," the big Fed said, trying to keep the strain out of his voice.

"Not quite. You heard about their sales rep who went sick out here?"

"It rings a bell."

"Our friend was sent to settle the account. You know his people are sticklers for balanced books."

And then some. "So I hear," Brognola answered.

"I was thinking that it might be helpful if we worked together, but discreetly. Common cause, that kind of thing. If we get tied up chasing leads, his company could come in handy."

"Will they play?"

"He's checking. If they turn thumbs-down, we'll have to reassess."

"Conditional approval then, but keep the accent on discretion, will you?"

"Right."

"Okay, I'll pass it on."

"How's Striker doing?"

"More or less as you'd expect. They've got a heat wave coming on."

Katz chuckled softly. "I'm expecting changes in the weather here, as well. The temperature's already going up a few degrees."

"Stay frosty."

"I'll do my best."

The link was broken, and Brognola cradled the receiver, cursing underneath his breath.

So, Phoenix Force had stumbled into the Mossad. A vengeance mission for the death of Asher Blum against the Vanguard, and their paths had crossed. The man from Justice reckoned he would soon be hearing all about the circumstances of their meeting in a classified report, perhaps some reference to a blowup in Berlin on television or the radio, before the paperwork came in.

They hadn't wasted any time in squaring off against the enemy, and that was fine, but Brognola was worried at the prospect of an independent agent mixing with the group. He trusted the Mossad to get a job done, never mind the odds, but the Israelis had their own priorities, wrapped up in payback more than half the time. They took shit from no one, but sometimes the commitment to biblical vengeance produced blind spots, a dangerous kind of myopia where other same-side players were concerned.

It would have been doubly hard for Katz to resist the overture, knowing his roots and his former ties to Israeli intelligence, but Brognola still trusted him to make the right decisions for his team. There was no question of Katz veering off on a tangent, discarding his mission in pursuit of some quixotic order beamed from Tel Aviv.

Still...

He considered the risk implied in one of Katz's remarks, concerning the value of Israeli contacts if their mission led them outside Germany. It was food for thought, with one end of the plot clearly anchored in Jordan and Iraq. At some point, they would have to consider a strike at the source, and any action in the Middle East would be easier to prosecute with Israeli support.

But would they have that support, when it mattered?

Throwing in with a Nazi-hunting Mossad agent was fine, as far as it went, but the big Fed had no guarantees that the Israelis would hold up their end when the time came. This was no carefully orchestrated diplomatic mission, complete with ambassadors and bargaining tables. Agents talking in the field could make an agreement in principle, each side meaning every word as gospel, and the rug could still be snatched from under them anytime by their superiors, safe behind the lines. Brognola had seen it happen too many times on the domestic level, and he didn't relish the thought of sending Phoenix Force out on a limb, when the chain saw might be coming up behind them.

He had agreed to pass the plan upstairs, but he was having second thoughts. Suppose the powers in Washington got jumpy, balked at throwing in with the Israelis on a covert mission, and the no-vote left his people dangling in the breeze.

Brognola made his choice, deciding that the buck would stop with him. That way, if anything went wrong, it would be his ass on the line, along with those who manned the trenches.

As it should be, right.

He rocked back in his swivel chair, scowling at the clock on the wall.

It was going to be one hell of a long, deadly day.

URI DAN WAITED while the international connections popped and crackled in his ear, familiar sounds from other forays in the field. It was hot, almost stifling inside the telephone booth, but he kept the door closed, watching the man who had been left to guard him. Slim, Hispanic, possibly a Mexican or Puerto Rican. Dan couldn't say for certain, and he didn't care.

They had accepted him, but only to a point. Approval had been granted from their own control, but the team's leader—himself an Israeli—made it clear that nothing about their original mission had changed. They weren't adopting Israeli priorities or objectives. Dan was welcome to cooperate, or not.

And if he chose to operate alone, what then?

He didn't think his new acquaintances, a true mixed bag, would kill him out of hand. If they were all Americans or all Israelis, then perhaps he would have felt more trepidation. Any one of them was capable, he knew that much, but their collective conscience seemed to draw a line between the necessary and unnecessary deaths.

He hoped so, anyway.

But, what if they decided Uri's death was necessary?

Never mind.

His problem, at the moment, would be selling his control in Tel Aviv on the idea of working with an unknown team, striving for common goals while maintaining some vestige of integrity and confidentiality.

Before he had a chance to concentrate on that, his call rang through and was answered on the second ring. He recognized Meyer Levin's voice at once.

"I'm calling on an open line," Dan said, trusting Levin to recognize his voice. It would be the least of many mental tricks the handler performed this day.

"I understand." If Levin was surprised to hear from Dan, he didn't let it show in his voice.

"Phase one of my assignment is complete. There has, however, been a complication."

"I am listening." More cautious now, but still no worry coming through. It wasn't Levin's way to show concern, no matter what went wrong.

"I have encountered others who appear to share our goals."

"And they are..."

"One of them is ours, or used to be."

"His name?"

"We have not introduced ourselves."

The surly grunt told Dan that his little joke was unappreciated at the other end. "The rest?"

"American, Canadian, a Briton, some kind of Latin."

"Mercenaries?"

Dan thought about it for a moment, coming to terms with a question that had lurked in the back of his mind, frowning as he finally made the decision on instinct.

"No, I don't think so."

"Then, whose?"

"The Company, perhaps. I can't be certain."

"Have they interfered with you in any way?"

He knew that it was time to shade the truth a bit, or risk an ultimatum from his handler that would prove impossible to satisfy.

"As I explained," Dan replied, "our interests seem to be the same, so far. I was surprised, of course, but grateful for the help."

"And you are wishing to continue." It wasn't a question.

"I am."

"To what effect?"

"I was dispatched to teach a lesson," Dan said. "We both knew it would be a temporary measure, at the best. This way, I see a chance to solve the problem, rather than postpone a reoccurrence."

"There are no solutions," Levin told him, sounding weary now. "We thought the problem had been solved in 1945, if you recall. Of course, that was before your time, but I assume you know your history."

"I do. It tells me that appeasement and half measures were the basic problem in those days. If someone had responded earlier and more emphatically before the Reichstag fire and *Kristallnacht*, there might have been no Holocaust."

"And so, no Israel?"

"We do not require a repetition of catastrophe to keep us strong."

"I hope you're right." The handler hesitated for another moment, making up his mind. "How do I know that I can trust these strangers?"

"You trust me. If anything goes wrong, the fault is mine."

"I should tell that to the Knesset, when you're gone?"

"When I am gone, old friend, feel free to tell them anything you like."

That brought a rasping laugh from Meyer Levin. Dan saw his handler, sitting in the basement operations room, chain-smoking, with the telephone receiver pressed against his ear. Meyer's eyes, the grayest part of him, would be as hard and cold as flint.

"So be it," Levin said at last. "You have my blessing, which I will forget at once if anything goes wrong. The great advantage of my age is a selective memory."

"I understand."

"Good luck."

It was a great concession from the gray man, something Levin had never said to Dan before. A minor nod to Fate, Jehovah, call it what you will. It was the first suggestion he had ever seen that Meyer Levin trusted anything beyond himself and the men and women under his command.

As for Uri Dan, he was no great believer. Not yet. But he was willing to give it more thought, when he had the time.

With all that lay ahead of him, Dan knew he would be needing all the help that he could get.

THE FAST-FOOD RESTAURANT on Olive Avenue in Burbank specialized in chili dogs and tacos, the sort of mismatched combination that appeared to be a minor fetish in the L.A. basin. The proprietors, in their infinite wisdom, had decided to call their establishment the Taco Dog, with outside murals that portrayed a dachshund wearing a serape and broad-brimmed sombrero.

Still, Bolan told himself, it could have been worse. They might have called it the Mexican Weenie.

Waiting for Janice Flynn to arrive for their meeting, he ordered the deluxe chili dog and was pleasantly surprised. The meal had come and gone, along with Dancer's self-imposed deadline, when he started to wonder what had gone wrong.

It could be anything, he realized—the phone rings with a windbag on the other end, the car won't start, she gets a speeding ticket on her way to the restaurant, a fender-bender blocks the street until a tow truck makes its way through traffic to dissolve the snarl.

All mundane explanations, none of them the sort that preyed on Bolan's mind. He was concerned about the other possibilities, the kind that spelled disaster for a comrade and, perhaps, for Bolan's mission.

The warrior waited ten more minutes, getting antsy as the time ran out, feeling suddenly exposed in the restaurant booth, picturing Janice under rough interrogation, giving up their meeting site. A team of gunners on the way to take him out.

Too soon.

Assuming the worst, Dancer's captors wouldn't have had time to break her...would they? Two hours since they had spoken by telephone, and Bolan had no way of telling where she had gone, what she had done—or what had been done to her—in the interim.

Two hours was a lifetime on the rack. Some rode it out, hung tough, and died without revealing anything of substance. Others cracked before their personal inquisitors got up to speed. Experience would be the crucial factor, outweighing all others, and Bolan frankly questioned whether Janice Flynn had been prepared to face the kind of punishment interrogators dished out when their hearts were in their work.

The warrior caught himself before his mind could shift into a roll call of the dead, familiar faces scrolling on the mental viewing screen. It would be premature to write the lady off before he found out what was wrong.

He paid the check and left a tip on the table, walking a half block south of the Taco Dog to reach a sidewalk phone booth. Tapping out Dancer's home number from memory, he kept his fingers crossed, hoping for an innocuous explanation, anything to lift the darkening cloud of dread.

He listened to the telephone ringing in her apartment. Three times. Five times. Seven. At ten, he gave up and dropped the receiver back in its cradle.

Janice had told him not to expect an answering machine. Working under cover, the convenience of having messages on tap was overshadowed by the risk of having the wrong messages available to certain ears. How to explain a call from her control or someone like Bolan, if Chet Blackmun or one of his cronies from the ARM should punch the playback button on her tape machine some evening?

No one home, and what did that tell Bolan?

Zip.

He stood and watched the restaurant for another moment, willing Dancer to appear, walking slowly back to his car when she didn't show. He ran the options in his mind.

One way to play it, he could wait and call back later, hope that Janice was all right and he could get in touch when she got home. Hanging out around the Taco Dog all afternoon wasn't an option, and she wouldn't have expected him to linger much past their appointed meeting time. He didn't know her home address, and what would he accomplish dropping by, in any case?

His best choice had some drawbacks, granted, but it seemed the only way to go if Bolan wanted anything approximating a definitive response. He drove a quarter mile before he found another public telephone with its directory intact. The blue pages gave him a number of the Los Angeles field office of the FBI.

He fed the telephone a coin, punched up the number and waited for an answer on the line.

It was a gamble, granted, but he had no other way to go.

12

Clay Nichols checked his dim reflection in the window glass, turning side to side as he admired his uniform, the semiautomatic rifle slung muzzle-down over his right shoulder.

Bitchin'.

For the first time in his nineteen years of life, Nichols felt like he belonged. The Aryan Resistance Movement gave him that and more, a sense of self-worth that went far toward healing the wounds of a cruelly dysfunctional family.

Not that Nichols would recognize the term "dysfunctional" in daily conversation, much less know the proper spelling if his life depended on it. He knew his father was a drunk who liked to punch the kids around, his mother little better in the old man's absence, taking out her personal frustration and fury on the only available targets. Teachers, counselors and social workers didn't give a damn. When Nichols dropped out of the eleventh grade and started hanging with a street gang, no one seemed to notice, much less care. It was dumb luck that he had managed to survive until the evening when he walked into a public meeting of the ARM and found what he was looking for.

Dumb luck, or fate.

The movement told Nichols who he was and where he came from. Not the burned-out slobs who called themselves his parents, but the deeper roots of racial identity, stretching back to a time when ancient history was still current events and Aryan warriors were committed to purging their homeland of the Demon Jew, together with his mongrel offspring.

History.

In school, it was the subject Clay had hated worst of any. These days he couldn't get enough—had even started reading for the pleasure of it, thanks to Justin Pratt, Chet Blackmun and the führer.

That was progress for you.

Clay Nichols had never gotten along well with blacks or Mexicans—he never got along much with anyone, for that matter—but now he understood why. His sense of racial pride and history taught him that his people were fighting for survival, and nothing less. The fate of humankind was hanging in the balance.

Now, it seemed, the war was heating up.

He couldn't talk to a brother in the movement for two minutes this morning, without hearing all about the attacks they had suffered overnight. Camp Victory in ruins, damn it, and Nichols had been there only once. The bookstore and the meeting hall were gone, a secret arms cache. Who knew what was next?

The latest flap had filtered down from Justin's office through the ranks. They had a traitor under lock and key this afternoon, no names as yet, but Nichols understood it was some bitch who hung around the movement's leadership. Before the day was out, she would be broken, spilling everything she knew about the enemy, and there would be a bloody reckoning.

Nichols hoped that he would be a part of it, when the time came.

Meanwhile, he was on guard, teamed with two of his brothers in arms to watch another of the movement's ammo dumps, an isolated house near Stone Canyon Reservoir, due north of the UCLA campus. He was ready for anything. It was the moment he had trained for, hoped and prayed for since the night of his initiation as a soldier in the ARM.

Turning from the window where his image was reflected, Nichols paced across the barren front yard of the property, barely glancing at the two jeeps parked in what amounted to a driveway. Not that you could really tell where dirt left off and gravel started. No one paid attention to maintenance around the place. Security was what counted.

The jeeps were twenty feet behind him, give or take, when one of them exploded, lifting off a cushion of smoke and flame. Jets of gasoline were spewed in blazing streamers, setting the second jeep on fire.

The shock wave knocked him sprawling, or it might have been the jagged shrapnel ripping through his legs and buttocks. Nichols lost his rifle when he fell, and he had no inclination to search around him for the weapon. Nothing mattered but the white-hot pain below his waist.

He heard the gunfire from a distance, muffled by the ringing pressure in his ears. Nichols didn't see his comrades die, wouldn't have cared if they were stretched out on the ground in front of him, close enough to touch.

Survival had a different connotation now, when he could feel his lifeblood leaking through his tattered slacks. How long before his consciousness began to fade beyond recall, and he was lost?

A rough hand gripped his shoulder and turned him over onto his back. Nichols almost lost it then, the pain washing over him in waves, drowning him. A slap across the face brought him back to a semblance of clarity, his dim eyes focused on a man who stood above him, dressed in camouflage fatigues. The muzzle of an M-16 was prodding him beneath the chin, forcing his head back, making him squint in the sunshine.

"Can you hear me?"

"Hear you?"

"Yes or no?"

"I hear."

"You want to live?"

"I do." Hating himself for the cowardice he displayed, Nichols was overcome by relief at the thought he might survive, regardless of the price.

"I have a message for the man in charge. You follow me?"

"A message."

"Right. You play delivery boy, and I'll put a tourniquet on this and call the paramedics. Fair enough?"

"A message."

"I want the girl, unharmed. The heat stays on until she's free. You got that?"

"Got it."

"Give it back."

"Unharm the girl. More heat, unless you get her back."

"That's close enough."

He barely felt the stranger tying off his mutilated legs, less pain than he expected from the dark man's touch.

"What girl?" Nichols asked, a portion of his mind clearing long enough to formulate the question.

"Never mind. Pratt knows. Just pass the word."

"Okay."

It seemed a small enough favor to ask in return for his life.

RAISING DANCER'S CONTROL on the telephone had required some fast talking at first, but Bolan was up to the task. The man identified himself as Special Agent Kitteridge, and he listened closely as Bolan introduced himself without names, explaining the circumstances of his call. They danced around the code words for a critical minute or two, before Kitteridge felt secure enough to part with the information that Dancer had left him a message, alluding to a "special source."

Could Kitteridge be more specific?

Reluctantly he could and was. Dancer had been looking at a black-bag job—illegal entry—on Chet Blackmun's apartment. All without Bureau sanction, of course. The modern FBI would never countenance—

Bolan had cut him off in midsermon, rolling out toward Blackmun's, not surprised at all when he found he was too late. It was too much to hope for that Janice Flynn had changed her mind. In that case, or if she had pulled the entry off without a hitch, he knew she would have kept their date in Burbank.

That meant trouble, and he knew only one way of dealing with a hostage crisis. Turn the heat up, keep it at a rolling boil, and hope that something broke in the enemy camp before they had time to damage the hostage beyond repair.

Another gamble, right, but it appeared to be the only game in town. The grim alternative meant cutting Dancer loose and going about his business as if nothing had happened. Writing her off, in effect. Bolan's humanitarian side refused to acknowledge that option, and he had practical reasons, as well.

If Dancer broke, spilled everything to Justin Pratt and company, his enemies would have at least a vague idea of who to watch for, where the next blow might be coming from. Bailing Janice Flynn out of her present jeopardy was as much a self-defence measure as it was an act of charity.

Or so the warrior told himself.

In fact, Bolan had never been able to turn his back on helpless prisoners, regardless of the risk involved in extricating them from danger. It was part of the person, dating back to Vietnam, that had seen Bolan christened "Sergeant Mercy" by the same men who knew him as the Executioner.

A callback to Special Agent Kitteridge had shaken loose some fresh targets, in addition to those already fingered by Dancer and the team at Stony Man Farm. Bolan had no shortage of options as he began the next, more intense phase of his Southern California blitz. It all came down to choosing your pressure points, applying the heat where it would produce the maximum beneficial result.

The weapons cache at Stone Canyon Reservoir was a natural choice for a place to begin. It stood to reason that the ARM wouldn't risk holding Dancer at a secret armory, and Bolan's personal reconnaissance confirmed that supposition. Of the three stormtroopers on the site, one clung to life when Bolan finished mopping up, coherent enough to carry the message home.

It was a start, but he was nowhere close to finished. His next stop was a print shop in Gardena, near Alondra Park, where racist pamphlets and newsletters were churned out for a variety of neo-Nazi and skinhead groups, including the ARM.

What better venue for sending a message to his enemies?

If necessary, he would run through every target on his list and then start over with a brand-new roster, whatever it took to set Dancer free and bring his chosen targets to their knees.

Scorched earth.

The only language predatory savages could understand.

JUSTIN PRATT WAS beginning to realize what people meant when they said a person was "beside himself." The anger and frustration that he felt were so intense, so overpowering, they seemed too much for a single brain or body to bear. Pratt felt as if he might explode at any moment, physically disintegrate like one of those blood-filled dummies you saw in the horror movies, spraying his essence all over the room.

The office hemmed him in, had turned into a cage, but Pratt was privately afraid to step outside. It wasn't the kind of fear he could discuss with comrades in the movement, when he had devoted the past few years to stiffening their collective backbone, preaching courage and honor at any cost, urging sacrifice for the cause.

Except that rhetoric was one thing, personal experience a completely different trip. For all his big talk, the arrests that he had logged for street fights with the dregs of humanity, Justin Pratt had never ducked a bullet in his life. He was responsible for several murders, more or less, because he had dispatched the shooters or he knew beyond the shadow of a doubt who pulled the trigger on a certain unsolved job, but he had never done the dirty work himself.

Or had it done to him.

That last part was the worst, undoubtedly. Pratt knew, or had convinced himself, that he could kill if it was called for. When the Day of the Rope rolled around, payback time for the Jew-loving race traitors across America, Pratt had every intention of leading the execution squads.

But that was later, somewhere down the road. It was the kind of thing you talked about and hoped for, like the spineless Judeo-Christians waited for Jesus to come back for seconds, but somehow it was always in the future. Waiting for you. Making no immediate demands.

What was that song that frizzy little redhead used to sing on Broadway? Always a day away, and that was the best thing about tomorrow, in Justin Pratt's books. He could harangue the troops and fire them up for battle, send them out to trash some fags or vandalize a synagogue, but his own binding promise to lead by example was always deferred. If anyone complained that he was slacking, Pratt could point to the importance of protecting your leadership, turn it around and fire back at the doubters with accusations of letting the movement down, falling down in the crunch and doing too little to make Pratt's golden day a viable reality.

Meanwhile, he pocketed their dues and bought the hardware, sharpening his tongue on hell-fire speeches to the faithful and the curious, making a name for himself in the press.

It shouldn't be supposed that Justin Pratt was in it for the money. Not exactly, anyway. His hatred for the Jews and muds was genuine, deep-seated, but he also understood that victors claimed the spoils in any conflict. When you were on top, you had your choice of houses, cars and women, treasure looted from the great museums and private homes.

Pratt knew his history. Hitler had already shown him how to rule an empire, but he had to win it, first.

And that, he realized, was getting harder by the moment.

It was Blackmun's fault, for trusting the bitch to begin with, talking out of turn about the movement's business when he had her in the sack. Demotion in rank would be the least of Chet's problems when they got the whole fiasco sorted out, but at the moment Pratt had more important problems on his plate.

The raids against his troops and installations, for example. It was bad enough the day before Chet caught his woman scanning the computer hit list of their enemies, and total chaos had descended on the L.A. basin since they put the bitch on ice. Pratt hadn't even grilled her yet, one of his primary concerns since Chet phoned the problem in, and now they had some kind of fucking psycho on a rampage, hitting everything in sight and leaving little messages behind, demanding the woman's immediate release.

Who was he? Even in the depths of Pratt's cultivated paranoia, he understood that the Feds normally refrained from waging open war against dissidents on American soil. It was unheard of for the cops and FBI to launch commando raids, torch public buildings, take no prisoners. The Bureau never pulled that kind of shit, not even in the 1960s when they went after the Klan with everything they had, disrupting marriages and framing righteous patriots as traitors to their race.

If it wasn't the cops, wasn't the FBI, then that left . . . someone else.

Pratt grabbed a decorative shell casing from his desk— one of the genuine Wehrmacht 88s, fired against the Allied troops at Normandy on D day—and hurled it across the room, knocking a photo reprint of the 1933 Nuremburg rally from the wall. The aimless destruction helped a little, but not enough.

Not nearly enough.

Bad enough that his own men were dropping like flies, his safehouses going up in smoke. Bad enough that someone on the outside seemed to know his business, recognizing when his people snatched the woman even before Pratt got to see her. Now, it was Woody Gainer on the line, near hysterics, babbling from his hospital bed about severing relations with the movement, frantic to protect his reputation.

Fine.

Fair-weather comrades would be remembered on the Day of the Rope, and Gainer's reward would be waiting for him on the gallows.

First, though, he had to get this fucking madman off his back, cut his losses and find out who the woman was working for. Slam the door on that leak before it bled their movement dry. But where to start?

The answer was so obvious, a blind man could have seen it.

Everything came back to the woman, and so would Justin Pratt.

Right now.

THE MONEY MAN IN DOWNEY was a minister named Noah Junken, pastor of the self-styled Church of Israel. Not that Jews were welcome in the congregation, mind you; Junken's flock was composed entirely of good, Aryan "Israelites" who traced their roots to the Garden of Eden via Western Europe and Scandinavia, judging fellow whites on their innate ability to show "color in the face" with a blush.

The Church of Israel met each Wednesday night and Sunday morning, Pastor Junken circulating plastic buckets through the congregation while he begged for cash to help him spread the word and salvage white America. Bolan had no way of knowing if the faithful realized a portion of their offerings each week were used to arm the Aryan Resistance Movement, but he suspected that few of them would raise any objection.

As a registered church, Junken's movement was technically exempt from filing tax returns, but law-enforcement sources placed the pastor's take at something over three million per year. Of that, an estimated 300,000 dollars made its way to the ARM in the form of cashier's checks and postal money orders signed with phony names.

The Church of Israel was beyond the reach of IRS investigators, at the moment, but its filing status wouldn't hold the Executioner at bay.

Bolan passed on the church itself, preferring not to give the racist movement a symbol of martyrdom, rolling on toward the Florence Avenue duplex where, he was informed by Special Agent Kitteridge, the pastor spent time with his mistress three days a week. If anyone asked, Junken would explain the visits in terms of "spiritual counseling."

This afternoon, the Executioner had a different agenda in mind.

He found the address, pulled into the driveway behind a year-old Volvo station wagon and switched the Ford's engine off. No sentries here, nothing to prevent him from circling around behind the duplex, slipping the back door's lock with a stiletto blade, easing his way across the threshold. Inside the kitchen, he put his knife away and drew the silenced Beretta from its armpit holster, following the muffled sound of voices to the bedroom.

The pastor was out of uniform when Bolan found him, stretched out on his back while a blonde half his age straddled his meaty hips, working up a sweat. Junken's eyes were closed, but Bolan had a hunch that he wasn't communing with the god of white supremacy.

He picked a target at random, chose the bedside telephone for practical reasons, and triggered a parabellum round that smashed the instrument's receiver, flinging it against the wall. The blonde stopped pumping and gave a little squeal that didn't sound like passion, swiveling to face Bolan with a shocked expression on her face. Without a word, she vaulted clear of the pastor's prostrate body, dropping out of sight behind the bed and staying there, her presence betrayed only by muffled sobbing.

Junken's eyes were open now, and he gaped at Bolan in the doorway, hiding his wilted phallus with one hand.

"Whuh...whuh...who are you?"

"Who I am isn't important," Bolan told him.

"Wh-what do you want?"

"Your worthless life, but I'll settle for your service as an errand boy."

"I...don't understand."

"You're in bed with the Aryan Resistance Movement," Bolan said. "You help them pay the rent, is that right?"

"There must be some mistake," Junken said, trying to bluff it out in spite of his obvious fear.

Bolan fired a shot into the mattress between Junken's

flabby legs, close enough to scorch the meat of his thighs. The pastor squeaked like a mouse in a trap.

"All right! It's true! Please, God, don't kill me!"

"I'm not God," the Executioner informed him. "I'm your judgment."

"You said take a message?" he asked desperately, looking for a way to wriggle off the hook.

"Tell Pratt I want the woman back, unharmed. Any damage done to her comes out of his lily-white hide."

"The woman, sure." He hesitated, frowning. "What woman?"

Bolan placed the still-warm snout of the Beretta flush against the pastor's forehead. "Do you really want to know?"

"No, sir!"

"I didn't think so." The warrior took the gun away, but left it where the naked man could see it angling toward his belly. "Just make sure you don't forget the message."

"No. I won't forget."

"You've got another phone around this place?"

"The kitchen, to your right."

"You know Pratt's number?"

"Yes."

"So move your ass and make the call."

He watched the pastor scramble naked from the bedroom, lurching down a narrow hallway toward the kitchen. By the time he heard the fat man's fingers tapping at the touch-tone wall phone, the Executioner was on his way through the living room, heading toward the front door.

Another ripple in the pond.

And Justin Pratt was in above his head already, even if he didn't know it yet.

13

For what it was worth, Janice Flynn knew exactly where she was. The Spanish-style house stood on Sherman Way, between Reseda and the Van Nuys airport, in the San Fernando Valley. Its occupants were members of the ARM she knew only as Jeff and Ted. It was their first time in the role of jailers, but they didn't seem to mind.

Chet Blackmun hadn't thought to use a blindfold once he knocked her down and tied her wrists behind her back with copper wire. He could have killed her then and there, but Blackmun clearly recognized the risks involved in lugging a corpse out of the apartment, so he draped a jacket across her shoulders, walking close behind her to hide the bound wrists and prod her along toward the car with his Colt .45 automatic. He made no effort to hide where they were going.

The more she thought about it, Flynn understood why Chet had taken no precautions with her transport. It wasn't the fact that he was in a rush, though that was true as well, once he had spoken on the telephone to Justin Pratt.

Chet didn't care if Janice knew where she was going, since he knew she was as good as dead. She had already seen too much, betrayed the movement by the very fact of breaking into Blackmun's flat and booting up the sensitive computer programs. There was only one penalty reserved for traitors to the ARM—death.

Unless . . .

Unless what?

She thought of Mike Belasko, sitting at the Taco Dog in Burbank while the deadline for their rendezvous slipped by. How long since Blackmun had surprised her? Could it be three hours?

She was losing track of time. She was unable to see her wristwatch, and there was no clock in the empty storeroom her captors had converted into a makeshift cell. No windows, either, which prevented her from trying to escape.

Her hands weren't quite numb, but they were getting there. She made a point of wiggling her fingers, trying to keep up the circulation. She had strained against the wire until she felt it cutting her, blood warm against her skin, but nothing seemed to help. Chet might be lousy in the sack, but he could bind a woman like nobody's business.

Belasko would be worried—well, concerned, at any rate—but how would he react? What could he do to help her now, in concrete terms? Would the Reseda safehouse be on any list of targets he possessed? And if it was, what were the odds that he would choose this place to look for her?

More to the point, how would her captors respond if Belasko did turn up gunning for trouble?

Flynn thought she knew the answer to that one off the top of her head. Jeff and Ted were tough talkers, trigger-happy at the best of times, and either one of them would be happy to waste her if Chet Blackmun didn't get there first. Hard luck, kiddo.

The knowledge of impending death was less terrifying, somehow, than Flynn had expected it to be. If anything, it seemed to strengthen her resolve, make her even more determined to resist when they got around to the interrogation.

And it was coming, she knew that much beyond a shadow of a doubt.

She had been caught red-handed, as it were, and they were bound to have questions. Why was she interested in the ARM's computer files? Who was she reporting back to? How much sensitive information had she passed on to her sponsors, over what length of time?

The good news was that she could take Chet Blackmun down with her. Stress the pillow talk, his bragging rap before and after sex. If it came out, in spite of her resolve, that he was working for the FBI, it would be Blackmun's fault for dragging a Fed into the fringes of the movement, letting her glimpse so many of the ARM's need-to-know secrets.

Above all else, she had to stall for time. Ed Kitteridge would have received her message by now; he knew she would be tossing Blackmun's pad, and when she dropped out of contact, the Bureau would react.

But slowly, cautiously. Perhaps tomorrow, or the next day. Maybe not until sometime next week.

Which meant that Flynn would be on her own.

Terrific.

She was suddenly distracted by a sound of footsteps in the corridor outside her Spartan room. She moved back to the single chair that was her only furniture and sat down, hands wedged in behind her, facing the door. It opened a moment later, and Justin Pratt entered the room. Blackmun and the live-in skinheads loitered behind him, filling up the doorway.

"So," he said, "I guess we need to have a little talk."

THE ARYAN RESISTANCE Movement's operational headquarters was a small house in suburban Bellflower, three blocks west of the San Gabriel River Freeway. There were no signs or posters, no swastika banners to announce the presence of a paramilitary racist group, but Bolan had doublechecked the address through Stony Man Farm and Special Agent Kitteridge at the FBI's Los Angeles field office.

There was no room left for doubt.

It was late afternoon when Bolan made his drive-by, circling around behind the row of houses to park his Ford in an alley barely wide enough to accommodate the weekly garbage truck. With any luck at all, he wouldn't be inside the target building long enough for his unorthodox parking to become a problem.

Bolan didn't bother changing into camouflage fatigues fo
the suburban strike. He wore blue denim, sturdy boots and
the same combat harness worn on his previous raids, sup
porting the Desert Eagle on his hip, with surplus magazine
for both side arms and the silenced Uzi submachine gun h
selected from the trunk.

All set.

There was a small gate in the fence behind his target, bu
a padlock held it fast. Bolan scaled the six-foot wooder
barrier without difficulty. No watchmen in the yard, but h
made haste, expecting an alarm of gunshots from the hous
at any instant.

Nothing.

The warrior wasted no more time on caution and sprinte
to the back door, where he launched a flying kick against th
latch and followed through into a small, untidy kitchen
Two men stared at him in amazement, one seated at th
kitchen table with a sandwich and a beer in front of him, th
other standing in front of the open door of a well-stocke
refrigerator.

Their guns were in view, but slightly out of reach, as Bo
lan made up his mind. He couldn't afford to leave these me:
behind him, and if they turned out to be the only Nazis i:
the house, he would accept the loss.

He took out the seated hardman first, because his weapo:
was closer to hand, and so a greater threat. A 3-round burs
left crimson tracks across the guy's chest and punched hir
over backward, flipping the lightweight breakfast table a
his feet came up underneath.

Target number two made a dive for the other visibl
weapon, hopelessly out of reach near the sink, and Bola
stitched him with a short burst from the side, slamming hir
broadside into the range with force enough to rattle the ad
jacent wall.

"What the hell are you guys doing in there?"

Bolan went to meet the questioner, coming face-to-fac
with a tall, freckled man in his twenties, blocking the hall
way that led to bedrooms on the left, a living room to th

warrior's right. The guy seemed unarmed, and Bolan took a chance, aiming low with the Uzi, cutting the man's legs from under him and dumping him facedown on the floor. A squeal of pain, in addition to the Uzi's muffled ripping sound, would alert any Nazis remaining in the house.

The Executioner headed toward the living room, moving with greater urgency now, homing on the sound of frightened voices. Going in he had them spotted, one tangled up on the couch, two others well out of their armchairs and diving for their weapons.

No time for choices. He took the gunner on his right with a rising burst that punched his target around in an arm-flapping spin, crimson spouting from a half-dozen wounds as he toppled and fell.

The couch potato never made it, still fighting gravity when a 3-round burst punched into his head at eyebrow-level and finished it.

Number three made it to his shotgun, jacking a round into the chamber as he turned, but Bolan got there first, drilling him with a burst that pushed him back into the corner, pinning him against the wall. A lifeless finger clenched around the shotgun's trigger, but the blast was high and wide, the dump of buckshot unleashing a fine plaster rain from the ceiling.

Bolan retraced his steps to the corridor, found the freckled Nazi lying on his side and moaning softly, one hand clutching at the muscle of his ravaged thigh. The warrior knelt beside him, let him see the Uzi up close and personal, demanding the wounded punk's attention.

"Justin Pratt. Where is he?"

"Left," the young man answered, gasping.

"One more time." The Uzi's muzzle came to rest beneath his chin and forced the Nazi's head back at a painful angle. "Where?"

"He didn't tell us. Ow, that— Wait! He left a number, just in case we had to call him."

"Give."

"I wrote it down. It's on a notepad in the kitchen, by the phone."

"You want to live?"

"I swear to God."

He found the notepad in the kitchen, taking it with him as he exited the house. The phone number could give him an address, but what guarantee did he have that Pratt would have gone to see Janice?

None at all.

As he went over the fence in back, he had a better idea.

And he could hardly wait to reach a public telephone.

JUSTIN PRATT WAS WORKING up a sweat, drawing strength from his anger, feeling an undeniable excitement at the same time. The combination kept him stoked, almost euphoric, and never mind the dull ache in his knuckles.

Janice Flynn sat in front of him, bound hand and foot to a straight-backed wooden chair. It had taken the four of them to strip her down, even with her wrists pinned behind her back, but Pratt agreed that it was worth the effort. Even with her blood-caked lips and nostrils, her left eye swollen almost shut, she was still something to look at.

Chet Blackmun had taste, when it came to women.

Too damn bad the stupid bastard couldn't spot a federal plant.

Chet's problems were behind him now. As soon as they had finished stripping the bitch and binding her fast to the chair, Pratt had drawn his pistol, slammed a point-blank round through Blackmun's skull and left his twitching body stretched out on the floor where she could see it. Let her know that he was deadly serious before they started with the questions, so there would be no doubt whatsoever in her scheming mind.

And she was tough regardless, Pratt had to give her that. He wasn't pulling punches when he hit her, rocking her head from side to side, landing the occasional body blow for diversity.

He felt Jeff and Ted watching him, still in awe of the way he had canceled Chet's ticket, and that was fine. Let his troops spread the word on their own, enhancing his reputation as a leader who took shit from no one, including his second in command.

He took a breather, stepping back and flexing his hands, holding them down at his sides.

"We can do this all night," he informed her. "You'd be surprised what we can do... or, maybe not. Why don't you save yourself some grief and tell me who you're working for?"

Pratt thought he knew the answer, but he needed confirmation, just to find out how much trouble he was in.

"Why don't you fuck yourself?" she asked him, managing a smile with lips puffed up to twice their normal size.

He laughed at her, knowing it would hurt more than another punch in the face. "Don't give me any notions, sweet thing. I've got boys here who would love a piece of you. That right, guys?"

Jeff and Ted were making barnyard noises, digging each other in the ribs like horny morons. Jesus, what a crew he had to work with when the chips were down.

"You're dead, regardless," he said, watching her face for a reaction, seeing none. "You know that, don't you? Question is, why should it be the hard way? Tell me what I want to know, and I'll make it nice and easy. There's no reason you should go through all this shit, unless you've got a thing for pain."

The telephone distracted Pratt, a shrilling ring from the kitchen. "Get that, will you?"

Ted was only gone a moment, coming back with a peculiar expression on his face. "Some guy for you," he said to Pratt. "Says you should take the call right now, if you want to live."

"What?"

"He said—"

Pratt shouldered him aside and stalked into the kitchen, lifting the receiver to his ear. "Who is this?"

"Pratt?"

"I asked—"

"I want the woman, Pratt. She's cost you plenty, as it is. She'll keep on costing you, until there's nothing left."

"I don't know what you mean," he answered, mindful of the possibility their line was tapped.

"Okay, play dumb. Is that the way you want to die?"

A moment's hesitation, then Pratt said, "I'm listening."

"All right," the deep voice told him, "this is what you do..."

14

The National Vanguard's Hamburg headquarters was located on Monckburgstrasse, a quarter-mile west of the main railroad station. The building occupied a corner lot, with windows facing north and east. If Gary Manning's information was correct, his target was a fourth-floor office suite, one floor below the penthouse level.

"Ready?"

Settled in the shotgun seat beside him, Calvin James was checking out the block. "As ready as I'll be," he said.

The team had split up for efficiency's sake, fanning out to strike different targets in a more-or-less synchronized fashion. Katz had been troubled, at first, by the thought of spreading his forces too thin, but the potential advantages had seemed to outweigh the risks.

For starters, fanning out cut down on travel time they would have wasted roaming from one town to another en masse. At the same time, if they pulled it off, they had an excellent chance to dazzle the opposition with footwork, presenting the facade of an omnipresent, inescapable nemesis.

They left the car together, locking it behind them for security. A light drizzle kept their raincoats from standing out among the various other pedestrians sporting ponchos or umbrellas, some with magazines or newspapers poised above their heads. A few passersby looked twice at Calvin James, surprised by his ebony skin, but the sight of American servicemen and international tourists was common enough in Hamburg that he didn't create a major stir.

They would remember James, though, and that was fine. It fit the program, letting leaders of the Vanguard know that they were marked, their status as defenders of the master race was being challenged where they lived.

Beginning now.

They waited for the traffic light to change and crossed the street with a dozen other shoppers, businesspeople, tourists. Manning was a step or two in front when they hit the sidewalk, closing on their target. Through the glass swinging double doors, across the lobby, they paused at the wall directory to verify their target's floor and suite number. They waited for the elevator silently, stepping in together when the car arrived.

Inside the elevator, both men took the opportunity to check the weapons worn beneath their raincoats. Manning had an MP-5 SD-3 silenced submachine gun on a shoulder sling, spare magazines in inside pockets, while James carried the shorter MP-5 K model.

Disembarking on four, they shouldered past a middle-aged man emerging from an insurance office across the hall. Two doors down, on the left, they reached their destination. The nameplate on the door translated to read the Germanic Cultural Preservation Society.

Right.

Manning was first through the door, a fair-haired receptionist glancing up at him with a smile, losing it as she saw Calvin James coming in on his heels. He let her see the submachine gun poking out from underneath his raincoat, waving her in the direction of the door.

"Get out. *Raus, bitte.*"

She started for the exit, doubled back to save her bag, and hit the outer hallway running. Perfect. They were on the clock now, knowing that her first priority, once she felt safe, would be a phone call to police.

How long? Five minutes maximum, allowing for the traffic on the street below. No time to waste.

They brushed past the receptionist's desk, bulled through a door marked Privat, breaching the Vanguard's inner sanctum. Two lanky skinhead types were slouched beside a hot plate, sipping coffee, when they saw Grim Death breeze through the doorway. One of them stood fast, too stunned to move, while his companion turned and bolted toward a row of cubicles, male voices emanating from behind partitions.

Manning hit the human statue with a short burst to the chest that slammed him backward, taking man and coffee maker down together in a clanking heap. The runner glanced back, breaking stride, colliding with the first partition on his left. That was all it took for James to drop him with a 3-round burst from his MP-5 K.

All hell broke loose inside the office, half a dozen members of the Vanguard scrambling for whatever sanctuary they could find. Fiberboard partitions were no match for copper-jacketed parabellum rounds, bullets ripping through the flimsy walls in search of human flesh.

On Manning's left, the nearest Nazi died before he had a chance to drop the telephone receiver he was holding, sliding from his chair as if his bones had turned to rubber, leaving crimson traces of himself behind. From the next cubicle down, a burly skinhead with his sleeves rolled up around his biceps burst into the narrow aisle, a Walther clutched in his fist.

Manning met the shooter with a rising burst that punched him off his feet with force enough to put his shoulders on the vinyl floor before his heels touched down. A dying tremor racked the skinhead's frame, and then the life ran out of him.

In fact, the raid took nowhere near five minutes. It was more like two and counting when the final target made his break for nowhere, both arms raised above his head.

The Phoenix Force warriors fired in unison, converging streams of automatic fire that swept the runner off his feet and propelled him headlong through the nearest window-pane. There was a crash of plate glass and a startled cry before he disappeared from view.

The elevator took them down, and they passed through the lobby without opposition. A small crowd of spectators had gathered on the street around a vehicle parked at the curb, the high-diver's legs and lower torso protruding from the shattered windshield.

Time to go.

The sirens had begun to wail, but they were blocks away as Manning turned east on Monckburgstrasse, bound for the autobahn leaving town. For the first time since they entered Hamburg, he could let himself relax.

But only for a while.

The campaign had begun, but it was far from over. And they had miles to go before they slept.

THE SECOND TWO-MAN TEAM, composed of David McCarter and Rafael Encizo, had drawn Munich as their target site. McCarter spoke enough German to let them pass in a pinch, but they stuck to maps for the most part, interacting with the natives only when they stopped for gasoline and sandwiches in Furth, on the drive south from Berlin.

The National Vanguard had no public headquarters in Munich, per se, but its local members interacted openly with functionaries of the German National Party, based on Widenmayerstrasse, overlooking the Isar River, near the Maximilian Bridge. While the party officially tried to divorce itself from racist violence, members of both groups had been charged with crimes including assault, desecration of Jewish cemeteries and arson.

It was time for things to change.

McCarter passed the target twice to get his bearings, once in each direction, checking the escape routes. The nearest open parking slot was three blocks distant, and the Briton made his choice.

"I need you in the car," he said, "to cover me."

"Say what?" Encizo's frown spoke volumes of concern.

"It's too far back to leave the car," McCarter said. "We can't be double-parking in the middle of the street, can we?"

"So I'll go."

"No good, old son. You don't quite fit the profile, if you get my drift."

Encizo snorted. "I'm not white enough, you mean."

"We're talking Nazis, Rafe. It's not polite society, and if you can't get through the door, there goes the job, all right?"

"I don't like this at all."

"Let's make it quick, then, shall we?"

He pulled around the corner, double-parking long enough to scramble out of the car, while Encizo slid over to take the wheel. The Cuban cranked his window down and stuck his head out, following McCarter with his eyes.

"Six minutes," he declared. "You're not outside, I'm coming in."

"Your choice," McCarter told him, crossing in front of the car and stepping onto the curb.

If he wasn't back on the street within six minutes, McCarter knew, the chances were he never would be. Not alive, at any rate, and there was nothing Rafael could do about it except to compound the problem, maybe get himself killed in a grand gesture of defiance.

Surprise was the key, hitting hard and fast where the enemy least expected it, putting everything you had behind the punch and making it count. McCarter would either make the tag, or he wouldn't.

And if he failed...

Forget that line of thought, he cautioned himself, pausing for a moment outside the smoked-glass doors. It was now or never.

From what he could see of the place, going in, it was much like any other political-party headquarters in Europe or America. Posters on the walls were bright with slogans, some of which McCarter couldn't read, and smiling faces that effectively concealed the hate behind their eyes. No swastikas were on display, nothing to suggest a hidden agenda aimed at the Jews, immigrants or other minorities, no excuse for the political police to drop in and shut the operation down.

Half a dozen party functionaries, all young males, were taking up space in the main room as McCarter entered from the street, all breaking off their conversations to face him with a mixture of curiosity and apprehension. More of the latter coming on as he flicked open his jacket, showing them his subgun with its built-on silencer.

McCarter didn't know these men from Adam, but he knew their type and what they stood for. He didn't bluff or threaten, didn't speak at all before he squeezed the automatic weapon's trigger, raking the room from left to right.

His first two targets died before they grasped the danger or reacted to the sudden threat, a stream of parabellum manglers blowing them away. The rest broke ranks and ran in all directions, panicked, leaping over chairs and tables in their path or thrusting them aside.

The Briton closed his heart to pity, kept on firing, replacing the spent magazine with a fresh one before he had finished the job. Shiny brass cartridges littered the floor at his feet, rattling away from his boots as he paced off the killing ground, confirming what he already knew.

He was backing away, fishing inside his pocket for a minigrenade, when the door to a back room flew open and two men popped out with semiauto pistols at the ready. McCarter triggered a one-handed burst from the hip, holding the SMG steady enough to drop the front man in his tracks. The other ducked back out of sight, pegging a poorly aimed shot in McCarter's direction, moving too fast to slam the door behind him.

The Phoenix Force warrior palmed the frag grenade, released its safety pin and lobbed the bomb across the threshold with an underhand pitch. He was retreating toward the exit when it blew, the shock wave cracking windows, smoke and plaster dust belching out of the storeroom in back.

The Nazi back there might still be alive, and that was fine. It wouldn't hurt to have a witness, someone who could spread the tale by word of mouth, demoralizing everyone he touched. In fact, McCarter wished that he had taken time to guarantee a lone survivor for that very reason.

Maybe next time.

Still under four minutes as he hit the sidewalk, moving to curbside in time for the pickup. Encizo swung in to meet him while groups of gawkers began to form on the street.

By now, someone would certainly be calling the police. No matter. They were on their way and rolling, free and clear.

"So, how'd it go?" Encizo asked.

McCarter shrugged and felt the submachine gun hard against his ribs.

"It went."

RUDOLF WETZEL HAD GROWN impatient, waiting for news of the next violent outbreak. Telephone lines were burning between GSG-9 headquarters in Berlin and counterterrorist outposts in Munich and Hamburg, trying to sort out the details. Officially the word was that a group of radical leftists—possibly a splinter group of the Red Army Faction— had declared open war on the right wing's most visible organizations.

Wetzel and his immediate superiors knew better, of course, and that was the rub.

He had joined the Grenzschutzgruppe initially to prevent acts of terrorism, not to stand idly on the sidelines and watch the violence proliferate. More to the point, it galled Wetzel to see foreign agents achieve what he and his own group couldn't.

Wetzel had no soft spot in his heart for Nazis, whether aging relics of the original party or their spiritual offspring of the National Vanguard and similar groups. The "new" breed of racists were responsible for dozens, perhaps hundreds, of crimes for which they would never be prosecuted due to lack of solid evidence. Lives had been lost, and property destroyed, with only a handful of convictions on minor political charges.

But that was changing. Overnight, since the arrival of the foreigners, Wetzel had seen the neo-fascists treated to a taste of their own bitter medicine. In Wetzel's mind, that punishment was long overdue.

And, as the Americans would say, he wanted a piece of the action.

Where to start? From the late-breaking reports on his desk, Wetzel knew the commandos had to have divided their force, enabling them to make coordinated strikes at targets situated miles apart. That much was obvious, but would they have abandoned Berlin altogether?

Wetzel didn't think so.

And if one or two of them were still inside the city, he could try to reach them at the Sylter Hof. Failing that, he still had a few other tricks up his sleeve.

He had already followed his orders to the letter, forming a liaison with the strangers and feeding them critical information. Anything more would be excessive, a violation of his mandate, potential career suicide.

He smiled at that notion, realizing that job security would be the least of his problems once he had cast his lot with the foreigners. They were efficient in their way, clearly courageous, but the odds were still against them. Taking on the Vanguard was one thing, but roping in the German National Party multiplied their potential targets—and committed enemies—by several thousands. All of this, and they were only five.

Would one more make a difference? *Could* he make a difference?

Perhaps, Wetzel thought, it was simply enough that he try.

Unmarried, childless, verging on complacency in his profession since the Grenzschutzgruppe brass had shied away from cracking down on far-right terrorists with all the force at their disposal, Rudolf Wetzel understood that he had little to lose.

Except, perhaps, for his life.

And what was that worth, really, if he had to mark time with his hands tied, waiting for strangers to drop in and do his job for him?

Not that Wetzel felt like throwing his life away on a lost cause, far from it. If he hadn't thought that victory was possible...

Wetzel checked his card file, found the number for the Sylter Hof and reached out for the desktop telephone.

He was prepared to take the risk, if for no other reason than to test himself. And in the process, he would teach these foreigners that not all Germans shared the Vanguard's racist views.

While he was at it, Wetzel thought he just might teach the Vanguard thugs a lesson of his own.

ELEVEN MILES outside Berlin, due north, the autobahn was flanked by forest, dark trees pressing close on either side. It felt strange, driving through the territory of the former German Democratic Republic without a thought to border guards or Stasi agents, but Katz concentrated on the highway, watching for landmarks. Rudolf Wetzel rode beside him, Uri Dan in back with the weapons.

Wetzel's call had taken Yakov Katzenelenbogen by surprise, but he accepted the GSG-9 agent's offer of help without hesitation. Three guns were better than two for the target Katz had in mind, and the German's knowledge of his native territory was bound to be useful. As for the motive behind Wetzel's change of heart, that was his business, no concern of Katz's as long as Wetzel pulled his weight.

"Ahead there, on your left," the German said. For emphasis he pointed out a narrow side road, leading to the west.

"I see it."

No one followed as Katz turned off the highway, picking up speed once the thick trees had cut off his view of the autobahn. From this point on, the danger lay ahead.

Their target was, ostensibly, a country retreat for business executives and their chosen guests. In fact, the only "visitors" were members of the Vanguard and the German National Party, selected in periodic rotation for sessions of illegal paramilitary training, disguised as hunting vacations or in-service "sensitivity training" to avoid the strictures of German anti-Nazi legislation. Well-placed bribes kept the camp's personnel informed of any "surprise" visits by police.

Unfortunately for the neo-fascists, they would have no warning of this day's unscheduled drop-in by Katz and his companions.

There was something to be said for throwing out the rule book when you went to war.

Katz found a turnout two klicks short of their final destination, nosing the car deep into a copse and killing the engine. The three warriors changed into camo fatigues provided by Wetzel, part of his contribution to their unsanctioned joint effort. The German had also brought along a submachine gun for himself and several hundred rounds of parabellum ammunition to supplement Katzenelenbogen's existing supply.

"All set?"

"I'm ready," Dan replied.

"And I," Wetzel added, cocking his submachine gun as he spoke, switching on the safety with his thumb.

"Northwest from here?" Katz asked.

A smile from Wetzel as he said, "I'll lead the way."

Katz fell in step behind the German, Dan bringing up the rear. It took the best part of an hour, darkness coming on, with shadows lengthening among the trees, slowing their pace in the last half kilometer or so, as Wetzel started watching out for booby traps and sentries. By the time they came within shouting distance of the target, lights were blazing in the compound, driving back the night.

They found a place on the perimeter, beyond the chain-link fence with razor wire on top, inside the tree line where the searchlights couldn't reach. Katz scanned the camp, a hundred meters and more from end to end, with sentries pacing off the wire at intervals, six men in all. He spotted several other figures, moving here and there around the camp, with no purpose Katzenelenbogen could recognize.

"I make it thirty-five or forty soldiers, maximum," Dan said. "The barracks and latrines give them away."

"Not soldiers," Wetzel told him. "Thugs and terrorists."

"Long odds, regardless," Katzenelenbogen said.

"I've seen worse," the Mossad agent told him.

"And I've been waiting for this chance too long to let it slip away," Wetzel said, flashing Katz a crooked grin.

And so it was decided. In another moment, they had sketched their basic strategy, choosing attack positions, arbitrarily selecting a jump-off time.

Dan and Wetzel had ten minutes to circle the camp under cover, taking up their places on the north and east, close to the perimeter. Katz would make his own approach from the southwest, completing the lethal triangle.

They were three against thirty or forty, assuming that the camp was fully occupied. If not, they just might catch a break.

And with a bit of luck, the three of them might be enough.

They had a chance, and that was all he could expect or ask for. Death was an occupational hazard, but Katz wasn't about to let it dominate his thoughts. He had a job to do, at any cost, and his commitment to the task was personal, a debt to the sacred memory of his ancestors.

There were worse things, he decided, than the sacrifice of life in such a cause.

Still, if he had the choice, Katz would prefer to sacrifice his enemies. If this turned out to be his final day on earth, the gruff Israeli wouldn't go alone.

He checked his watch. Two minutes left, and it was time for him to move. He clutched the silenced MP-5 SD-3 submachine gun in his one good hand and struck off through the trees.

15

Josef Buhler lighted a fat cigar and leaned back in his lounger, blowing a plume of fragrant smoke toward the light fixture overhead. He propped his feet on the corner of his desk, his alligator shoes polished to the point that Buhler could have stretched a little to behold his own reflection in the leather.

To the casual observer, had any been present, Buhler presented a classic portrait of relaxation, an affluent businessman taking his ease at the end of the day. Perhaps he had concluded several major deals that afternoon, taking his competition to the cleaners and still never breaking a sweat. He would be thinking of the night ahead, by now, his wife or mistress—maybe both—anticipating his arrival with a fine bouquet of flowers, tickets to the symphony or theater.

They would have been mistaken.

Josef Buhler was the chairman of the German National Party, widely praised by its supporters as a conservative voice of Teutonic nationalism, reviled by its enemies as the forerunner of a Fourth Reich in reunified Germany.

For his own part, Buhler thought of himself as a patriot, struggling against near-hopeless odds with the best interest of his fatherland at heart. To Buhler, that meant standing on principle, telling his own brand of truth about the decadent "liberals" who were driving his nation to ruin. He made no apology for his pointed attacks on perverts and radical feminists, third world invaders who sapped German resources and polluted the racial stock, "ex"-Communists and other radicals who still saw socialism as the yellow brick road to a godless utopia.

Josef Buhler had a vision for the future of his country, as clear as crystal in his mind. He couldn't share its details with the general public yet, while certain laws dictated in the aftermath of World War II were still in force to silence him, but there would come a day when he could speak the truth, uncensored by his enemies.

When that day came, he would be ready, and the staunch majority of purebred Germans would respond. Buhler knew his people, trusted in their judgment to erase a half century of leftist propaganda and grasp the essence of his truth.

In the meantime, there were countless smaller battles to be fought and won.

Until recently, Buhler's struggle had been a war of votes and words, with the occasional back-alley skirmish to satisfy his younger, more impetuous disciples. In the past twenty-four hours, though, it had become a literal death struggle, with no holds barred.

The change troubled Buhler, not least of all because his own life was riding on the line. His public speeches frequently alluded to the possibility of martyrdom, but it had always been a mere rhetorical device for Buhler, a means of stirring his audience to cries of outrage . . . until now.

In the space of a day, his perspective had changed, the sudden violence hitting home. His comrades in the National Vanguard were clearly outmatched, unequal to the task of running their enemies to earth, and the police showed no inclination to involve themselves beyond perfunctory investigations after the fact.

And for the first time in his thirty-seven years, Josef Buhler had been forced to recognize his own mortality.

He had no clear idea of who was stalking him, or why, but he couldn't escape the notion that his latest tribulation was connected to his covert dealings in the Middle East. It was the Vanguard's business, really, but the plan had Buhler's personal endorsement from the start, and he would be hard-pressed to draw a line between his party and the Vanguard, if it came to that. Their memberships had mingled to the point that one was virtually indistinguishable from the other, save for their respective uniforms in public demonstrations. Members of the German National Party leaned toward business suits and formal evening wear, while younger Vanguard stalwarts liked their combat boots and khaki, showing off for the young women who swarmed around them like flies drawn to honey.

Buhler could remember being young, the hot blood in his veins. It was a different age, of course, with far less freedom of expression for the patriots who recognized their nation's leftward drift. These days, police were less inclined to press the issue of a simple speech or pamphlet, most especially in the districts where his party held a clear majority.

And they were growing every day, would keep on growing, gaining strength, unless...

The kind of violence he had witnessed recently could ruin everything, destroy the middle-class consensus he had labored to achieve these past four years. It was incredible, preposterous, to think that Buhler's whole lifework could fall apart within the space of hours, cast aside like so much litter on the shoulder of the autobahn.

Preposterous, but true.

He needed help—or reassurance, at the very least. A reassuring word would let him keep his goal in sight.

And that meant he would have to call the Arab. Buhler saw no way around it. He drew deeply on his cigar as he reached for the telephone and pressed the button for an outside line.

BARBARA PRICE SAT on the front porch of the main house of Stony Man Farm, facing north across open ground toward the airstrip, the forest and the invisible track of Skyline Drive beyond. She saw it all and registered next to nothing, her concentration worlds away.

The word from Southern California was sketchy at best, Striker moving too quickly for regular check-ins, Jack Grimaldi's sideline reports barely keeping up with the action

They knew that Katz had divided Phoenix Force to execute a round of whirlwind attacks on the enemy in Germany, his own private blitzkrieg, but they ran well behind on the details, tapping links at Interpol and GSG-9 for periodic updates.

Mostly Price felt left out of the action, worried that any real help she might render would come too late. Such feelings were an occupational hazard for rear-echelon troops, her own distress exacerbated by personal feelings for Bolan.

She wouldn't have changed him for the world, not really, but at times like this she almost changed her mind, caught herself wishing he could give it up, accept a safe advisory position at the Farm, perhaps in Washington.

And then what?

Nothing.

Price's own experience had taught her the futility of trying to derail a personal commitment on the scale of Bolan's. She had come up the hard way herself, in a male-dominated system, proving herself without resort to quota systems or "minority" set-aside programs, coming up through the ranks to stand as the mission controller at Stony Man Farm. It had taken balls, at least in the figurative sense, but she couldn't lay claim to anything approaching Bolan's years of sacrifice.

She heard the door open behind her, the familiar sound of Aaron Kurtzman's wheelchair gliding up beside her. "Got some news in from Berlin," he said.

She waited, shifting in her seat to face the man they knew as Bear.

"Looks like they've got a new man on the team," he said. "Their contact out of GSG-9 decided to jump into the game."

"What got him off the fence?" she asked.

"No telling. If I had to guess, I'd say he got fed up just watching from the sidelines."

"Right. I know the feeling."

"You know the drill. They also serve—"

"Who only stand and wait," she finished for him. "So I've heard."

"We're getting there," Kurtzman said.

"Yeah? I hope so."

"Place your bets, I'm telling you."

"It's not a game."

"I heard that rumor, Barb."

She looked at Kurtzman in his chair and cringed. "I'm sorry."

"I'll pretend I didn't hear that."

"Right. Okay."

"You know, the night they came to get us, even when the smoke cleared, there was no way I could picture any future for the project. We were finished, any way you tried to shake it out. Forget about the casualties. I mean, they burned us, blew our cover all to hell. You don't come back from that, no way at all."

"Except, you did."

"We didn't," Bear corrected her. "*He* did it. Striker. Just like that, he rolled the opposition up and it was done. Except it's never really 'just like that,' you know? He started out with nothing, worse than nothing, and he brought us all the way back, better than before."

"He isn't Superman," she answered, smiling gently.

"No, I've never seen him leap tall buildings in a single bound. With Jack to fly him, maybe."

"And he isn't bulletproof," she said.

No answer.

"I'd feel better if we had some kind of handle on the men behind this thing." She faced back toward the airstrip, which was nearly lost to sight in twilight shadows. "Even knowing the Iraqis are behind it somehow, what is that supposed to tell us?"

"We'll keep working on it," Kurtzman promised.

"Beautiful. Another week or two, we just might have a name."

"Don't sell our frontline people short. They're doing more than kicking ass out there."

"I know. The trouble is, I want it all."

Carmen Delahunt came through the door behind them, her fiery red hair in sharp contrast to the white smock she wore over a conservative suit. Recruited by Kurtzman from the FBI computer mill at Quantico, Delahunt still had an air of the Bureau about her, from her attitude to mode of dress.

"We've got a new squeal from the coast," she told them both. "I think you'd better check it out."

TARIM SUDAIR HAD DONE his best to put the German's mind at ease, but it was difficult, from such a distance. Buhler's people had been taking steady, numbing punishment since the day before, and they were still without a clue to the identity of their opponents. It was worrisome, to say the least, and yet...

The slim Jordanian took solace from his own position as a middleman. He was a mercenary, strictly speaking, even though he shared the resolution of his colleagues that the state of Israel should be crushed, and he had lined his pockets from their various transactions—not to mention the profit logged by his government.

It would have been ideal, except for the adversity that had been haunting them the past few days.

Sudair had been inclined to shrug the convoy ambush off, dismiss it as a fluke, until the violence had erupted in America and Germany. There was no doubt that someone had identified their foreign allies at the ambush site, deciding to pursue them on their own home ground.

Good news, bad news, as the Americans would say.

The good news: King Hussein's regime—and, more importantly, Tarim Sudair himself—appeared exempt from the attacks that had beset their Western partners in crime. Sudair and his immediate superiors were safe, at least so far.

The bad news: while their enemies remained anonymous and faceless, they couldn't protect themselves with maximum efficiency. The mayhem stalking Southern California and Berlin might find its way back to Amman tomorrow, or the day after.

Sudair had grown up with war and rumors of war, generally involving the Israelis, but this was the first time the violence had threatened him personally. Even in his youthful military service, after basic training, he had managed to land a noncombatant support assignment, protecting himself in the event of fresh hostilities.

This time, though, there seemed to be no sanctuary, no safe haven from their enemy. If he could range at will between Los Angeles and Germany, striking synchronized blows on two continents, it would be vastly premature for Tarim Sudair to call himself secure.

But what to do?

Running was out of the question. Sudair had his pride, to be sure, and there was no real danger yet...was there? Amman was untouched by the spate of attacks, even though the bloody cycle had begun days earlier on Jordanian soil.

Were there unseen enemies around him, even now? Observing him, perhaps, and laying out their strategy? Sudair dismissed the thought, or tried to, reminding himself that he had taken measures to protect himself in his dealings with Baghdad, no public meetings, only guarded conversations on the telephone. His visits to the camps had been circuitous, but if there was a leak among his so-called friends perhaps a traitor in the ranks...

Sudair considered the possibility, deciding that the leak—if there was a leak—had to lie somewhere close to home. Perhaps across the border in Iraq, where many dissidents still schemed against Saddam Hussein, or even in Jordan. It was no secret to anyone that the Zionists had recruited spies in every walk of life, seducing them with gold or other favors, picking their brains in defense of the parasitic Jewish state. There had been so much covert business with Iraq since Operation Desert Storm, it would have been miraculous if nothing was reported to the outside world.

Sudair didn't believe in miracles.

The only person he could absolutely trust, from this point on, would be himself. In dealing with the others, East or

West, Sudair decided he had to keep his guard up even more than usual, in case one of his "comrades" was a Judas.

How best to protect himself?

He had already taken out insurance in the form of numbered foreign bank accounts, skimming a marginal percentage from the Iraqi transactions for himself whenever possible, salting it away against the prospect of some unforeseen disaster. His government position gave him access to emergency transport at any hour of the day or night, on ten minutes' notice.

If the game began to fall apart, Sudair would simply cut and run. His dedication to the covert war on Israel and her Western allies took a back seat to his sense of self-preservation. He knew the slogans, could repeat them in his sleep, and while he certainly despised the Zionists as much as any other Arab, he wasn't a suicide commando, begging God for the opportunity to throw his life away.

Nearly half a century had passed since the state of Israel was carved out of Palestine and forced upon the natives of the region, coming up on fifty years of overt and guerrilla warfare, and the Arabs had nothing to show for it but ever-expanding refugee camps and graveyards. There might, indeed, be victory to celebrate one day, but Sudair wasn't about to hold his breath until that day arrived.

It would be nice to see the Zionists destroyed, but what would the victory mean to Sudair, in concrete terms? If Jordan managed to regain the West Bank and Jerusalem, he didn't plan to move there. It was doubtful he would even go to visit the recaptured territory—sand, rocky hills and hovels he could see within a short drive of his downtown office, if he felt the urge to be depressed.

Not likely.

Tarim Sudair despised the Jews, oh, yes, but he was in the struggle for himself, and no one else. If he had been American or better versed in Western slang, he might have said that he was looking out for number one.

Who else would do the job, if he didn't?

The latest news from Germany was bad enough that he felt moved to pass it on. They would resent the disappointing bulletin in Baghdad; it would make his contact angry... and the thought produced Sudair's first smile since everything had started going wrong.

The best way to relieve depression was to share it, and Sudair felt almost cheerful as he reached out for the telephone.

IT WAS FIFTEEN MINUTES past quitting time when Hal Brognola took the call. He seldom got away on schedule. Problems piled up around the office, each demanding personal attention from the man in charge. The crew at Stony Man was only part of it, his covert warriors in the field a relatively small percentage of the troops at his command. Still, as the afternoon wore on, Brognola found that he could think of little else.

The phone call from Virginia on his private line made it worse.

He picked up midway through the second ring.

"Hello?"

"You got a minute, Chief?"

He knew that Aaron Kurtzman wouldn't call to pass the time of day. "I'm switching on the scrambler," the big Fed replied.

"Same here."

The five-inch metal cube was tucked inside the upper right-hand desk drawer. When he switched it on, an amber light informed him that his office telephone was now secure. The green bulb, winking on an instant later, verified the scrambled link to Stony Man.

"What's up?" Brognola asked.

"We got another flash from Striker. I thought you'd want to know."

"Let's hear it."

"There's a problem," Kurtzman told him. "Striker's contact from the Bureau was a woman."

"Was?" Brognola felt the short hairs bristling on his nape.

"Poor choice of words, I hope. They smoked her out a while ago. We don't know how, and I'm not sure it matters. Striker's pulling out the stops to get her back."

"He would. What kind of backup is he getting from the Bureau in L.A.?"

"I take it he's in touch with her control, some kind of informational exchange on targets, this and that. The brass hats want her back, of course, but there's no way they're jumping in to play our kind of game."

"It's just as well," Brognola said. "They'd only get in Striker's way."

"I've got an open line to Able Team," Kurtzman stated, coming up to the crux of it. "If you want me to, I can extract them in the next half hour, stick them on a plane."

Brognola didn't hesitate. "Too late. Whatever Striker's planning, he'll be into it by now. We don't need Able picking up the pieces, one way or the other. Wait and see what happens."

"Sure. Okay."

"You think I'm wrong?"

The CEO at Stony Man was silent for a moment, pondering the question. "No," he said at last. "I just hate sitting on my hands."

"Stay close in touch, whatever breaks."

"Will do."

Brognola severed the connection, frowning as he switched the scrambler off and closed the drawer. It came as no surprise to anyone that Bolan would extend himself to help his contact when she stumbled into unexpected danger. Still, it was troubling to think of Bolan's federal ally in enemy hands, perhaps already spilling everything she knew.

And what was that, exactly?

Bolan would have told her nothing that could hurt the team. As for her control in the FBI's Los Angeles field office, he would know only what the Washington brass chose to share. Damned little, if he knew the gray men in their offices on Pennsylvania Avenue. The Bureau wouldn't want its agents tainted any more than necessary with Brognola's covert war.

And that was fine.

He thought of calling Leo Turrin and decided not to bother. The big Fed could worry for the two of them until he had more solid information to report. He had watched Bolan work in the past, when there were innocent lives at stake, unleashing everything he had to keep the pressure on his enemies till something broke.

Recalling Boston and Miami, from the old days, Brognola could almost sympathize with Bolan's current opposition.

Almost, but not quite.

The lady Fed's predicament might be coincidence, a fluke that would have happened even without Bolan's arrival on the L.A. battlefield. No matter. Striker was in the midst of it now, and Brognola knew he wouldn't rest until the books were balanced.

Or until he died in the attempt.

SHIRAZ NAJAF WAITED for his chauffeur-bodyguard to switch off the limousine's engine and circle back to open his master's door. Expressions of gratitude were misplaced with subordinates, and Najaf's watchdog would expect no thanks for the simple performance of his duty. Pushing past the man in uniform, he moved along the flagstone walkway to his house.

Inside, the house was cool and dark. He lived alone, with no wife or children to distract him from his duty. Servants catered to his every need at home. When he required a woman—rarely, these days—it was a simple matter to obtain one for an hour or a night.

This night, Shiraz Najaf had more pressing matters on his mind.

It had been four days since the Iraqi convoy had been ambushed in Jordan, nineteen men massacred by unknown enemies. That had been cause enough for concern, but the surprise eruptions of violence in America and Germany, targeting their reluctant allies, had given Najaf a sleepless night. And now, the call from Buhler in Berlin, badgering the Jordanians for some assurance that his own domestic problems would be solved.

As if Tarim Sudair could reach out from Amman and stop the killing in Berlin or Hamburg. It was foolish, but Najaf couldn't afford to let his allies feel that they had been abandoned. A continued market for Iraqi goods and laundered cash depended on Baghdad's ability to maintain a solid front, keeping faith with its allies. If he couldn't help the German fight his battles, there might be another way.

He was distracted for a moment by another matter of concern. The South American connection wasn't a problem yet, since the violence hadn't reached his drug connection, but Najaf was apprehensive. Anything could happen in a world where nameless, faceless enemies came out of nowhere, wreaking havoc on the best-laid plans of men with everything to lose.

And what could Shiraz Najaf do to save the day?

His manservant hovered close behind him, wise enough to hold his tongue, accepting the jacket and tie Najaf handed to him almost without thinking. The man was animated furniture, nothing more. Najaf trusted him as he would a cat or dog, secure in the knowledge of the fear he inspired with a harsh word or stony glance. He shared no secrets with the household staff, discussed no sensitive matters in their presence, but it was more a matter of rank and protocol than security. A servant who betrayed him would live to rue the day he was ever born.

But he wouldn't live long.

Najaf had spoken to his immediate superior about their problem, trying to minimize the damage suffered by their foreign allies without sugarcoating the matter. He had received instructions to proceed at his own discretion, within limits, of course. The Baghdad regime wasn't well-known for encouraging personal initiative.

Najaf had conceived the plan on his own, knowing in advance that any credit for the scheme's success would be claimed by Saddam Hussein and his circle of intimate advisers. It was only if the plan went wrong that Najaf would be acknowledged . . . on the day of his execution.

So be it.

Najaf had faith in himself, and if his life depended on the success of his plan, that simply meant he must not fail.

It was simple—at least until you ran into an enemy intent on wrecking all that you had worked for over months on end. A different story, if the raids had taken place in Jordan or Iraq. In that event, Najaf could use his network of informers, squeeze the petty criminals in Baghdad and environs to produce a name, description, something he could use. Since Desert Storm, he had no reach to speak of on the European continent, nothing at all in the United States.

Still, he wasn't entirely without friends or resources. The Jordanians could help, to some degree, and he could press the Iraqi consulate in Berlin, have them on stand-by in case Buhler needed a place to hide.

God help them, if it came to that.

Najaf wasn't yet ready to concede defeat, by any means. He knew the value of perseverance, having seen his homeland fight back from the destruction inflicted by American air power in 1991. His own contribution had played no small part in that recovery, opening pipelines for Iraqi exports despite the oppressive United Nations embargo, and he had been duly rewarded in turn.

It would be helpful if the would-be warriors in America and Germany could do their part, unleash the terror they had promised against the Zionist parasites. The Germans had made a good start of it, with their elimination of the Israeli consular official, but everything after that had been chaos.

Ironically it might be the South Americans who saved them, after all. Najaf had no personal interest in the drug traffic one way or another, except as it could help his own cause in the broader scheme of things.

And now, he thought, it just might make the crucial difference.

Sweet irony, with the Americans bogged down in their never-ending "war on drugs," blissfully unaware of a dagger aimed at the heart of their nation. No one, from the White House to the street agents of the DEA, would suspect Iraqi involvement in what lay ahead . . . or the ultimate goal of their hidden enemy.

It pleased Najaf to have a secret hidden up his sleeve. He wouldn't be intimidated by the CIA, the Seventh Fleet, or anything else that Washington could throw against him.

A tiny scorpion could kill the largest elephant with a strategic sting. There was a lesson to be found in nature, if one only took the time to learn.

Shiraz Najaf was learning every day, and he wasn't afraid. Not yet.

Bolan had selected the meeting ground himself, giving his
adversaries no option. He was looking for a combination of
cover and combat stretch, room to ramble without giving
anything away, and five minutes with the Triple-A street
map had made up his mind.

Marina del Rey.

His choice was pragmatic, as well as strategic, putting
Justin Pratt and the ARM off guard with a surprise shot
below the belt.

Marina del Rey was, according to Bolan's federal sources,
a primary port of entry for cocaine smuggled into California by the Aryan Resistance Movement.

Whiter living through chemistry, right.

Bolan could remember the "old days", when far-right
extremists made much of their personal opposition to vice
in general and drugs in particular. In recent years, paramilitary groups ranging from the Ku Klux Klan to the American Nazi Party had climbed on board the cocaine
bandwagon, and Pratt's ARM was no exception. In Bolan's mind, it reinforced the moral bankruptcy of his neo-
Nazi opposition... and it also granted him a point of lev-
erage for his crucial bid to free Janice Flynn.

Pratt's drug boat, purchased for the ARM under a phony
name, allegedly using the proceeds from an armored-car
robbery in Utah, was a thirty-foot cabin cruiser called the
Patriot. She made bimonthly runs from L.A. south to To-
copilla, Chile, a bare 150 miles from the Bolivian frontier
and well within the reach of heavily armed drug caravans.

Customs inspections had turned up nothing, so far, but DEA was on the case, committed to pulling the *Patriot*'s plug.

As far as Bolan was concerned, the DEA had missed its chance.

His word to Justin Pratt had been concise, no energy squandered on threats or meaningless argument. "Last chance," he had said. "If you want to save the *Patriot*, I'll meet you at the dock. One hour, on the nose. You bring the woman, safe and sound. Blow this one, and you don't get any second chance. Scorched earth, you read me? Ashes all the way."

No chance for Pratt to phone ahead and lay a trap at the marina. Bolan had recognized the area code when he dialed the man's number, opting to draw the Nazi leader out instead of trying to sniff him out, risking Dancer's life or missing her entirely on a hasty rescue bid. His call to Pratt had been completed from a phone booth two blocks north of the marina, near the intersection of Venice and Lincoln boulevards. He was a short drive from Marina Mercy Hospital, no problem for the meat wagons that would be dispatched to fetch the losers in an hour's time.

Bolan had no illusion about Pratt coming alone, much less unarmed, and he hadn't insisted on the point. If anything, more targets made his mission that much easier, allowed him to inflict the maximum potential damage on his enemies. Civilians were a problem, but the docks were sparsely populated on this weekday afternoon.

In gang-ridden L.A., Bolan thought, the sudden outbreak of a firefight might not even come as a surprise.

He found one guard aboard the *Patriot*, a burly skinhead, twenty-something, whose double-digit IQ was reflected in his eyes. He was tall and muscular, his weight lifter's physique displayed in a formfitting tank top and butt-hugging shorts.

Bolan was on deck before the sluggish watchman noticed him, as he came up from below. "Whadda you want?"

Conversation was a waste of precious time, so Bolan stepped forward rapidly and rapped him on the temple with the Beretta, checking the area for witnesses before he dragged the unconscious watchman behind a barrel on the pier, out of sight.

It took him less than sixty seconds to prepare the plastique charges with their radio-remote detonators keyed to the firing transmitter in his pocket. Bolan used enough C4 to lift the *Patriot* a foot clear of the water, trusting the combustible furnishings to help out by incinerating whatever remained after the initial blast.

There were no drugs on board, and Justin Pratt could rob another bank or armored car to get himself a brand-new boat, but the Executioner didn't intend the vessel's demise as a killing stroke against the ARM. If anything, he meant for it to serve as a diversion, something to distract his adversaries when the shit hit the fan.

The rest of it would be skill and luck, in roughly equal measure: skill required to pick his targets out and take them down on cue, without endangering the woman he had come to save; dumb luck in terms of how his enemies deployed themselves, how well and swiftly they responded under fire.

Thus far, he hadn't been impressed by the performance of the ARM in combat, but he shied away from anything resembling overconfidence. The warrior knew his capabilities and limitations, but he couldn't speak for gunners he had never seen before. Unless you fought the same man every time, there was an element of doubt in each and every battle, going in.

Still, there was nothing he could do but forge ahead and give it everything he had.

The warrior took up his position, double-checked his arsenal and settled back to wait.

"SOMEBODY WANTS to see you," Pratt told Flynn when he'd returned to the interrogation room. "Wouldn't leave his name, but that's all right. We made a deal."

"What kind of deal?" she asked him. Swollen lips and parched vocal cords gave her an old woman's voice, sounding like something from the grave.

Close enough.

"The way it plays, I trade you off for certain property your friend is holding. Give and take, you follow me? Too bad we don't have any time to finish off our little chat. That's life."

There was a glint of recognition in the woman's eyes, but Pratt didn't have time to grill her for his adversary's name. It made no difference now, regardless. In an hour—less—Pratt would have the bastard in the palm of his hand, alive or dead.

And God help the wild man if he fell into Pratt's clutches alive. There were no points given for raw nerve in this game, not with all the ARM had riding on the line. It was winner-take-all, and he meant to be the last man standing when the smoke cleared.

Mr. X could take their deal and shove it up his ass.

"We're going for a ride," he told the skinhead roomies. "Out to the marina. I want twenty of the best to meet us at Olympic and Sepulveda, east of the airport, in fifteen minutes. No questions, no arguments. Nobody heads for the dock on their own. You got that?"

"Got it," Jeff replied, already moving toward the kitchen telephone to make the necessary calls.

"One other thing," Pratt said to his remaining brown-shirt.

"What?"

"You've got plastique here?"

"Sure. How much you need?"

Pratt scrutinized the woman for another moment, making his decision. "Two, three pounds should do it. And a motion detonator. Can you rig that in a hurry?"

"Motion's easy," Ted informed him.

"No mercury. Some kind of an electric charge."

"Can do."

"So do it."

"On my way."

The plan had come to Pratt halfway between the kitchen and interrogation room. An inspiration, really, lifting the initial weight of shock and depression from his shoulders, letting him breathe in something approximating comfort.

Losing the *Patriot* was one thing. Pratt hoped he would be able to save the cabin cruiser, even thought he knew its usefulness was coming to an end. The Feds pegged it now, and he would have to scuttle the boat one day soon, get what he could from the insurance and find himself a new vehicle for importing the shit that kept his domestic operations afloat.

And one day, perhaps, if his alliance with the rags bore fruit, he might be able to phase out the drug trade entirely.

Except that it was so damned profitable, all around. And it allowed him to remain in touch with precious friends south of the border, men he admired almost to the point of reverence.

Enough for now to lay his trap and make it stick. If he lost the *Patriot* in the process, it would be a reasonable price to pay for taking out his unknown enemy.

Pratt's little surprise would make all the difference in the world.

"I guess we'll have to get you dressed," he told the woman, watching her and gloating at the first faint signs of hope. "Too bad, you know? We could have had ourselves a party, once you loosened up a little bit. I know Ted and Jeff are going to be disappointed. They always like leftovers."

"Fuck you," she told him, getting her nerve back now that relief was in sight.

"Maybe next time," Pratt answered. "We haven't got the time right now, you want to meet your friend. I don't suppose you'd like to tell me who he is?"

No answer this time, glaring at him like he was the lowest piece of scum on earth.

"Suit yourself. I'll get your clothes, and you can dress yourself. No tricks, or it will be dead meat your friend collects at the marina. Are you reading me?"

"I hear you."

"Fair enough."

Dead meat. Pratt liked the sound of that.

Before another hour was out, there would be meat enough to go around.

BOLAN SAW HIS ADVERSARIES coming, four sedans in single file, filling up his field of vision as he tracked them with the compact glasses. They took their time approaching the marina, rolling in two minutes ahead of the deadline, refusing to be rushed.

How many guns in four cars? At least a dozen, probably sixteen, perhaps twenty-three if he left room for Janice. An army, any way you broke it down.

Bolan expected a trap, but he wouldn't allow himself to consider the worst-case scenario, that Pratt and company would come without the woman, simply dump her corpse somewhere along the way and go for broke with everything they had.

He had positioned himself thirty yards from the *Patriot*, in direct line of sight to accommodate his remote detonator. The duffel bag at his feet was unzipped, granting Bolan easy access to the M-16 A-1/M-203 combo weapon and peripheral hardware inside. A utility shed provided him with cover at the moment, placing the warrior midway between the marina's parking lot and Pratt's cabin cruiser.

Where the battle would take him from that point was anybody's guess.

He watched and waited, saw the last two cars in line break off before they entered the parking lot proper. Doors swung open, disgorging three gunners from each car, while the drivers remained with their vehicles.

The Nazis had opted for casual street clothes this time out, nothing to draw attention from casual passersby. There was no hardware showing, but Bolan noted the prevalence of heavy flannel shirts and windbreakers, worn in defiance of the muggy weather. There was something to be said for concealable weapons, at least: no risk of long-range fire from high-powered rifles, unless the drivers were marksmen, hoping for a lucky shot from the parking lot.

If they were using side arms, sawed-off shotguns, even submachine guns, Bolan would be starting out with an advantage. The M-16's greater range gave him better reach, while the 40 mm M-203 grenade launcher added muscle to the package, something extra in the crunch.

It demanded more concentration now, tracking the foot soldiers on their approach and keeping watch on two remaining cars at the same time. The hardmen were fanning out as they approached the waterfront, taking their time, trying without much success to look as if they belonged at the marina.

The two unloaded vehicles fell in line once more behind the point car and its escort, completing the chain. The lot itself was almost empty, giving Pratt and company their choice of spaces near the water. Bolan stood and watched them lining up, three of the drivers backing into adjacent slots, ready for a swift departure at need. The lead car stood apart, separated from the rest by close to thirty yards.

He reached inside the duffel bag, never taking his eyes off the enemy, extracted a mixed bandolier of rifle magazines and 40 mm rounds and draped it across his chest. The weapon came next, already locked and loaded as he flicked the safety off.

Downrange, the former second car in line was disgorging its passengers. Four in all, still no hardware showing, and they hung near the car, waiting. The other two drivers were out of their vehicles now, but they kept their places, standing near open doors, clearly on edge.

There were stirrings at the separate point car now. Bolan checked his flanks again—no way for his opponents to come up behind him unless they went into the water—before he focused on the primary target. He recognized Justin Pratt from his photos. Two hulking skinheads rode with him.

And Janice Flynn.

One of the skinheads helped her out of the car, half dragging her, letting him see that her hands were secured somehow behind her back. Bolan raised his field glasses, focused on her face and felt a low snarl rising in his throat as he surveyed the damage. Someone had tried to clean her up, but there was nothing they could do about the bruises, cut lips, or the left eye swollen nearly shut.

He wasted no time wondering what else she might have suffered in enemy hands. Janice was alive, and she was here, almost within his reach. Fifteen gunners ranged against him, which was nothing that he couldn't handle with sufficient concentration and a bit of luck.

Bolan watched as they put Janice back in the car, front seat, Pratt leaning in behind her for a moment. Giving her last-minute instructions or warnings? No matter. The Executioner was ready, and it all came down to the mechanics now, split-second timing.

Pratt was out of the car and facing the marina, flanked by his two human pit bulls. The fair-haired racist spread his arms and raised his voice, calling out in the general direction of the *Patriot*.

"All yours," he shouted. "Keys are in the car."

He smelled the trap, nothing specific, no more or less than he had expected coming into the set. It struck him that the keys probably *were* in the car. And why not? Ideally they would seek to remove him from the neighborhood of the marina and their drug boat, let him run a little, box him in and kill him somewhere else.

Would there be other cars on stand-by, somewhere out of sight but close enough to pick him up the moment he left the parking lot? Or, would the gunners simply wait until he neared the waiting car before they cut him down?

Again, it made no difference. Bolan had his own plan working, his own surprise lying in wait for the enemy. No time like the present to put things in motion.

He rose from his crouch, left the field glasses and empty duffel behind as he stepped out from cover, letting them see him near the utility shed. He had the opposition spotted and their positions filed away, as he began to move along the pier.

JANICE FLYNN HAD BEEN allowed to dress herself, and it occurred to her that she was going home. Well, not directly—there would be reports to file, debriefings for the next few hours, at least—but she was on her way.

What had Belasko done to win her freedom? It came as a surprise to her that he would have deviated from his schedule to effect a rescue, when they barely knew each other.

Flynn checked that train of thought before it carried her away. There would be something in the game for him, of course. Humiliating Justin Pratt, if nothing else, rubbing the would-be Hitler's nose in defeat one more time before . . . what?

Her head was throbbing with a brutal ache that kept distracting her from her primary focus on survival. She knew Pratt well enough to understand that he wouldn't take one more defeat lying down. A new sense of dread enveloped her, warning her that Pratt was bound to have one last trick up his sleeve, a plan to turn the game around and crush Belasko flat.

Crush her, while he was at it.

Pratt was finished, if he let her go. There would be murder charges to start with, for gunning down Chet Blackmun in her presence. Separate counts of kidnapping and assaulting a federal officer would be the frosting on the cake. She knew enough to shut down the Aryan Resistance Movement and send at least three dozen of its die-hard members to the penitentiary for ten or fifteen years apiece. Illegal weapons and explosives, drugs, armed robbery, conspiracy—you name it.

There was no way Pratt could let her live. No way at all.

The shoebox clinched it.

Pratt was gloating, showing her the heavy block inside that looked like clay and smelled like marzipan, the twelve-volt battery and snarl of brightly colored wires. She didn't understand the firing mechanism, how it was supposed to work, and Pratt didn't enlighten her. He was all smiles as Ted came up behind her with the handcuffs, fastening them tight enough that she knew her fingers would be numb in minutes.

The drive from Reseda to Marina del Rey took forty minutes, following the San Diego Freeway most of the way. Flynn rode in the back seat, Justin Pratt beside her with the shoebox in his lap, Jeff and Ted in the front seat with their guns. They stopped off at Olympic and Sepulveda, picking up a three-car tail that stuck with them the rest of the way.

As they pulled into the marina parking lot, she didn't know what to expect. There was no sign of Belasko, nothing to betray his presence. Around them, gunners from two of the tail cars were fanning out, forming a picket line to cut off his escape.

They parked some distance from the other cars, Ted and Jeff climbing out with their hardware concealed. Pratt dragged her out of the car on his side, and she knew he was showing her off. Still no sign of Belasko, but she imagined she could feel him watching.

They stood together in silence for a moment, Flynn watching for any flicker of movement among the silent boats, but there was nothing. Was Belasko even there?

Another moment, and Pratt steered her back toward the car, into the front seat this time. Sitting on her hands, the handcuffs truly cutting off her circulation now, she felt herself begin to tremble as he reached behind her, came back with the loaded shoebox and placed it on her lap.

Pratt raised the lid, reached in and flicked a switch on the homemade detonator. Flynn half expected it to start clicking, but nothing happened. Pratt was grinning as he replaced the lid.

"I wouldn't jump around too much, if I were you," he said, displaying extra caution as he backed out of the car and eased the door shut.

So that was it. Some kind of motion sensor. Flynn felt her blood run cold.

Pratt stood beside the car, spread his empty hands in a gesture of mock surrender and addressed himself to the marina at large. "All yours," he shouted. "Keys are in the car."

The ARM leader had reached the other cars, where several of his men were waiting, by the time Belasko showed himself. A man in miniature, reduced by distance, stepped from behind some kind of shed positioned halfway down the dock. From where she sat, Flynn recognized the weapon in his hands and knew that he had come prepared to take the bastards with him, if he fell.

Except that he would never have that chance, once he was seated in the car with Flynn and the bomb positioned in her lap. There were at least a dozen ways it could go sour, anything from accidental jitters to a bullet smashing through the window to knock her sprawling where she sat. From the weight of the box on her lap, she knew there was sufficient power there to leave a smoking crater where the car now sat.

Two dead for the price of one, while Justin Pratt stood laughing on the sidelines, nothing left to bring him down.

Belasko was closer now, moving with cautious, measured strides, his automatic rifle leveled at Pratt and company from the waist. Another twenty yards remained until he reached the car and lost it all.

Unless...

The lady made her choice, tears welling in her eyes.

No way.

No goddamned way at all.

She took a deep breath, held it, then bucked her hips.

Her world disintegrated in a blazing field of white.

You NEVER HEARD the shot that killed you, Bolan thought. An old truism from the military, accurate or otherwise, which made him wonder if he might have missed a gunner somewhere. One was all that it would take, a single shot to drop him in his tracks.

But no one fired. His enemies were waiting, biding their time, perhaps intimidated by the hardware he was carrying.

He kept the rifle-grenade launcher dead-level on Pratt and the six gunners around him, thinking he could take them all—or most of them, at any rate—no matter what befell him next. Unless a head shot killed him instantly, there would be time for him to trigger a grenade and to go down hosing them with automatic fire. A measure of retaliation, at the very least, if he could pull it off.

It was much too slick for comfort, Pratt surrendering without a fight, a broad smile on his face. It had to be a trap, with all those gunners waiting in the wings, but where was the trigger. What was the plan?

The car was clearly part of it. Behind the wheel, with Dancer at his side, it would be open season. There was nothing but Pratt's interest in the *Patriot* to see them past the line of gunners. Letting Dancer go would basically destroy the Aryan Resistance Movement, never mind Pratt's hunger for revenge against the man who had already caused him so much grief.

And the answer to that was simplicity itself: Pratt had no plan to let them go. In fact, the trap had already closed, but Bolan couldn't see its detailed outline yet.

The waiting car...

He shot a glance at Janice, saw her staring at him from behind the windshield, her eyes fierce in her swollen, discolored face. It almost seemed that she was trying to beam him a telepathic message, but Bolan's receptors were down. He couldn't make that necessary contact, read the crucial message in her mind.

His eyes slid back to Justin Pratt and company, keeping them covered. He missed Dancer's final, convulsive movement, didn't see the car explode so much as feel it, a rush of superheated air that made him squint and duck his head, bracing for the shock wave that battered him a heartbeat later.

Staggering, he saw the flaming ruin of the car touch down on melted tires, smoke billowing in oil-black clouds. The driver's door was blown clear of the wreckage, skimming like a giant Frisbee across the parking lot, where it smashed into the side of another parked vehicle. A secondary blast from the fuel tank sent the trunk lid flying, launching the car's spare tire airborne like a fiery comet.

Bolan's ears were ringing, but he heard the sudden crack of gunfire loud and clear, bullets snapping around him, gouging splinters from the wooden dock.

He fired by reflex, triggering a high-explosive 40 mm round toward Pratt and his storm troopers, dodging to his right toward a low-slung sailboat lying at anchor. The warrior's headlong dive carried him across the foredock, dropping him into the cockpit.

Behind him, in the parking lot, the world had gone to hell, men screaming and a second car in flames.

And all at once, it felt like home.

17

Yakov Katzenelenbogen checked his wristwatch one more time, confirming that the others should be in their places, ready to proceed. Full dark had overtaken them, except within the compound, where strategic floodlights held the night at bay. A pilot passing overhead would certainly have noted the illumination, but a treetop-level pass would be required to spot the roving sentries with their automatic rifles.

Time.

In combat, it always came down to time, the critical factor that no man could ever control. One false step, one fuzzy calculation, and the best-laid plans of any fighting man went down the crapper. If luck was with you, only the careless warrior went down. In the worst-case scenario, he took others with him, sometimes the whole outfit, lives thrown away on the tick of a clock.

Unless you got it right.

Katz left the shelter of the darkened trees, worming his way down a slight incline, following the natural contour of the ground. He timed his movements, picturing the others as they did the same, advancing on the wire. The nearest sentry was some thirty meters away and had his back turned.

He'd have to make it quick, before he lost his edge.

It turned out that the lights were actually in his favor for the first few moments. They provided fair illumination for the camp, but none had been directed at the trees outside the wire. The sentries walked their beats, but they were in the same position as a man who tried to spot a prowler in his backyard, staring from the window with the bedroom lights behind him.

Strategy.

The wire cutters were a recent acquisition, three sets purchased at a hardware shop before they left the city. They made short work of the chain-link fence, their faint snipping noises barely audible from ten feet away. Rudolf Wetzel and Uri Dan would be performing the same delicate surgery at different points on the perimeter, watching the nearest sentries for a sudden stiffening or other change of attitude that would betray alertness to the danger close at hand.

Katz finished clipping, a simple flap that let him wriggle through. Inside the wire, he drew his knees against his chest and let the makeshift gate ease shut without a telltale jingle of the wire. He left the clippers on the grass, no longer necessary, and shifted the MP-5 SD-3 submachine gun to his good left hand.

The nearest sentry had his back turned, dragging on a cigarette, the smoke drifting in a haze around his head. He'd hunched shoulders, one of them supporting a Steyr AUG assault rifle on a sling of military webbing. Katz had risen from his prone position to a crouch before the lookout glimpsed the movement from a corner of his eye—or had he merely sensed the close approach of death?

Whatever, the guy began to turn, the cigarette still dangling from his lower lip, his right hand clutching at the AUG. The rifle's stubby "bullpup" configuration gave him an advantage, better balance and a shorter barrel, but he was starting out one jump behind, with everything to lose.

Katz hit him with a rising burst from thirty feet, watching the sentry's khaki shirt pop and recoil from the impact of his parabellum rounds. The guy was dead or dying as he fell, gravity and backward momentum combined to take him down, but his index finger still had enough life in it to trigger the Steyr. The rifle stuttered half a dozen rounds that missed Katz by a good three yards.

And that was all it took.

A warning shout went up on the perimeter across from the Phoenix Force leader, redundant with the sound of gunfire ringing in his ears. Around the compound, sentries were converging on the point where Katzenelenbogen stood... until all hell broke loose.

It would be Wetzel, he decided, since the mini-Uzi Uri Dan was carrying was silencer-equipped. The weapon made a high-pitched rattling sound, immediately followed by a bleat of pain. The running sentries lost their focus in a heartbeat, torn between two widely-separated targets. Katz could almost sense their rising panic, feel them losing it, but there was still no end of danger here.

He was outnumbered nine or ten to one, with no immediate visual contact with his allies.

Time to move, before they pinned him down.

Katz left the fallen sentry where he lay, unleashing a burst in the direction of two gunners racing toward him. He followed the fence and set off running for the cover of the nearest bungalow.

URI DAN HAD WRIGGLED halfway through the fence when everything began to break around him. He had been delayed while two young sentries stood and chatted near the fence, unable to proceed until they moved away, and even then he had to work with caution to avoid unnecessary noise.

And he was getting there, slowly but surely, when the roof fell in.

The burst of automatic fire wasn't exactly a surprise—he knew what they were there for, after all—but Dan had hoped to find himself a more secure position by the time it hit the fan. Instead, the flap of chain-link fence was draped across his waist like some pathetic parody of armor, more a hindrance than a help.

He powered forward with his elbows, digging at the grass, gripping the silenced mini-Uzi with sufficient force to blanch his knuckles. Rapid glances to his left and right showed Dan the sentries who had slowed him down, both sprinting for the far side of the compound now to join the fight.

He shot the nearest of them, squeezing off a 3-round burst, remembering the young man was a Nazi as the guy stumbled and sprawled on his face. Dan pivoted to the left and saw his second target moving out of range, declined to chase him with a burst that might call more attention to himself before he was prepared.

They each had preselected targets, splitting up the fascist compound into wedge-shaped slices, like a pie, but Dan was well acquainted with the way things started to unravel in the heat of combat. Something had already gone awry, perhaps a sentry dropped too late to keep his finger off the trigger, and their enemies were on alert now, scurrying around the compound, shouting questions, curses, calling for directions from their leadership.

Another automatic weapon stuttered somewhere on his left, near the perimeter. The German counterterrorist? He had no way of telling, but the outburst seemed to draw some of the Nazis off their single-minded rush across the camp in search of different targets.

The Mossad commando took advantage of the moment, sprinting toward the cover of a shed that housed the compound's generator. There had been no guard outside the building when they made their first reconnaissance, so long ago, but would they have one now?

He had to take the chance.

A glance around the corner revealed no one. He duck-walked along the east wall of the shed, feeling terribly exposed on every side. Another step would bring him out of cover, and he knew the move would have to be coordinated, swift, no thought of turning back.

And no time like the present to begin.

He surged around the corner, index finger on the Uzi's trigger, finding no one to absorb the burst of parabellum slugs. The shed's door was unlocked, a simple latch, and in another heartbeat Dan had shut himself inside.

The generator's noise competed with the sound of gunfire from outside, but it was no real contest. Dan drew his side arm, stepping closer to the generator as he chose a target point.

The motor.

He fired two quick rounds at close to point-blank range, and the two-stroke motor cut out. The naked bulb above his head went dark, and when he turned in the direction of the door, there was no glimmer underneath it from the floodlights spotted around the camp.

Step one completed.

Groping toward the door, he hesitated for a moment, listening to angry shouts as the defenders suddenly went blind. They would have no luck trying to repair the generator under fire, but Dan took out some insurance by palming a grenade and yanking out the safety pin. He tossed the lethal egg across his shoulder as he hit the door and kept on going, running in a crouch to make himself the smallest possible target for stray bullets.

The explosion rocked him, and something like a giant hand between his shoulder blades pushed him to his knees. He came up dodging to his left, saw muzzle-flashes in the night like fireflies and resisted the urge to return fire before he was sure of his targets.

Thirty fascists in the compound, maybe more. It wouldn't do for Dan to shoot his only friends by accident.

In his imagination, Dan could smell the Nazis, tracking them in darkness by the stench of death that emanated from their very flesh. A fantasy, of course, but if it served him, he wouldn't complain.

It was poetic justice, in a way, as if the Nazis had assassinated Asher Blum with the specific aim of bringing Dan here to keep a date with destiny.

It wouldn't be the same as meting out rough justice to the men behind the Holocaust, but most of them were dead now, or about to die. This newer generation of the same old plague had been dismissed by many self-styled experts—even some Israelis—as a group of children playing morbid games. If all the world ignored them, they would simply go away.

And if they didn't, then what?

Uri Dan believed he knew the answer to that question, saw it written in the record of atrocities committed by "black" terrorists—the opposite of "red," in European parlance—and he also reckoned the solution should be plain for all to see.

If not before the death of Asher Blum, at least this night.

A running figure loomed in front of Dan, and there was time for him to recognize the khaki uniform before he brought up the Uzi. He hammered three rounds through the runner's chest and dropped him on his back.

A small down payment on account, for justice.

Dan moved on, a silent hunter in the darkness split by muzzle-flashes, sniffing out his human prey.

BRUNO LAUCK HAD protested angrily when Gerhard Kasche ordered him to leave Berlin and take two dozen of their soldiers with him. Guns were needed in the city now, when they were facing unknown enemies, but Kasche had been unyielding. It was critical, he said, that they retain a strike force in reserve, prepared to move the moment that their enemies were finally identified.

And, Bruno read between the lines, if they weren't...

The day had been interminable, and he wasn't looking forward to the night, afraid that he would have to drink himself to sleep. All thoughts of sleep were banished now, as Lauck crouched in the doorway of his bungalow, a Walther P-38 automatic clutched in his hand, waiting for a target.

More than ever, now, he wished that he was back with Kasche in Berlin, and he was shamed by the thought, an implication of cowardice he couldn't deny.

His troops were badly rattled, taken by surprise to start with, blinded as the generator blew and all the lights went out. There was no hope of firing them again; Lauck knew that much from the explosion of the generator hut. Repairmen would be useless to him, even if they had a chance to work all night without getting their asses shot off.

A number of his men were firing wildly, aimlessly, and Lauck knew that he should call them off, but something stopped him. Was it fear, the nagging thought that any sound he made would bring a bullet homing on his position?

Of course, the chances were that none of them would even hear him, with the weapons hammering away. It made a satisfactory excuse—or might, to others—but the truth was that his vocal cords seemed frozen. He was trembling, and the night was far from cold, the chill of autumn weeks away.

The fear.

Raw hatred for the enemy boiled up inside him while he scanned the darkened camp for targets, following the muzzle-flashes, wondering which weapons—if any—were in the hands of his enemies.

A bullet slapped the wall two feet above his head, and Lauck scuttled back around the doorjamb, hissing a startled curse. Recovering from the initial shock, he told himself the near miss was a fluke. No one could see him in the dark and target him deliberately. Without an infrared device . . .

The fear was coming back at him again. He held the Walther out in front of him, aiming at the bungalow's doorway, as if he expected his enemy to come barging in at any moment and attack him physically.

He caught himself, disgusted with the fear that left him cringing in the darkness of the bungalow. He felt emasculated, worse than useless. Nothing could redeem him now, unless he seized control once more, reasserting himself. These were his troops, pledged to liberation of the Fatherland, and he was leaving them to struggle on their own instead of showing them the leadership they needed and deserved.

Sudden anger coupled with embarrassment to purge Lauck's fear. The trembling in his legs began to fade as he edged toward the doorway. He had to get out with his men, had to lead them by example. There was still a chance to bring some order out of chaos in the compound and destroy their enemies.

There had to be!

He was rising from his crouch when running footsteps crunched the soil outside his bungalow. A boot heel scraped on the wooden steps, then a body filled the doorway, errant moonlight glinting on the barrel of an automatic rifle.

Lauck fired on reflex, two rounds aimed directly at the center of the gunman's body mass. Explosive impact from the parabellum bullets took his target down without a grunt of protest, likely dead before he hit the floor. Lauck stood above him for a moment, making sure, before he knelt to check the gunner's pulse.

A sudden, chilling doubt came over him.

He had to know.

Lauck palmed the lighter from his pocket, flicked it with his thumb and held the small flame close to his late conquest's face. Instant recognition, Horst Something-or-other, and he cursed bitterly as the orange flame winked out.

No matter.

Accidents would happen, and no blame accrued without a witness. Lauck was on his own, and who could say that Horst hadn't been shot by one of their opponents?

Push him back out the door for insurance, to keep matters hazy, and move on from there.

Horst seemed to weigh a ton in death, though he looked slender in his uniform, bright crimson soaking through the khaki blouse in front. Lauck found he couldn't push the corpse, would have to drag it with his hands cupped underneath the dead man's arms—and that, in turn, meant he was backing through the open doorway, unprotected, while the battle raged around him.

Never mind. The only way to do a job was to forget about the risk and simply do it.

Barely through the door, he felt a presence on his left. There had been no sound of running feet this time, but Lauck knew instinctively that there was someone standing there, watching him. He dropped Horst on the wooden steps and straightened, his right hand gliding toward the Walther as he turned.

No recognition this time, in the moonlight, as he faced a total stranger. The features were difficult to make out, to tell for certain if his enemy was a Jew, but the Nazi had no difficulty making out the automatic weapon aimed directly at his gut.

The sound that slipped between his teeth was closer to a whimper than a snarl, but Lauck had his pistol, its muzzle rising, sweeping toward his target. Any second now—

A giant fist struck Lauck in the solar plexus, driving him back and down to the wooden floor. He lost the Walther, barely felt it slipping from his fingers. It almost felt as if someone had pulled a plug in his feet and drained the critical sensation from his body, leaving him an empty shell.

So dark, so cold.

But for the first time since the shooting started, he wasn't afraid.

He closed his eyes and let the darkness carry him away.

RUDOLF WETZEL BRACED his MP-5 K submachine gun in a firm two-handed grip and hosed his two young adversaries with a rattling figure eight. The Nazis went down in a snarl of arms and legs, one of them squeezing off a short burst from his Steyr automatic rifle as he fell. The bullets struck his comrade, slapping into flesh, but there was no reaction from the dead man draped across his legs.

This was Wetzel's first real mission in eighteen months, and he felt the adrenaline pumping, inducing a state of near euphoria that he would have to watch, if he wanted to live. The blood rush that accompanied mortal combat was deceptive, imparting a false sense of security—even invincibility—on the battlefield.

Still, it was good to be back for as long as it lasted. As long as he lived.

And death was a real possibility, Wetzel realized, with the odds stacked so heavily against them. They had done all right so far, and the Israeli agent made their work a little easier when he destroyed the generator, blacking out the camp, but it would still come down to stacking bodies, killing one-on-one.

Or two-on-one, he thought, and stepped around the lifeless bodies of his enemies. There were more where those two came from, dodging willy-nilly all around the compound, some of them firing at shadows, perhaps at one another.

That was fine with Wetzel, let them thin the herd a bit with "friendly fire," as the Americans would say...but what of his companions? Keeping track of anyone amid the chaos was a virtual impossibility. He knew where they had entered, more or less, but after that...

A bullet whispered past his face, and Wetzel went to ground. The nearest bungalow was twenty feet away, and he veered in that direction, crawling over grass worn bare in spots by boots and truck tires, hoping that the shot had been a simple stray. If someone had him spotted from the darkness, tracking him, he would be finished here and now.

He made it to the bungalow without another bullet coming close enough to worry him. The wall felt good against his back, a tiny measure of security, but Wetzel dared not let himself relax. He had no time to waste and everything to lose if he let false security replace the caution that had carried him this far.

Behind him, in the bungalow, he heard the scuffling sound of footsteps, and muffled voices. Two men, at least; perhaps more. Another chance to trim the odds.

Wetzel plucked a V-40 minigrenade from his belt, dropped the pin and held the safety spoon in place as he edged his way around the bungalow. A peek around the corner showed him that the door was standing partly open, offering a gap of several inches.

Could he make it? There was one way to be sure.

He broke from cover. A short burst from his machine pistol slammed the door back, widening his target gap, and he lobbed his grenade through on the run. Inside the barracks, someone tried to drop him with a hasty rifle shot, but

Wetzel kept on going, triggering another burst from his subgun as he put on the speed.

The blast was more or less contained, but the windows blew, and Wetzel felt the hot breath of the concussion on his neck. He stumbled, almost went down, but somehow kept his balance, dodging toward the next bungalow in line.

YAKOV KATZENELENBOGEN lobbed the frag grenade, then backpedaled in the darkness, counting down the seconds in his mind. He hit a shoulder roll and came up firing with the MP-5 SD-3, a short burst to suppress incoming fire. In front of him, three Vanguard riflemen were charging at him, unaware of the hand grenade.

One of the gunners was directly over the grenade when it exploded, and the blast nearly ripped him in two. The spray of shrapnel dropped his nearest comrade in a writhing heap, but number three kept coming, off his stride but still determined on the kill.

Katz met him with a rising burst that tripped the gunner and dropped him onto his face. Another burst to keep him there, and Katz was moving, spotting targets on the run and pinning them with short, precision bursts.

Random gunfire along the camp perimeter was slacking off. Several of the bungalows were in flames, the firelight showing the Phoenix Force leader a trail of scattered bodies across the compound. He couldn't begin to count the dead while watching out for living adversaries, but it seemed to Katz there had to have been two dozen Nazis down, which left—

Twenty meters in front of him, across the camp, another bungalow exploded. The initial flash showed Uri Dan, retreating from the shattered structure, ready as a burning scarecrow leaped from the wreckage, flapping wings of flame as if in an attempt to fly. The man from Tel Aviv unleashed a 3-round mercy burst, propelling the Nazi through an awkward somersault that wound up with the dead man stretched out on his back.

Another ragged burst of fire on the perimeter to the left drew Katz's attention. He turned in that direction and saw Rudolf Wetzel standing near the line of vehicles that was the compound's motor pool. The GSG-9 agent stood out in the open, tracking with his submachine gun, but he drew no fire.

Silence had descended like a cloak, as if someone had pulled the plug and brought all action to a grinding halt. Katz rose from his crouch, half expecting a new round of firing to start at any moment, but nothing happened. He stepped toward the center of the camp, showing himself and waiting for the others to join him, each man checking the fallen Nazis as he passed, prepared to fire if anyone showed signs of life.

All was quiet, as still as death.

"Is that the lot, then?" Wetzel asked.

"Unless you spotted any on the run," Katz replied.

"Who had the time?"

"In that case," Dan remarked, "I would suggest that we—how do you say?—haul ass."

"That's what we say," Katz answered. "And it's not a bad idea."

At that, he spent another moment pondering priorities, but there was nothing more for them to do around the camp. It would have been a relatively simple thing to torch the buildings still intact, but Katzenelenbogen hadn't come this far to simply burn a row of empty bungalows.

His comrades would be making for Berlin with all deliberate speed, perhaps already waiting for him there. They had delivered a resounding blow against their enemies, but more were still at large. The battle was not over yet, by any means.

"Let's go," he said at last, and led his two companions toward the waiting, darkened trees.

18

As soon as Bolan hit the sailboat's deck and rolled into the cockpit, he had one hand at his waist, a finger mashing the panic button of the radio-remote transmitter clipped to his belt. The plastic box made no audible sound, but its signal got through to the nearby detonators, loud and clear.

Within a second and a half, the *Patriot* disintegrated, Bolan's plastique charge erupting below deck with the force of a pent-up thunderclap, blasting up through the cabin and bulkhead like a giant fist. The superstructure of the boat dissolved into a cloud of giant splinters, wafted on a tongue of flame that leaped nearly thirty feet into the air. Adjacent craft were damaged, listing badly, while the *Patriot* burned to its waterline.

The Executioner rose to a crouch and reloaded his 40 mm grenade launcher on the move. Downrange, one of the ARM vehicles was belching oily smoke from the first direct hit, the other two scarred with shattered windows and gouged bodywork. Two men were down beside the cars, a third on his knees, cradling his bloodied head in his hands, while the others took to their heels.

The *Patriot*'s explosive demise shocked Bolan's targets into fleeting immobility, and that was all he needed for a start. He fired another HE round and cut loose with a long burst from his M-16 before the grenade struck the pavement. Two of Pratt's skinheads took the 5.56 mm tumblers chest-high, going down without a hint of grace, and then the grenade exploded in the midst of the survivors. Razor-sharp shrapnel drilled into the Nazis, and they flopped on the asphalt, screaming.

Two gunners crawled along the ground, dragging shattered limbs behind them, and he caught them with a blazing figure eight that punched them over onto their backs. Dead silence reigned for a moment on the killing ground, and his imagination kicked in with a scream from Janice Flynn that he had never really heard. He glanced back at the shattered hulk of the sedan where she had died short seconds earlier.

To save him? Possibly—or, was it just a booby trap that blew ahead of schedule? In the last analysis it made no difference to the Executioner. All bets were off, and he would grant no quarter to his enemies.

Scorched earth.

He scanned the killing ground in search of Justin Pratt, ticked off the bodies he could see, found no one with a close resemblance to the leader of the ARM. Was Pratt the headless corpse stretched out beside the car where Bolan's first grenade had landed?

No, the tattered clothes were wrong.

Which meant that he was still alive, perhaps retreating from the field at that very moment.

A couple of the outlying gunners broke the momentary trance, unleashing bursts of automatic fire from their position on the fringes of the parking lot. The first few rounds were high and wide, but they were getting there, a second burst gouging divots in the gunwale of the sailboat where Bolan had taken refuge. More weapons blasted at him, a half dozen or more peppering the small craft from bow to stern, ripping the furled sails to tatters and spraying the narrow cockpit with jagged splinters.

The Executioner flattened himself on the deck, pushing off with his feet toward the stern, where the craft was moored to its berth. The move he had in mind was risky granted, but remaining where he lay was tantamount to suicide. Within the next few moments, one or more of his assailants would begin to take advantage of the cover fire advancing for the kill, and once they closed the box he would have nowhere left to go.

That made it now or never, do or die.

The move, when it came, could have done credit to an Olympic gymnast. Bolan pushed off from the deck with one hand and both feet, twisting in midair and rolling toward the starboard rail of the craft as he brought his left hand back to the rifle-grenade launcher combo. The M-203 belched its 40 mm round with a muffled popping sound, lost in the staccato rattling of the M-16. The weapon's minor recoil helped with his momentum, taking Bolan to the rail and over, dropping out of sight behind the gunwale as his HE round impacted in the parking lot and detonated in a ball of flame.

It had the feeling of a clean miss, but the shot would serve its purpose if it kept their heads down for a few more moments, while he finished the audacious gambit.

Eighteen inches to the water, give or take. He splashed down on his back and sank immediately, kicking hard to the surface, gulping air. He held the rifle overhead, water streaming from the barrel, knowing it was built to function in the worst of combat circumstances. By all rights, a dunking shouldn't foul the weapon, though long-term immersion was strongly discouraged. As for any rusting, Bolan's contest with the ARM would be decided, one way or the other, long before corrosion had a chance to form.

Determined not to fail when he had come this far and lost so much, he pushed the weapon out in front of him and started kicking toward the pier.

JUSTIN PRATT WAS LEARNING how it felt to spin a dream and watch the whole thing disintegrate before your very eyes. In fact, it might not be that bad—the bitch was dead, at least, and even though a number of his troops had joined her, there were still enough in fighting trim to finish off their enemy—but he could see no end of trouble coming from their free-for-all at the marina.

Ideally it should have been quick, if not precisely clean. Chet Blackmun's bimbo and the stranger in the car together, peeling out, and *Bang!* The end of all Pratt's troubles in a rising cloud of smoke.

But, no.

He had to give the woman credit for her courage when it counted. It was too bad she had been a traitor to her birthright, selling out her race. He could have used a breeder with that kind of nerve and loyalty, but there was no point crying over spilt blood.

What mattered now was finishing the job, eliminating her connection on the spot, and he could see it going down the tubes. Not lost, exactly, but the grim snafu potential was there, staring him in the face, his attack force cut in half and dwindling while he watched.

The target had reacted swiftly to the blast, unleashing an explosive charge without the slightest hesitation, hosing Pratt's bodyguards with automatic fire from his assault weapon. Pratt was already diving for cover when the grenade went off, hugging the asphalt as a giant hand picked him up and slammed him back to earth a heartbeat later, driving the breath from his lungs and leaving him empty. He knew what it felt like to drown, but there was no time for convalescence on the firing line, when he could die at any moment.

At the same time, a second blast had taken out the *Patriot,* some kind of time bomb or remote charge triggered by the enemy. The boat had cost Pratt sixty thousand dollars, earning three or four times that amount in eighteen months, but that was over now.

It was stunning, how the best-laid plans could fall apart before you saw it coming. Master race or not, there came a point where circumstances and coincidence stepped in, and they could kick your ass unless you had a backup plan in readiness.

Just now, Pratt had his thoughts and hands full trying to recoup their early losses, nail the lid down on his adversary's coffin while they had a chance. Before the bastard turned it all around and managed to escape.

Before he killed them all.

That was impossible, of course, one man against so many...but how many of his men were still alive? Two were down beside the cars, including Jeff. Ted was wounded, kneeling in the open, both hands pressed against a forehead streaming crimson. That left three still capable of fighting and another six on the perimeter. With nine guns still behind him, he could...what?

Pratt circled to the rear of the demolished vehicles, keeping his head down, barking commands at the three dazed members of his entourage who were close enough to hear him without a shout.

"Get under cover, damn it! Don't just stand there!"

They were moving, breaking toward the clubhouse twenty yards away, and Pratt was watching from his covered vantage point when their antagonist unleashed another high-explosive round, followed at once by another burst of automatic rifle fire. Pratt ducked before the charge went off, but he could picture the destruction, echoed in the rising scream, cut off almost before it started, swallowed by the heavy blast.

He was still on his knees, huddled behind the third car in line, when something like a giant spider struck the pavement several feet away. It lay there, twitching, legs up toward the sky, and Pratt could feel his stomach rolling as he recognized the object as a severed human hand.

There was another burst of fire from the direction of the pier, and he kept his head down, giving the rifleman nothing to shoot for. Let him waste his bullets on the dead or dying, anything at all, while Pratt's surviving troops closed in and cut him off.

Assuming they were still in place and hadn't run for cover at the first explosion. Pratt craned his neck and he could see one of the skinheads, waddling in a crouch across the blacktop, one hand out to keep his balance while the other gripped a sawed-off shotgun at his side.

If one was sticking, maybe there were others. He had dropped six guns outside the parking lot before they pulled the caravan inside, and six could be enough, if they would only keep their wits about them.

It was time to move. He could accomplish nothing from his present hiding place, unable to communicate with his surviving men. Emerging from the cover of the cars would be a risk, but Pratt had no viable alternative. He could remain in place and wait to die, or he could gamble on his own intelligence and speed.

No contest.

Pratt put his head down, braced himself and came out running for his life.

BOLAN SURFACED underneath the pier, chest-deep in sea water, clutching the nearest pylon to support himself. Above and behind him, several weapons were still blasting the bullet-scarred sailboat, snipers apparently uncertain that the warrior had given them the slip. Staccato automatic fire was punctuated by the loud blasts of a shotgun, but the rounds were falling well away from Bolan's hiding place.

He took a breather, counting off ten seconds in his mind. That was enough for his assailants to begin their move, aware that they were running out of time before somebody in the neighborhood dialed 911 and brought police cars with their sirens screaming.

Now.

He worked his way beneath the pier, open on both sides, with automobile tires mounted as bumpers to avoid damaging craft in their berths. Coming up on the other side, he found himself sandwiched between a thirty-foot cabin cruiser, on his right, and another sailboat. The cruiser lay between Bolan and the marina clubhouse, with the parking lot beyond.

It was ideal.

He draped the M-16 A-1/M-203 over his shoulder on its sling and sidestroked toward the cruiser's bow, an anchor rope down in the water. Bolan scrambled up the rope in seconds flat, rolling over the low rail and onto the deck, keeping the cabin between himself and his enemies. The assault rifle was dripping but functional, and the Executioner pushed it in front of him as he crept along the deck. He used the last-minute lull to palm a fresh 30-round magazine, shaking it dry before he slipped it into the rifle's receiver. Then he slotted another 40 mm high-explosive round into the grenade launcher's firing chamber.

Ready.

The hostile fire had slacked off momentarily, the snipers closing in to find a better angle of attack. Still prone, he peered around the corner of the cabin cruiser's wheelhouse, spotting two men on the pier, with two more hanging back to cover their approach. Four showing, and at least another two beyond his line of sight, unless they had decided to evacuate the scene.

Six brownshirts and their boss remained. Without a shot at Justin Pratt, he knew the game wouldn't be finished in Los Angeles.

Not yet.

But he would take what he could get, for now, and play it one step at a time.

He stayed low, lining up the first mark with his assault rifle, framing the gunner in his sights. Twenty yards, give or take, and Bolan thumbed the fire-selector switch to semiautomatic for precision work.

The first goon never saw it coming. He was edging toward the bullet-riddled sailboat, half crouching with an Uzi submachine gun in his hands, when Bolan shot him in the chest. One 5.56 mm tumbler slammed his target backward, arms outflung, his weapon dropping with a splash into the nearby water. Sprawling on the pier, the gunner's body quivered to the rhythm of his fading heartbeat for an instant, then lay still.

The Executioner was already tracking toward a new target, the first mark dismissed from his mind. The nearest backup shooter saw his buddy drop, but he had no fix on the source of danger, seeming to believe the killing shot had emanated from the ruined sailboat. He pumped a shotgun blast in that direction, wasted, and was waiting for the enemy to show himself when Bolan squeezed off two quick rounds and finished it.

The Nazi gave a violent jerk on impact, dropping to his knees as blood pumped through his shirt from ragged entry wounds. Another moment, and he toppled slowly forward on his face, deadweight surrendering to gravity.

That left two in Bolan's line of sight, but both of them were falling back to save themselves, his angle fading fast. He moved the fire-selector switch to full-auto, charging out of cover as his adversaries tried to cut and run.

He fired a 40 mm high-explosive round, going for altitude, dropping the grenade some fifteen feet in front of the moving targets. One runner took the full force of the blast head-on, the impact lifting him completely off his feet and throwing him in a backward vault that left the man in a crumpled, broken heap. His sidekick took a shrapnel hit and went down on all fours, shaking his head like a groggy wrestler, scrabbling after the weapon he had dropped.

Bolan moved to the cabin cruiser's stern and stepped onto the dock. A drifting pall of smoke obscured his vision, but it worked both ways, providing him with marginal security against the threat of snipers in the parking lot.

One down but still alive, at least two others unaccounted for.

And Justin Pratt.

Above all else, the leader of the ARM would have to die.

He moved along the dock, heading toward the parking lot and clubhouse, past the riddled sailboat and the bodies of his fallen enemies. His mind was focused on destruction. He had no illusion that eliminating Justin Pratt and his surviving brownshirts could restore the loss of Janice Flynn. Payback had its limitations, but the job remained unfinished. His eradication of the ARM wasn't a simple matter of revenge.

It had to do with justice and preserving civilized society

A MAJOR PART of leadership was knowing when to cut your losses. Justin Pratt had learned that much from history, examining the trials and tribulations of his heroes during generations past. No less a godlike figure than the führer had mistaken courage for judicious wisdom at the gates of Stalingrad, and one mistake could ruin everything.

One slip could get you killed.

It didn't take a rocket scientist to tell him he had lost control of the situation, and it was time to go before he wound up like his soldiers on the pier.

Pratt's vehicles were wasted, but it made no difference. Los Angeles is a city on wheels, and anyone who couldn't shag a ride somewhere, somehow, deserved to die. Survival of the fittest was a rule both near and dear to the Nazi's heart, and he was bent on demonstrating just how fit a member of the master race could be.

He was still without a clue to his enemy's identity, but that could wait. He meant to live and fight another day, and that meant getting out of the city—out of the country, perhaps—until things blew over.

Fortunately hiding out wasn't a problem. He had friends south of the border, Blackmun's friends and fellow white men, who would welcome him with open arms. He could relax awhile and let the dust settle around L.A., pull some strings to find out who was stalking him. Let the Feds earn their paychecks for a change, instead of hounding patriots with trumped-up charges generated by the Zionist Occupational Government in Washington. Fine irony, if the police and FBI wound up protecting Pratt's interests for a change.

But in the meantime, he would have to look out for himself.

It had required some goading, pulling rank to get his people off their butts and moving toward the sailboat where the enemy had taken cover, but he pulled it off. He still thought they could pull it out, despite the losses they had suffered, finish off the bastard while they had him trapped and get the hell away from there before the squad cars started rolling in.

So much for confidence.

He knew that they had blown it when their adversary popped up on a different boat, across the dock, and started picking off the remnants of his strike force. Two or three men were left, and Pratt couldn't afford to stick around and see if one of them got lucky.

Pratt was up and running when the next grenade went off, abandoning his soldiers to their fate. If one of them could pull it out, so much the better. Pratt would buy the trigger-man a new Mercedes, give him Blackmun's vacant office in the movement, maybe even kiss his ass at Hollywood and Vine... but something told him that wasn't about to happen.

Not with this guy.

He was like some kind of one-man army. Could it be one man behind the damage Pratt had suffered in the past twenty-four hours, a wild man with guns up the ass and no fear of death?

Christ, what Pratt could do with ten or fifteen men like that at his command. With Pratt's brain, his apocalyptic vision, and the kind of muscle this guy threw around, they could make history.

Forget it. Pratt would *be* history, if he didn't get away from the marina soon.

He fled the parking lot, running north on Lincoln Boulevard, traffic slowing in response to the drifting clouds of smoke and the sounds of gunfire. Leave it to Los Angelenos, gawking in a free-fire zone. At times, he thought the whole damned town was populated with morons and maniacs in equal proportions. It made L.A. a fertile recruiting ground, no shortage of bullyboys and true believers ripe for the picking, but what Pratt really needed at the moment was a ride.

He found the taxi two blocks north, its driver just emerging from a doughnut shop on the corner. Pratt yanked the back door open, piling in before the guy could wedge his bulk behind the wheel.

"Off duty, pal," the cabbie told him, talking with his mouth full.

"Fifty bucks on top of what the meter reads, if you can take me where I need to go."

The driver grinned, revealing chocolate crumbs between his teeth. "It's like I said, let's hit the road."

THE WOUNDED NAZI SAW Mack Bolan coming through a veil of blood, and his lips drew back in a wordless snarl, his fingers groping for the shotgun at his side. A 3-round burst from the Executioner's M-16 ripped through the kneeling figure's chest and slapped him backward.

Someone was firing from Bolan's left. He swung in that direction, moving toward the sound of gunfire, reloading the M-203 launcher before he spotted his target. A slender blond with mirrored shades dodged back toward the marina clubhouse, an Ingram submachine gun thrust in front of him and laying down a screen of cover fire.

Too little, far too late.

Bolan triggered the HE round, standing fast as it arched toward the target and detonated on impact, propelling a twisted rag-doll figure through the plate-glass window of the clubhouse, there and gone.

The shout from the warrior's flank was fear and outrage, mingled in a wordless cry that drew his attention to another adversary. Buckshot rattled toward Bolan's position, but the Executioner had already dived through a forward shoulder roll.

He came up firing from the hip, his first rounds punching through the legs and pelvis of a gunner standing twenty feet away. The wounded Nazi fell across his line of fire as Bolan held down the rifle's trigger, the copper-jacketed tumblers whipping his target through a spinning, flopping sprawl.

Sudden stillness descended on the killing field. The warrior was aware of traffic slowing at curbside, drivers rubbernecking, scoping out the scene of mayhem. Sirens were already wailing in the distance, answering the crisis call.

Bolan had to go, but he couldn't leave until he checked among the dead for Justin Pratt. Deliberately retracing his steps, he visited the bodies in the parking lot, turning each one over to reveal slack faces, eyes glazed in death.

The would-be Hitler of Los Angeles wasn't among them.

Bolan muttered a curse, standing on the field of death and breathing gun smoke, waiting for the flush of unproductive rage to pass. He scanned the sidewalks north and south of his position, picked out various pedestrians with nerve enough to venture close, but none of them was Justin Pratt.

His target had evaporated. Gone.

And that left Bolan's work unfinished in Los Angeles.

He started back in the direction of his waiting car. The flow of traffic would retard police response, provide the lag time he required to slip away. He hesitated by the burned-out hulk of the sedan that held the pitiful remains of Janice Flynn.

A shameful waste, for which the man responsible would have to pay.

He might not get the bill today, but it was coming, payable in blood.

And when that tab came due at last, the Executioner would be there to collect.

* * * * *

The heart-stopping action continues in the second book of The Terror Trilogy: Cleansing Flame, *coming in July.*

Join Mack Bolan's latest mission in

THE TERROR TRILOGY

Beginning in June 1994, Gold Eagle brings you another action-packed three-book in-line continuity, the Terror Trilogy. Featured are THE EXECUTIONER, ABLE TEAM and PHOENIX FORCE as they battle neo-Nazis and Arab terrorists to prevent war in the Middle East.

Be sure to catch all the action of this gripping trilogy, starting in June and continuing through to August.

Available at your favorite retail outlet, or order your copy now:

Book I:	JUNE	FIRE BURST (THE EXECUTIONER #186)	$3.50 U.S. $3.99 CAN.	☐
Book II:	JULY	CLEANSING FLAME (THE EXECUTIONER #187)	$3.50 U.S. $3.99 CAN.	☐
Book III:	AUGUST	INFERNO (352-page MACK BOLAN)	$4.99 U.S.	☐

Total amount	$_____
Plus 75¢ postage ($1.00 in Canada)	$_____
Canadian residents add applicable federal and provincial taxes	
Total payable	$_____

To order, please send this form, along with your name, address, zip or postal code, and a check or money order for the total above, payable to Gold Eagle Books, to:

In the U.S.
Gold Eagle Books
3010 Walden Ave.
P. O. Box 9077
Buffalo, NY 14269-9077

In Canada
Gold Eagle Books
P. O. Box 636
Fort Erie, Ontario
L2A 5X3

TT94-2R

**Adventure and suspense in the midst
of the new reality...**

JAMES AXLER

DEATH LANDS®

Rider, Reaper

A peaceful interlude for Ryan Cawdor in the mountains of
New Mexico becomes a blood-soaked game of survival as Ryan's
idyll becomes a mission of revenge. His quarry on a cross-desert
manhunt is the General, a man who grimly prepares to destroy
his pursuers.

Hope died in the Deathlands, but the will to live goes on.

A biochemical weapons conspiracy puts America in the hot seat. Don't miss

STONY MAN™ 11
TARGET AMERICA

The Army of National Independence—ANI—is a radical separatist group using terrorist activities to "free" a captive Puerto Rico. When they plan a master strike that will send shock waves through the world, STONY MAN races to break the chain of destruction.

BATTLE FOR THE FUTURE IN A WASTELAND OF DESPAIR

AURORA QUEST

by **JAMES AXLER**

The popular author of DEATHLANDS® brings you the gripping conclusion of the Earthblood trilogy with AURORA QUEST. The crew of the U.S. space vessel *Aquila* returns from a deep-space mission to find that a devastating plant blight has stripped away all civilization.

In what's left of the world, the astronauts grimly cling to a glimmer of promise for a new start.

Available in July at your favorite retail outlet.

**A new warrior breed blazes a trail
to an uncertain future in**

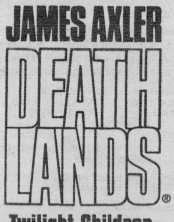

JAMES AXLER
DEATH LANDS®

Twilight Children

Ryan Cawdor and his band of warrior-survivalists are transported
from one Valley of the Shadow of Death to another, where they
find out that the quest for Paradise carries a steep price.

In the Deathlands, the future looks terminally brief.

Don't miss out on the action in these titles featuring
THE EXECUTIONER, ABLE TEAM and PHOENIX FORCE!

The Freedom Trilogy

Features Mack Bolan along with ABLE TEAM and
PHOENIX FORCE as they face off against a communist
dictator who is trying to gain control of the troubled
Baltic State and whose ultimate goal is world supremacy.

The Executioner #61174	BATTLE PLAN	$3.50	☐
The Executioner #61175	BATTLE GROUND	$3.50	☐
SuperBolan #61432	BATTLE FORCE	$4.99	☐

The Executioner ®

With nonstop action, Mack Bolan represents ultimate
justice, within or beyond the law.

#61178	BLACK HAND	$3.50	☐
#61179	WAR HAMMER	$3.50	☐

(limited quantities available on certain titles)

TOTAL AMOUNT	$	
POSTAGE & HANDLING	$	
($1.00 for one book, 50¢ for each additional)		
APPLICABLE TAXES*	$	_____
TOTAL PAYABLE	$	_____
(check or money order—please do not send cash)		

To order, complete this form and send it, along with a check or money order for the
total above, payable to Gold Eagle Books, to: **In the U.S.:** 3010 Walden Avenue,
P.O. Box 9077, Buffalo, NY 14269-9077; **In Canada:** P.O. Box 636, Fort Erie, Ontario,
L2A 5X3.

Name: _____
Address: _____ City: _____
State/Prov.: _____ Zip/Postal Code: _____

*New York residents remit applicable sales taxes.
 Canadian residents remit applicable GST and provincial taxes.

GEBACK5